Praise for
Kissing Your Ex

"*Kissing Your Ex* unfolds with the quiet intimacy and unaffected candor of a late-night conversation over a couple of bottles of wine . . . a touching meditation on the risks and realities of dreams, on what is lost to time and damage and human fallibility, and what endures." —Tim Farrington

"Brooke Stevens has written a book that is at once old-fashioned and contemporary." —Gabriel Brownstein

Praise for the Novels
of Brooke Stevens

"Riveting" —*Chicato Tribune*

"Stevens's ability to create empathetic characters is impressive . . . a book that won't be easy to forget." —*The Dallas Morning News*

"Stevens has created a work of page-turning intensity . . . nearly impossible to put down." —*San Francisco Chronicle*

"Nothing short of astounding." —*Boston Herald*

"Earnest and fabulous . . . richly imagined." —*The Washington Post Book World*

continued . . .

Written by today's freshest new talents and selected by New American Library, NAL Accent novels touch on subjects close to a woman's heart, from friendship to family to finding our place in the world. The Conversation Guides included in each book are intended to enrich the individual reading experience, as well as encourage us to explore these topics together—because books, and life, are meant for sharing.

Visit us online at www.penguin.com.
Learn more about the author at www.brookestevens.com.

Kissing Your Ex

BROOKE STEVENS

NAL Accent
Published by New American Library, a division of
Penguin Group (USA) Inc., 375 Hudson Street, New York, New York 10014, U.S.A.
Penguin Books Ltd, 80 Strand, London WC2R 0RL, England
Penguin Books Australia Ltd, 250 Camberwell Road,
Camberwell, Victoria 3124, Australia
Penguin Books Canada Ltd, 10 Alcorn Avenue, Toronto, Ontario, Canada M4V 3B2
Penguin Books (N.Z.) Ltd, Cnr Rosedale and Airborne Roads,
Albany, Auckland 1310, New Zealand

Penguin Books Ltd, Registered Offices: 80 Strand, London WC2R 0RL, England

First published by NAL Accent, an imprint of New American Library,
a division of Penguin Group (USA) Inc.

First Printing, July 2004
10 9 8 7 6 5 4 3 2 1

FICTION FOR THE WAY WE LIVE
REGISTERED TRADEMARK—MARCA REGISTRADA

LIBRARY OF CONGRESS CATALOGING-IN-PUBLICATION DATA:

Stevens, Brooke.
    Kissing your ex / Brooke Stevens.
        p. cm.
    ISBN 0-451-21202-9
    1. Triangles (Interpersonal relations)—Fiction. 2. Divorced
women—Fiction. 3. Atlanta (Ga.)—Fiction. I. Title.
    PS3569.T447K575 2004
    813'.54—dc22   2003024390

Printed in the United States of America

PUBLISHER'S NOTE
This is a work of fiction. Names, characters, places, and incidents either are the
product of the author's imagination or are used fictitiously, and any resemblance
to actual persons, living or dead, business establishments, events, or locales is
entirely coincidental.

BOOKS ARE AVAILABLE AT QUANTITY DISCOUNTS WHEN USED TO PROMOTE PRODUCTS
OR SERVICES. FOR INFORMATION PLEASE WRITE TO PREMIUM MARKETING DIVISION,
PENGUIN GROUP (USA) INC., 375 HUDSON STREET, NEW YORK, NEW YORK 10014.

For Karen

Acknowledgments

For editorial insight and support, I thank Nina Aron, Carla Bigelow, Francesca Lia Bloch, Emily Buchanan, Marco Capalbo, Jon and Andrea DePreter, Sharon Guskin, Alexis Hurley, Isabelle Lousada, D. Mara Lowenstein, Brendan O'Connell, Chris Pratt, Craig and Lu Marcus, Peter Ohlin, Oren Rudavsky, David Shifren, Lyde Sizer, Jonah Winter, Kim Witherspoon, Celia Wren, Marvin Zimble and Sondra Zimble.

And to my wonderful agent, Laurie Liss, thank you for the many hours you put into this manuscript.

And to my editor, Leona Nevler, and her assistant, Susan McCarty, for making it all possible in the end.

. . . I loved her against reason, against promise, against peace, against hope, against happiness, against all discouragement that could be. Once for all; I loved her none the less because I knew it, and it had no more influence in restraining me, than if I had devoutly believed her to be human perfection.

—*Great Expectations,* Charles Dickens

A man is more likely to let a relationship suffer in order to hold on to his sense of self, while a woman is more apt to let her identity suffer to help strengthen it.

—*Passionate Marriage, Keeping Love and Intimacy
Alive in Committed Relationships,*
David Schnarch, Ph.D.

Chapter One

As I opened the door into my office that morning, I noticed a Federal Express package next to my computer, not the usual slim kind for the graphic art department, but one with a little heft. I stared at it a moment and then shook my raincoat of water and hung it up in the closet. It had been raining outside, a pleasant Georgian spring shower. I slipped on a dry pair of socks and shoes, pulled a comb through my wet hair, and then walked back over to my desk and picked up the package to examine it under my lamp. The label was addressed to me at Barnes Advertising Agency here in Atlanta, but there was no name under SENDER, just a typed street number from Brooklyn.

I shook the box—it wasn't light—and then pulled the tab to one side. The first thing my hand touched was a blue-and-yellow hardcover edition of *Alice in Wonderland*. Turning it over, I saw that it had been published in the twenties and the illustrations were those of John Tenniel; some were black-and-white and some were touched up with color. The drawings depicting the Queen of Hearts, the Cheshire Cat, and Alice were grotesque, yet delicately rendered, and quite beautiful. Gently closing the book, I pushed it aside and reached back into the package.

My fingers brought out a large postcard with a photograph of a long, slender white beach leading out to a point surrounded by a soft blue ocean. The beach was banked by bluffs and tropical forest. There was nothing handwritten on the back of the card, just a few words in the corner about the beautiful Caribbean sunsets. I was not sure what connection this could possibly have with the book, so I felt inside the box again and this time slipped out a present wrapped in handmade paper. Silk-screened on the paper were blotchy mermaids. My name, Maddy Green, was printed neatly on a card under the ribbon.

I was mystified. The package seemed like the sort of thing that a secret admirer might send, but I'm not the sort who inspires secret admirers, or crushes for that matter, particularly since reaching the grand old age of thirty-seven. Nor was there any other special occasion that I could think of that might inspire such a surprise. Valentine's Day had come and gone over a month ago. As I reached back in the package, the telephone rang and a gruff voice broke me out of my state of wonder.

"Ah, Ms. Green." The caller was a client, a manufacturer of suntan lotion and a cigar smoker, I imagined, though I'd never met him. "I'll leave it to your better judgment, but isn't this orange bikini actually a bit more noticeable than the girl's tan? We're not selling the bikini, you know." As head of the art department, I was used to getting calls like these, which were more about personal contact than anything else. In as personable a voice as I could muster, I told him that I would tone the bikini down and then e-mail him the copy.

I felt inside the package again and drew out a letter-size

envelope and a few snapshots held tight with a rubber band. The top snapshot was a sun-warped Polaroid with a blurry, almost underwater-like background and a white fingerprint-stained border. There I was, fourteen years old, smiling, a bubble of saliva clinging to a network of flashing silver wires. Nestled like an infant in my arms was my West Highland terrier. My mother was standing next to me, her big, dark-rimmed seventies glasses shaped like small televisions, her arm resting on my bony shoulders. Behind us in the green blur, my summer camp's dock jutted out into a lake.

Turning it over, I discovered a smudged note penciled on the back.

The second cutest picture of Maddy Green of all time. To be auctioned off at Sotheby's when she's a famous painter.

A yellow Post-it fell from the package. Scribbled in red ink were the words:

Sorry about breaking our agreement . . .
                                        Jack

For an instant my world came to a standstill, a little like a freeze-frame in an action movie—not that my life is exactly that. I hadn't heard a word from Jack in over three years despite all that we'd been through together, and we'd been through a lot. The agreement the note referred to was made at the time of our separation, when the two of us firmly resolved not to talk to each other until we were both back on our feet, whatever that meant. I had seen Jack's signature on the divorce papers, but that was about it. The silence thereafter was deafening.

I reached for a letter opener and slit open the envelope with my name on it. Jack's handwriting was never neat—he had no sense of a horizontal line even when there was one. The words he'd penned looked like they were melting down the page.

Dear Maddy,

I've written much longer versions of this letter and thrown them away. Sorry to shock you. I've done what I said I would—tried my hardest to forget what we had together, but I've come to the conclusion that we were simply too close for that to ever happen. Maybe this is not the case with you; maybe you've moved on, found somebody you're happy with. If so I wish you the best and apologize for this interruption.

I'm writing to ask you something, but first I do want you to understand this is not merely a wild impulse; I've spent many months thinking about it. I'm wondering if there's any way we could open up lines of communication again. I'd love to talk to you or to see you. I'd even fly down to Atlanta for the day just to have lunch with you. I've got this crazy idea that if things work out, we might go somewhere for a weekend, someplace beautiful that neither of us has ever been to, just to see what it's like to be around each other without all that history of ours. But at the moment I'll settle for just a phone call from you. Maddy, I'm asking you this because I love you still and miss you and I now know something that I didn't before. The closeness that we shared together for all those years is far too precious to lose. Yes, we had our problems like all couples, but our love for each other was different—it was a wonderful gift.

Would you call or write to me if you get a chance?
Here are my telephone numbers and e-mail. Until
then, I'll be waiting anxiously to hear from you . . .

Love,
Jack

I stared at Jack's signature. I too had once thought about going somewhere new with him to shake the past, but it never occurred to me that this was anything more than a fantasy, the breaking of some unwritten rule that all exes everywhere know about. And yet something about this idea had that vague familiarity of the inevitable, as if I had known all along that no matter what I did after our separation, no matter how hard or far I ran, I would eventually come back to him. The problem was complicated: Our divorce was amicable. There was none of the usual bitterness.

I stared at the contents of the open package scattered before me—still in disbelief.

My eyes went to another picture. I was in his arms, one arm around his neck. Snow covered the rocky summit of Mount Lafayette in the White Mountains where we were standing. Jack looked as he often did back in his twenties— red-cheeked and out of breath, as if he were trying to take in as much of the world as possible. His wavy black hair was snow-coated, as were his eyebrows and the little fuzz over his lip. My knitted wool cap was all but covering my eyes, and my two long braids were resting on the shoulders of my parka. I was looking up at Jack and blushing.

I remembered how the day in New Hampshire began, lifting our packs on our backs and setting off through a warm, light green valley at the base of Lafayette. Though it was late spring in the valley, we knew that the weather at the summit could be volatile and so we'd brought along plenty of winter clothes. A tin cup tied onto the back of Jack's pack made a pinging sound as we followed the trail of smooth rocks and black earth through the shade of aspen and pine. I was so happy to be alone with him after all the craziness of our life in New York. I wanted to grab him and pull him against me and tell him how happy I was. But he was making me laugh, telling me a story about his eccentric family.

The air became cooler as we rose in elevation, and the pine trees were gnarled and windswept. Across the wide valley we could see the remains of snow avalanches in the ravines of Mount Garfield and spots of melting snow and grass on the closed ski trails of Cannon Mountain. Finally we climbed out above the timberline just under the clouds and followed the zigzagging trail up the slope of boulders and broken rocks that led to the summit. The clouds were moving quickly and breaks of sunlight and shadow raced up the rocky slope. We stopped and shared a big chunk of chocolate from the general store in Franconia, both of us leaving teeth marks on its sides before wrapping it in cellophane again.

Then it happened; a black cloud swept across the surrounding peaks and smothered the trail. First sleet and then snow began to fall. Blinded, we barely made it behind a boulder for shelter. I sat down next to Jack, but he pulled me onto his lap and held me around the waist as the snow gathered in our hair and piled up on our laps. The storm grew fiercer with that hollow whistling sound and I could feel the sting of ice against my ears. It was frightening; hikers perished in spring storms like these.

Then the cloud blew off the mountain and the sun came out again and a blanket of wet snow lay around us so bright that we had to shade our eyes with our hands. We laughed at each other, still giddy with fear. We knocked the snow from our pants and jackets and climbed the rest of the way up, holding each other for balance. On the summit we dropped our gear and went to a wall of rocks facing east. The air was clear, the clouds gone, and we could see seventy-five miles across the untouched Pemigewasset Wilderness to Mount Washington. It was breathtaking—the many bright snowcapped peaks of the Presidential Range while far down in the valley the wilderness was the light green of spring.

Jack took out the chunk of chocolate again and handed it to me. Then he lifted his camera and tripod from his pack and asked me to stand against a rock so he could focus. I stood there watching him, nibbling at the chocolate and blinking from the bright light.

He kept staring into the lens, focusing and refocusing. It was unlike him; he was anything but meticulous. Then he began walking toward me, and the next thing I knew, he had fallen in the snow at my feet—or at least I thought he had.

Suddenly I realized he was holding something out to me. Between his fingers I saw a silver ring with three inset sapphires and a diamond, an antique from the twenties.

At first it seemed like a stupid, corny stunt—we were never into tradition of any kind.

"Maddy . . . I've been meaning to ask you something . . ." He was more nervous than I had ever seen him. I too was trembling.

"Jack—are you crazy?" I said, and leaped into his arms without finishing my sentence and kissed him. We continued kissing passionately until Jack began to stagger and we tumbled into the snow, laughing.

Five years later on our wedding anniversary in a bar across the street from our apartment on the Lower East Side of Manhattan, Jack pulled an envelope out of his bag and laid it on the table. He was always the master of small surprises. Opening it, I slipped out the photograph that I now held in my hand for the first time. I had no idea that he had used a timer.

I set the picture down on my office desk and picked up the present decorated with handmade paper. Unwrapping it revealed a small white box with a label of gold lettering: FRANCONIA GENERAL STORE, FRANCONIA, NH. I opened it.

"Chocolate?" I suddenly heard. I quickly slipped my hands over the photographs and letter and looked up. Andrew Barnes stood in the doorway of my office—he was the last person in the world I wanted to see this. "What's this, a secret admirer, Maddy?" He was tall with black hair, beautiful smooth eyebrows, and a sharklike jaw. We'd been dating for close to six months and things were just starting to get serious.

"It's nothing," I said. He stepped toward me and I attempted to shield the package with my arm. "Hey, Andrew, please." I glared at him and he stopped in the middle of the room, staring down at my desk. Then he turned and walked briskly out of my office. "Now, wait a minute," I called. I went to my door. He turned the corner far down the hallway near the executive offices. I continued down the hall and peered around the corner. His door was closed and his secretary, Ms. Lavender, was at her station. She was a tough woman in her sixties who dyed her brittle hair a crisp black and painted her fingernails an intimidating shade of magenta. She liked being the boss's secretary—Andrew Barnes was the Barnes in Barnes Advertising of Atlanta. She raised her waxed eyebrows at me. I knew better than to proceed. I returned to my office and closed the door.

I read the letter over again, slowly this time.

I'd even fly down to Atlanta for the day just to have lunch with you. I've got this crazy idea that if things work out, we might go somewhere for a weekend . . .

It was a lot to register at nine o'clock on a Monday morning. I tucked everything back into the package and slipped it into my desk. I had plenty to do that morning.

At noon I pushed my long hair behind my ears and strolled down the hallway to Andrew's office—I was accustomed to lunching with him on Mondays, but his door was shut and I came face-to-face with Ms. Lavender. She was tapping her nails on her desktop.

"He's out with a *very* important client—for the rest of the afternoon," she said. "I guess he didn't tell you."

"Actually, he did," I lied. "It just sort of slipped my mind."

She grinned and I smiled, knowing she had won, and then I returned to my office to get my umbrella. I really needed some air.

Chapter Two

By the time I arrived home that evening the clouds were gone and vapor was rising from the drying pavement. I parked my car under one of the elegant, wide-branched poplar trees along my street in Lullwater Park, opened the back of my station wagon, and took out a bag of cat litter and a frozen dinner. The sun was setting and birdsongs were echoing against the neighboring houses. The grass in my yard was usually the longest and rattiest in the neighborhood, a botanist's dream of flowering weeds, from dandelions to violets. I never minded the appearance; after all, I took the apartment after moving here from New York because of the building it was in—a decaying, Faulknerian mansion that looked like it belonged on a winding country road in the heart of Yoknapatawpha County.

Opening the front door to my building, I saw my mail organized in neat piles on the foyer table. My charming eighty-year-old landlady, Penny, the same woman who refused to comply with our neighbors' wishes to mow weekly rather than monthly, sorted the junk from my bills and personal letters. Small gestures like these were one of the reasons we'd become close so soon after I moved in. Penny never cared about what others thought of her, and yet she had exquisite taste and a wry sense of retro. Two years ago, when I arrived from New York, she helped me repaint and decorate the large, rambling apartment on the second floor to my liking. On my days off from work, the two of us would drive around town to tag sales and thrift stores and scour shelves for an offbeat lamp or chair from the forties or fifties. She was born in Atlanta, and her knowledge of the city's history was both personal and grand. She talked about the Civil War as if Sherman's march were still smoldering somewhere on the horizon.

There were windows with diamond-shaped panes leading up the carpeted stairs to my apartment on the second floor—the sills needed painting and some of the fogged glass was cracked. I loved the ecclesiastical atmosphere—the intricate wainscoting and crown moldings—as if it represented the collapse of some magnificent era of the past. Climbing the stairs, I could hear the scrambling of my dogs' nails against the parquet floor and the occasional squawk of a parrot. Soon after settling in here I began assembling a small menagerie. All the extra space in my apartment—the two bedrooms, the narrow servant's room, the walk-in pantry, and the many nooks and crannies along the hall— begged for life of some sort. It so happened that the neighborhood newspaper ran pictures of the strays of St. Francis's Animal Shelter only two blocks away. It was love at first sight with a one-eyed pug named Popeye and then later a dachshund named Charlie. Charlie cost me an arm and a leg because he needed an operation on his back to save him, and Popeye already limped around with a metal plate in his hip. I had to carry both of them up and down the flight of stairs to my apartment to walk them. I also took on an African Gray parrot named Cynthia whose owner had abandoned her when Cynthia lost a wing after a window sash dropped on her. The shelter had warned me that she was antisocial, but she seemed to know quite well that I had saved her life, riding on my shoulder like a wounded sea captain, guiding me by pulling at my ear.

The moment I opened my door, nuzzling snouts and wagging tails besieged me, and I knelt to greet them. I could see the answering machine blinking across the room. Climbing to my feet, I nearly stumbled over my tabby cat, Bella—a sticking point prior to my separation from Jack. We'd found her as a nearly newborn kitten under a parked car on Stanton Street one night years ago—so young that she shook as she walked. In the end Jack gave in—there was a no-pets clause in the lease of his new apartment—and Bella had ridden down here to Atlanta with me, clinging to the back of the seat in the cab of the overly packed U-Haul. I rubbed her far too large belly until she was adequately hypnotized and then reached over and pressed the PLAY button.

"Maddy, I felt a little awkward at work this morning. I didn't mean to just walk into your office like that, but now I do think it's in my rights—not as your boss or whatever you insist on calling me—but as your boyfriend. Who the heck's sending you chocolate?"

I lifted the telephone and dialed Andrew's number as I scooped Bella into my arms. He answered on the first ring.

"Sorry about that—just kind of freaked out or something," I said. "I chased after you. I don't know if you heard me."

Andrew was silent. "So who sent the chocolate? He obviously knows you well."

"My ex-husband—"

"I knew it. You said you weren't in touch anymore."

"I haven't heard from him in three years." Once again it occurred to me how strange that was—after spending almost fifteen years together.

"Then what's going on? What's the urgency? I mean, FedEx?"

"Jack's got a terrible habit of putting the past on a pedestal. He really should see a shrink about it, but he's stubborn. Really, Andrew, I promise you it's nothing to worry about." I laughed a little and tried to change the subject, but a call came in on his other line.

"Hold a minute, would you?" he interrupted me, and then put me on hold. After a long silence, he said, "Hey, Maddy, got to take this. Okay?"

I said nothing.

"Listen—I do have to take this. I'll call you back a little later—sound good?" He hung up.

For a moment, I stood above the telephone, at a loss as to what to do. I considered calling him back, but decided I'd better play it cool. I didn't want to push things. I opened Cynthia's cage and she limped over to my finger and then onto my shoulder. I sat down on my couch, a beautiful down piece from the forties that I had picked up for a song at an estate sale soon after I first moved in.

Three years earlier I was standing on the corner of Prince and Broadway in Soho with Jack, having sealed our agreement to end communication between us. Tears were in our eyes as we kissed one last time, then turned and walked our separate ways. I was late for work and so I rushed for the R train, trying to imagine where my life was headed. Divorce wasn't my idea. I would have done almost anything to make things work out back then. But it was my idea to cut communication. I was just six months shy of my thirty-fifth birthday and harboring a serious dream of

having children and starting a family. I was in no position
to do things halfheartedly.

Within a few days, I signed a sublease for an apartment
on the Upper West Side and gave up the lease to our rent-
stabilized apartment—this in spite of the fact that the rent
had barely risen in twelve years. It was early spring, a good
time for new beginnings—at least I hoped. Over the next
few months I met new friends, dutifully attended parties,
art openings—any sort of gathering of faces. As summer approached I decided to spend some of my savings on travel.
In July I took a bike tour to the Mediterranean, first to
Greece and then to Turkey, and later that same month I
ended up on a raft trip on the Snake River in Idaho. After
returning from Idaho, I purchased an old Volvo station
wagon from a girlfriend. Traveling seemed like the best way
to keep my sanity, and so I began taking trips out of the city
on the weekends. I did meet the occasional man—at the luggage carousel at JFK or a bed-and-breakfast in the Berkshires—
but most of them came to me through friends. Perhaps it
was just too soon after my divorce, or perhaps they were the
wrong men, but I couldn't imagine spending more than one
or two evenings with any single one of them. If my frequent
trips in and out of the city taught me one thing, it was that
leaving New York was a lot easier for me than returning to
it. I had too many memories there, and besides, I'd had a
run-in with Jack that put a new spin on things for me—Jack
had already met a woman he was serious about, serious
enough to hold hands with in public. New York could be a
very small city when you were hoping not to bump into
somebody.

That winter I began researching other cities to settle
down in. I spent a weekend in Montpelier, Vermont, loved
the people but not the weather, another one in Boston, a
pretty city, intellectually stimulating but deceptively provin-

cial. A trip to Taos, New Mexico, was most convincing, and I would have taken the plunge if not for my parents' living on the East Coast. Then I began reading about Atlanta. The more I learned about it, the more I liked it. It's a historical city with culture and plenty of physical beauty, and it's also the home of one of my closest friends, Jennifer Stone. I flew down to spend a week with her and her husband and right away fell in love with the city. Before returning to New York, I borrowed Jennifer's car to go apartment hunting. That's when I spotted a sign in the yard of this rambling old building. Any number of famed literary mansions came to mind—*Absalom, Absalom!* or *Wuthering Heights*. I knocked on the door, and in less than an hour I held a signed lease in my hand. I flew back to New York and began making arrangements for my move.

Life opened up for me as I settled into Atlanta. The Georgian summer came roaring in, but there was plenty of shade on my street and that colorful weedy lawn, and I had the feeling that the Southern pace would make it all seem bearable. I spent the first few months looking for a job in a leisurely manner and living off my savings. By August, though, I was starting to carry a balance on my credit card; my job hunting became a little more real. I began having second thoughts about my move. Then, in late September, I saw the ad in the *Atlanta Journal-Constitution* classifieds for a graphic designer at Barnes Advertising. I called and made an appointment for an interview.

Barnes Advertising occupies the top two floors of one of those corporate tombstones in the downtown district with darkly tinted windows. It's a lobbyless building, no doormen, no fake potted plants in the corner or even a place to wipe your feet before stepping from the underground parking lot into the elevator. I arrived for my first interview at eight-thirty in the morning feeling optimistic, despite the handful of other women filling out applications in the lobby. By noon, after a grueling round of job interviews, I was shaken. The interviewers all seemed like corporate guinea pigs, as soulless as the very building they were in. I thought for sure they would notice the vibe I was giving off—*I'm not one of you and never will be.*

Maybe my interviewers were impressed by the fact that I had lived within shouting distance of Madison Avenue for over a decade, but as the day went on, they kept passing me on up the chain of command until I was to meet the man, the headman, Andrew Barnes, founder and CEO of BAA, Barnes Advertising of Atlanta.

It was four in the afternoon by the time I was shown to Barnes's secretary, Ms. Lavender. She seemed surprised by my arrival, and then unsettled and then downright unnerved by it. Mr. Barnes was *very, very busy,* she said, as if I were foisting myself upon his fragile back, but he would be with me shortly; then she showed me into his office. I was sure by that look on her face that my makeup was starting to wilt, and so I tried to correct that in the reflection of one of the framed prints on the wall.

I had somehow expected the CEO to be an old white-haired man who'd built the company from scratch over a fifty-year period, but instead a man no more than three years older than I appeared. He was tall and moved agilely, like a basketball player, and I knew in a flash that he was eligible. I was also sure he wasn't my type—he was wearing some sort of cologne, not a terribly offensive one but a cologne just the same. His conservative suit told me that he had the ability to make people feel uncomfortable when he wanted to. He shook my hand too firmly, apparently forgetting that I was a woman. Then he looked me up and down, as if he were taking notes about my appearance. Finally he sat down across from me, opened my folder, and began to

read my résumé. I studied him. He looked a little like the
actor Peter Gallagher, though taller and a bit more handsome. He started nodding his head. I had no idea what could
be on his mind.

"Let's see, disillusioned art student with an advanced
degree, making good with the one marketable skill she
learned in college—PhotoShop."

"That's me," I said. I couldn't tell if he was trying to be
intimidating or funny, but at least he was insightful.

"Your letters of rec are pretty good." He still hadn't
looked at me, and I was starting to wonder if he was actually afraid of letting our eyes meet. I pushed my long,
straight brown hair behind my ears. "Thing is, Ms. Green,
you haven't really worked for a large company before. All I
see are small outfits—you don't happen to have a case of
corporate resentment, do you?"

"I've had every other type of resentment, but I don't
know if I've—"

"Other kinds, like what?"

"Oh, you name it. Male resentment, female resentment . . . umm, big-car resentment—I have a small car, you
see, and I think SUVs should be banned. They're dirty—
there are no air-pollution standards for them, they're dangerous to other drivers, let alone their occupants, and most
of all they're aesthetically abhorrent." I tried to laugh but
Andrew barely smiled, and I wondered how on earth I had
done the one thing you're never supposed to do in job interviews: complain. I was also quite sure he drove an SUV
himself.

There was a long pause as he continued to study my résumé. I was sure I'd sealed my fate.

"Tomorrow at nine," he said. "How does that sound?"

"Tomorrow? Yes, that would be fine."

He stood up, still without meeting my eyes, and he

blurted out my salary as if it were set in stone. I was never good at asking for more, but I think I must have known something in some deep, unconscious way. I named a much higher figure. He acquiesced without hesitation.

I saw plenty of Ms. Lavender for the next six months—she took it upon herself to manage the coffee station in a ruthlessly stripped-down, dictatorial fashion, complete with rationing and sudden inexplicable curfews—but not much of Andrew.

Then one morning Ms. Lavender showed up at the entrance to my cubicle with a handwritten note between the clutches of her magenta fingernails. She let the note fall to my desk, turned around, and left.

Green,

  We need to lunch today to discuss overall job performance.

                                                            Barnes

I knew that he lunched with his employees on occasion, and yet I was surprised that his invitation was so impersonal. A postscript noted that he was out of the office for the morning but would meet me at the restaurant.

I read the note over several times. I was pretty sure I was doing a good job, but I was still a bit unhinged.

I found him already at the table, studying the menu, a glass of beer next to his napkin. He smiled at me briefly and then went back to reading. After we both finished looking at our menus, he finally allowed our eyes to meet. It was the first time he'd ever looked into my eyes, and I was still curious whether he'd summoned me here to mete out some sort of punishment.

"I wanted to tell you, for a disillusioned art student,

you're doing a fabulous job. I also wanted you to know that you're now head of the art department."

I laughed a little—people often mistake me for being younger than I am. I have a narrow face and large eyes and fine, light brown hair that I push behind my large ears, and I think it's the combination of these four things, large ears notwithstanding, that makes me look deceptively younger. "How do you know that a disillusioned art student would want to be head of anything?"

"Your next paycheck will convince you."

"Aren't you supposed to ask me if I want that position?"

"All right, do you want to be head of the art department?"

"Yes," I said. "And thank you." I ordered a root beer from our waiter—and Andrew drank his beer.

"So now that you're part of management, tell me about yourself," he said.

"You already know most everything about me," I said, feeling suddenly confident. "How about you?"

He seemed taken aback that I had turned the tables on him. "Let's see . . ." He thought for a while. Then he turned and looked directly at me once again. "Do you want to know what I can't stand about advertising?"

"Sure," I said and smiled.

"I can't stand it when the people who do it claim it's an art, because it's not. It's just a matter of creating illusions that deceive people into buying products."

"Isn't all art about illusions?" I said, playing devil's advocate, though I agreed with him wholeheartedly.

"Yes, but only to get at some kind of truth. The last thing in the world an advertisement cares about is truth. Advertising is far more concerned with deception—which is nothing more than a euphemism for lying. Believe me, I've been at it for almost fifteen years." Suddenly he soft-

ened his tone of voice. "There now, I've said it, and please
don't go running back to work telling everybody that I think
what we do is phooey."

I smiled.

"But I do like what I do," he went on. "Not so much the
advertising but the managing of people. There are many ad-
vantages to being the boss, you know. Not that I don't make
plenty of stupid mistakes. I hate having to discipline people—
I really do—but I do like helping people."

Though Andrew could be intimidating to his employees, he was also fair and quite generous. One had to really
try to get fired by him.

He began talking about what he liked about some of the
employees.

"And Ms. Lavender?" I asked.

"Lavender's been with me for years," he said. "She's an
incompetent, but I hired her because she told me in our interview that she loves Westerns. She's seen every Western
ever made, I can assure you, and she knows the credits like
the back of her hand. Try her. Ask her who was the sound
man in *Red River*. I've been to her house—she has a life-size
statue of John Wayne in the corner of her living room that
lights up and talks." He smiled. "She's been with me since
the beginning—and she'll most likely bury me."

We ordered lunch, and when he saw me hesitate over
ordering a glass of wine, he encouraged me to order the
most expensive one.

"Now it's your turn," he said.

"Well," I said, thinking. "You weren't entirely on the
mark when you called me a disillusioned artist. I love doing
art—provided it's with kids."

He smiled. "Is that what that mention of the Puppet
Garage was on your résumé?"

I was surprised that he'd remembered or even noticed that—it was tucked away on the last page, under HOBBIES.

Started and ran a not-for-profit art center for children in Brooklyn called the Puppet Garage. Applied for and received state and federal grants. The Puppet Garage became the afternoon hangout for many children who would otherwise have been playing on the street.

"What gave you the idea to do something like that?" he said.

"Well, sometimes you get tired of taking yourself so seriously—especially when there are carbon copies of you everywhere in the city. You know, speckled paint in your hair and jeans. White V-necked T-shirts. A slightly worried look on your face, as if you're grappling with the politics of your next installation or your sixteen-foot canvas. An occasional cigarette just to reassure everybody that your art is more important than your health."

"You did all that?"

"I didn't do the installations, and my canvases were small enough so that people could hang them on their walls if they were so inclined. But I was spending a whole lot of time thinking about myself, and I really got tired of that—has that ever happened to you?"

"God, yes. On a daily basis."

"Well, after I quit, I decided to renovate and paint an old garage on Atlantic Avenue in Brooklyn. I posted a few flyers in the area, but most of the kids showed up on their own. At one point there were about forty regulars in there."

"So you had puppet shows?"

"A few—mainly it was just a place for kids to make things."

He stared at me a moment with his beer in one hand. "I bet your art was a lot more original than you gave yourself credit for."

His cell began ringing. He answered it quietly, mumbled a few yeses, and then slipped it back into his jacket pocket.

"Damn, I hate to cut this short, but I've got to catch a flight," he said, rising. "This was great." He left before I had time to stand up. I walked back to the office thinking about our conversation—not only had I just been promoted, but I also felt I had a rapport with a boss who had so far been remote.

Later that afternoon, after I had settled into work, Ms. Lavender suddenly appeared at my cubicle and signaled me to follow with one of her magenta nails. She did not seem the slightest bit pleased with wherever she was taking me. She walked down the hall and opened a door—it was an empty office with a great view of the city.

A few days later Andrew came into my new office with a personal project that he said he would pay for out of his own pocket. It was to design invitations for a fund-raiser that he was throwing at his house for the Big Brothers program of Atlanta. He asked me if I could do it after hours, and I agreed to it. After the invitations were designed and printed up, he handed one to me and told me he'd be delighted if I could come, but that he would certainly understand if I didn't. "You might get a kick out of the kids," he said. "You can also witness one of my few talents: bamboozling people into donating money."

On a Saturday afternoon I followed directions to a suburban neighborhood across town. Most of the houses along Andrew's street were brand-new colonials, far too new and grand for my taste. I had the feeling that his house would be even more of the same, so I was pleasantly surprised when I found his number posted on a tree. There was an old, lichen-covered stone wall and a gravel driveway leading up a slight grade to a two-story house, a Cape. I've always been fond of Capes; I grew up in one. This one was particularly beautiful. It had been renovated and expanded with large, multipaned windows and a spacious annex with skylights and a long stone terrace. The landscaping and gardens gave it a Japanese feel.

After I parked under a carport of lattices covered with magnolias, a high school boy took the keys from me, and I followed the sound of rock music to the backyard. There was a moonwalk back here, and several picnic tables covered with hamburgers and pizzas. Andrew was standing in the middle of about thirty children, mostly black and Hispanic, some as young as five or six years old. He wore jeans and a funky Bob Dylan T-shirt. A boy on his shoulders kept messing up his dark hair so that most of it was standing on end. He looked like an entirely different person out here, far more relaxed and more like a friend of mine. The other children were trying to pin something on his rear end—a bumper sticker that said DANGEROUS GAS—STAY BACK FIFTY FEET. All the kids were shouting for his attention; they had a nickname for him, Mr. Cuckoo.

Then he caught sight of me. "Hey, there," he said. "Show some ID and that guy over there will serve you a root beer."

"Very funny—*Mr. Cuckoo*," I said.

"Hey," he said, smiling. "That's strictly confidential."

I smiled and then turned and waited in line for a root beer, wondering if it was a coincidence that he'd mentioned root beer or whether he'd remembered it from our lunch. Then I noticed a table with art supplies on it set up on one of the terraces of the Cape. I looked back over at Andrew. The children were climbing over him as if he were a jungle gym.

Guests began arriving, some of the more prestigious people in town, by the look of them, including some of the press. After shaking himself free Andrew stepped away, threw on a nicer shirt over his T-shirt, and then stumbled into the crowd to play host. Right away he drew me in and began introducing me. "This is my new art director, Maddy Green, one of the reasons our forecast is so good this year."

Andrew seemed to move fluidly from children to adults. At one point in the afternoon I overheard a little scene between him and a tearful six-year-old who had bumped his head in the moonwalk.

"Do you know why they call me Cuckoo?" Andrew said, kneeling next to the boy. "Just this morning I wore my shoes on my head and my hat on my feet, and when I stepped out my door to go to work, I slipped, right over there, landed right on my head, just like you did. Look," he said, and when the boy leaned over to examine the bump on Andrew's head, Andrew grabbed him and tickled him.

It was a cute story, and Andrew returned him to the moonwalk smiling. The rest of the afternoon I found myself watching him whenever he was around children. He really had a knack with them, and he must have had a knack for the adults too—they seemed to be donating far more money than they had anticipated.

At the end of the party I noticed quite a mess scattered about the yard, and I volunteered to stay and help him clean up. He asked me if I would stay for dinner, and soon he was giving me a tour of his house. It turned out he'd designed the layout of the annex with all its windows and skylights and completed the finishing work himself, like the cabinetry and ornamental molding; even his houseplants seemed to complement the landscaping outside. His bookshelves were lined with classics and serious contemporary.

He opened a bottle of wine and then began throwing together the ingredients for a light pasta dish. Over dinner I learned that he had lived in New York for two years back in his early twenties. I also learned that he had been married and divorced. I told him that I was divorced as well.

"Hard feelings?" he asked.

"In a way."

"Everyone has them. And I've been through it twice."

"You must be a pro," I said.

"Oh, right, I've been honing my skills," he said. "Actually it doesn't get any easier the second time."

I was glad that he didn't offer me details about his woes, because I felt no desire to share my own. The conversation went on to other subjects that evening, and I didn't leave his house until close to midnight.

The following Monday at work, I saw on the company calendar that he would be out of the office on business for two weeks. I was relieved; I wasn't sure what it would be like seeing him in the setting of the office after our intimate conversation. I kept remembering the way he was with the children. I've noticed that most men either talk down to boys or become overly serious with them and take it upon themselves to teach them lessons. But I detected nothing patronizing in Andrew. He was a much more attractive prospect than I'd given him credit for at first.

By the end of the week I began to miss him, and yet I also began to feel uneasy. It was as if the better I felt about him, the more certain I was that he didn't feel the same way about me. I spent most of my days in his company under his jurisdiction; perhaps he acted this way with all of his employees; maybe it was all part of his being the boss. Toward the end of the second week, I was sure I had only imagined his attraction to me. Then one afternoon just before he was to return, I opened an e-mail.

Hi, Maddy,
    I know that I'm throwing caution to the wind by
saying this, but I keep thinking of our conversation at
dinner the other night. All right, I'll come out and say
it. I had a great time with you and I'm really looking
forward to seeing you when I get back. Andrew.

I hadn't felt that excited since leaving New York.

Twenty minutes passed and Andrew still hadn't called
me back. The most unsettling thing about it was that I had
the feeling that the call he had taken was unimportant—
only friends had his number. I didn't quite know what to do
with myself. I took Cynthia off my shoulder and put her
back in her cage. Then I took the microwave dinner I'd
brought home out of the freezer. Most of the time I love to
cook, but I had already done this for myself three times that
week. When I took my dinner from the microwave, I turned
on the television and while eating watched a *Seinfeld*
rerun—Kramer was playing ball boy at the U.S. Open.

I was in no mood to laugh. I turned off the set and dialed Andrew. To my surprise the answering machine picked
up. "Hello?" I said. I assumed he was screening his calls.
"Andrew, are you there? Hey, where are you? I thought you
were going to call me back? Did you go out?"

I hung up, a bit baffled. I was planning on apologizing
and inviting him over. Now I was just getting angry. There's
nothing I hate more than game playing—maybe because I'm
not good at it. If you feel something, out with it, get it over
with. No time for the high school runaround, the hard-to-get
thing. If I learned one thing from almost ten years of marriage, it's that everything destructive about love comes from
lies of one kind or another. Even the very small, innocent-
looking white lies take their erosive toll. Everything in love
is about trust.

Another half hour passed, and I was doubly unsettled. I picked up the phone and dialed his number again.

"Hi, it's me again," I said on the tape. "Listen, barring something terrible, it's just not cool saying you'll call right back and then not. Call me when you get in." I hung up and stood there next to my dining room table with my arms crossed.

I could see Jack's package on the other side of the table; the spine of the *Alice in Wonderland* book was sticking out. I flipped it open and my eyes landed on the second paragraph:

> *So I was considering in my own mind (as well as I could, for the hot day made me feel very sleepy and stupid) whether the pleasure of making a daisy chain would be worth the trouble of getting up and picking the daisies, when suddenly a white rabbit with pink eyes ran close by me.*

I knew exactly why Jack had included this book. At the time of our separation, we nearly bought a run-down old house perched on a hill in upstate New York. It was a fabulous place, a grand edifice as impractical as a clipper ship in a pond, but affordable because the previous owners—two sisters, we were told—had turned some of the rooms into a warren for rabbits, white rabbits to be exact, and nobody bothered cleaning up after them. When a real estate agent gave us a tour of the place, we noticed that the eccentric owners had left behind ragged copies of *Alice in Wonderland* on almost every other shelf. In the margins of one of these copies, I discovered the diary of one of the sisters, Maggie Comane. I learned that the two women were not sisters at all, but lovers who had fallen passionately in love when they were young. Then one of the lovers, Gwen, died and was buried on the property. Only months after this burial, Maggie began losing her already tenuous hold on reality. Three times she attempted suicide, and each time she was revived and saved. It was Maggie who set the rabbits free in the house eventually, and it was she who abandoned them when she set out on a journey—a kind of inner quest to find meaning in life without her lover. I found her life fascinating. She was crazy in many ways, but as imaginative as any of the well-known artists I admired at the time. I'd often wondered whether Jack and I would still be together had our offer on the house been accepted.

The telephone rang and I was on it immediately, sure that it was Andrew. But it was Jennifer. She asked me what was new, and I began telling her about my day as if it were uneventful—not a mention of Jack. I loved her; she was my oldest friend. Talking to a best friend, I've noticed, is nearly synonymous with complaining. If you can't really moan about your troubles to her, then she's simply not a best friend. That said, a tension had crept up between Jenny and me two years ago when I moved down here. I confided in her that I still had a secret yearning for Jack, and she told me that wasn't cool. Thereafter there was a subtle shift in our relationship; I continued complaining to her, but in a strategic manner.

I asked her about Max, her two-and-a-half-year-old, and about her mother-in-law, with whom she was in perpetual battle. I was always the good listener for her, even though I envied her situation as a mom.

"So did he propose?" she said suddenly, referring to Andrew.

"Jenny, give me a break. We hardly know each other yet."

"He knows your situation," she said. "Your situation" was Jennifer's euphemism for my age—I was pretty sure she was counting off the months just like I was.

"That's none of his business, at least at the moment." Sometimes I wanted to tell her that it was none of hers either. I knew she meant well, but she sometimes crossed the line, like the time she'd said that I was boxed into a corner. I'd exploded at her.

"If he doesn't soon, he's going to have to answer to the toe of my Prada."

"He's not even answering his own phone at the moment. He's probably got other prospects."

"Oh, Maddy, that man would lie down in busy traffic for you if you asked him to."

After hanging up, I cleared off the table. It was true that there were plenty of other women who would go out with Andrew at the drop of a hat. I wondered if he wasn't on his way to see one of them right now. I tried not to think about that, then realized I was staring at the contents of Jack's package on the table. One of the photographs was sticking out under the *Alice in Wonderland* book. I reached over and picked it up.

This one was taken just after we met on the campus of Oberlin. I was standing with my back to the camera on a flat quarry rock at the edge of a lake, my hands in the back pockets of my jeans. As I stared at the picture, I recalled the details of that day—I'd ridden to the lake on the handlebars of Jack's bike—and I knew exactly how I was feeling the very moment the picture was snapped—a lightness in my chest, a floating feeling. I was breathing fast, not from physical exertion; it was simply the feeling of being in love for the first time in my life. Turning the picture over, I saw Jack's scraggly handwriting: *Cricket—Oberlin, Ohio.*

Chapter Three

I arrived at Oberlin my freshman year accompanied by my parents in the front seat of our Ford station wagon. The car was packed floor to ceiling with duffel bags, suitcases, and cardboard boxes, and there were two trunks strapped to the roof. Even then I was incapable of leaving things behind. I'd brought a sweater and two hats' worth of hand-dyed merino yarn, an old-fashioned Brownie camera, half a dozen framed antique sepia portraits of women from the Roaring Twenties, and my prize find—a bicycle with balloon tires and chrome fenders. Most of the clothing was thrift-store finds that I'd altered with my cumbersome old Singer sewing machine to fit my thin frame; the sewing machine was also in the car. My favorite item was an old suede jacket with a silk lining that I'd taken from another jacket. It may have been the smell of new clothes or the mere fact that the colors hadn't seen the sun, but I simply did not want to own anything unless it had already been around the block. School rules had required me to leave my Westie, Mack, behind. I'd called and fought with the administration about that, had even considered deferring, but in the end I knew I could not stand another year in such a cloistered home as ours.

After unloading the station wagon and meeting my roommate, my parents took me out to lunch to bid me farewell. I can still remember all the nervous anticipation of that meal: Freedom was just a few bites away. Before departing, my mother embraced me warmly and told me that she sincerely hoped that I'd "find happiness here." She didn't mention the word *boy,* but I knew that was exactly what was on her mind. Despite our close relationship, I'd done nothing to allay her anxiety about my lack of dates in high school. Her greatest fear was that I might be gay, and I just couldn't bring myself to comfort her about that. The truth was, quite a number of boys asked me out, but never the ones I was interested in.

I'm an only child. My father is a career officer for Travelers Life & Annuity in Hartford, and my mother is so involved in volunteer work in our town that she rarely strays beyond the malls in Farmington. There's nothing terribly exciting about their relationship except the fact that they actually do love each other. My overserious, taciturn father once admitted to me that he was born without a creative bone in his body. His one redeeming feature, at least in my eyes, was that he seemed perpetually amused by my mother. He thought of her as funky, merely because she once painted our living room an unusual shade of green—sea foam, I think it was.

While I was growing up, we had our routines as a family. On Saturday afternoons my father and I would watch old movies. Spencer Tracy, Katharine Hepburn, and Jimmy Stewart—other than my mother, these were the only people who could truly animate him. At age nine, I knew practically every Hollywood star and director of the thirties and forties. On Sundays we attended Mass together, and then later the IHOP just outside of town. I enjoyed our little rituals right through high school—even after I began questioning our priest and the whole notion of the Church. The only bone I had to pick with my parents was that our house was far too neat and quiet, but I figured out ways around that. By the time high school rolled around, I was into baby-sitting and child care the way most kids are into video games. I was famous in my neighborhood for converting half of our garage into a small arts center for kids, not unlike what I did in Brooklyn years later. A dozen six-foot-tall papier-mâché masks bedecked the carport. There were art tables set up against the walls with piles of construction paper, fabric, boxes of half-used craypas. I owned a vast collection of children's books and wooden toys that I'd found at the Salvation Army or at garage sales. On weekends, my overalls were always covered with paint and glue and scraps of yarn, and so were the children who came wandering in and out of the place.

At Oberlin my habits barely changed. I took a part-time job in a day-care center and ended up baby-sitting for my teachers on the weekends. It wasn't until two months into that first semester that I kind of woke up to the fact that once again I had avoided meeting boys. I also happened to be rooming with one of the more socially active girls on campus. By fall break, Jennifer had already acquired and broken up with two boyfriends and was working on a third. I was starting to wonder where the heck I'd gone wrong.

Then one day late in the fall, I was on my way out of class when a boy in a wrinkled tweed jacket glided up to the science building, hopped off his bicycle, and let it coast into the grass without even turning around to see where it fell. I stared at his bike in the grass—it had chrome fenders and balloon tires like mine. Everywhere I turned after that I saw him. At school dances I saw him onstage in a rock band, though he couldn't sing or play an instrument; he just jumped around a bit and banged on a tambourine. He had wavy black hair that he kept pushing behind his ears. He seemed more confident around groups of people than anyone I'd ever seen. While taking a walk on a Sunday morning, I looked up to see him sitting on a musty old couch on the porch of a funky off-campus house with six other boys. They were leaning back, tipping the couch on its back legs. Strewn across the yard were all the signs of a raucous party the night before, including a keg of beer in the shrubs. I wondered how on earth he'd made so many friends so quickly; he and his companions seemed like they had known each other since kindergarten, though he was a freshman like me. His name, which everyone seemed to know, was Jack Martin.

As far as I could tell, the only place on campus Jack never put in an appearance was the library. Not until one evening before midterms when I saw him stroll in looking a little flustered—as if he were unfamiliar with the setting. He dropped his books on the other end of the long table, unwrapped a stick of gum, and began to chew loudly as he read. The smell of cinnamon filled the library. Jack was one of those guys whose presence is constantly felt no matter where he ends up. He kept rustling around in his seat as if this were the first time in his life he'd been made to study and everybody in the school should know about it. I could not keep my eyes off him. Close up, he was handsome in an unconventional way—bushy black Middle Eastern eyebrows set off by ivory skin and the kind of attentive eyes that made him seem a bit wiser than most. He kept tossing his unkempt hair out of his eyes between cracks of his gum. Gazing at him, I tried to put myself in his shoes. He didn't seem to care at all about how he looked or what he wore, yet every stitch of clothing, from his faded T-shirts to his black Converses, seemed the height of fashion.

He suddenly looked up. Our eyes met and locked, and I did everything in my power to turn away. He had caught me in the act of staring.

By the time I did look back to my page, it was too late. I tried to appear to be deeply concentrating, but I could feel myself being examined. Out of the corner of my eye I saw him get up and walk around the table until he was only a few feet away from me.

"Excuse me. I was wondering if we know each other," he said.

It was a strange question to be asking. He knew very well that we didn't know each other. I shook my head a little too hard.

"Then may I ask you a question?"

I nodded and kept my eyes down on my book.

"Why are you always staring at me?"

Blood rushed to my face. "I'm not. I was just looking at that portrait behind you."

"That's a landscape, not a portrait."

Slowly I let my eyes rise. The painting of a muddy, steamy Lorraine County dairy farm did not even closely resemble a portrait. Our eyes met again, and this time he was smiling in an almost naughty way.

"I'm sorry. I thought it was a portrait," I said.

He continued to stare at me confidently and I continued to blush. "I think—though I could be wrong—but I think you're going to fail art history."

"I'm not taking art history," I said. I was too embarrassed to realize that he was trying to be funny.

"Now what do you say we get a beer at Scruffy Murph's? This library scene stinks."

"I've got a fifteen-page paper due in two days—American lit. It's a prerequisite."

"Okay, sure, *prerequisite*. But if you do change your mind—and I highly recommend you do, *considering*"—and he raised his eyebrows—"we'll be there until nine." He exited the library, leaving his pile of books on the table.

My fingers were trembling as I picked up my pen. To say that I'd made a total jerk of myself seemed an understatement. I immediately tried to bury myself in an essay on the presence of katydids in Faulkner's descriptive passages. Several months earlier I had noticed a profusion of these insects in *As I Lay Dying* and *Absalom, Absalom!* and mentioned it to my teacher in conference. "Maddy, that's brilliant," my teacher exclaimed excitedly, as if I'd discovered a new continent. "That's your paper topic. And remember, a *genius* such as William Faulkner includes everything for a reason—even bugs." If I had perfected one thing back then, it was pleasing teachers. I didn't know who I hated more—my teacher for getting so excited about these bugs or myself for pointing them out to him.

I kept thinking about what Jack said before departing, "considering," and then the raising of the eyebrows. To this day I'm particularly sensitive to rolling eyes and raised eyebrows. Considering what? Had he invited me out to make fun of me? If I was sure of anything, it was that I wasn't his type and never would be. I didn't smoke, didn't wear berets, wore a bra under anything lighter than one of those Peruvian sweaters (and still do), and I was terrified of even the most remote possibility of a minus sign to the right of an A.

I kept reading, or tried to, but Jack's pile of books scattered on the other side of the table haunted me like a lonely dream. Then I did what I felt was one of the braver things

I'd ever done in my life—dropped my pen, closed the volumes of critical essays on Faulkner, and ran out of the library to my dorm. I threw on a cotton blouse with soft, worn threads, a hand-embroidered vest that I'd picked up at a tag sale in town, and then a pair of jeans that I'd kept alive with patches for years. Slipping on my favorite suede jacket, I dashed across the campus square to town.

Scruffy Murph's was a bar that I always believed to be a hangout for town drunks. At all hours of the day, the reek of stale beer and greasy fries threatened to sweep you inside. Behind the dirty windows, the first two letters of the neon Reingold sign were out so that the sign perpetually read INGOLD. I opened the big wooden door and peered through the smoky room. Old men with crooked necks, swollen Adam's apples, and Uriah Heep–like postures were craned over the bar under a blaring television. I decided that if murderers and thieves hung out anywhere in Oberlin, Ohio, this dingy hole was surely the place.

Backing toward the door, I was about to leave when I heard boisterous laughter, not the kind that issues from the raspy throats of old men or hardened criminals. Along the walls at the booth tables I noticed students, some of the hippest on campus, apparently having a grand time.

"Maddy, ah, you made it," Jack said, appearing from the darkness to one side. He took my elbow and ushered me over to an empty booth. I was surprised to see him and even more surprised that he knew my name. "Beer? No, wait a minute. That *wasn't* a question." Minutes later he was sliding an ice-coated mug across the table as he sat down opposite me. This gave me just enough time to become even more suspicious about his motives for asking me here.

"How did you know my name?" I said.

"Let's quickly come to an agreement that neither one of us pretends that we don't know the other."

I laughed nervously. "I don't know you. I don't even know your name."

"Inside sources say that you are thinking of dropping your lit classes for studio arts. I'm going to side with the little chorus that says make the move."

"Who told you all this?"

"You're especially partial to Kit Kat bars—some people think you must own stock in the company."

"God, what did you do—hire a private eye?"

"When I like somebody, I check them out—simple as that."

"How do you know you like me?" I was about to get up and walk away. "You don't even know me."

"Those pointed white tennis sneakers you wear say it all. They're cutting-edge."

That was one part of my outfit that I didn't care for. I was convinced he had invited me here to jeer at me. I laughed uncomfortably. "God. I don't want anyone checking me out."

"Sorry," Jack said. He introduced himself and began talking about his life—not in a smug way, since his life seemed to be as much about others as about himself. The effect of it was to calm me down. Jack had taken a year off before college, hitchhiked all over Europe, and worked on a cargo ship that took him back to the States. He told me hilarious anecdotes about all the crazy characters he'd met at sea. The more I listened and laughed, the more taken by him I became, until I suddenly found that I was nervous in a different way than before. I was afraid that he was going to put me on the spot and discover how naïve I really was.

"You're a traveler too, aren't you?" he said.

I put my palms against my temples as if I were working on a difficult math problem. "No. I used to go to summer camp in Maine. . . . It was an"—I couldn't think of what to say—"an outdoor thing."

"An outdoor thing?" He laughed. "I meant *abroad,* but I suppose summer camp *does* count."

"I've always wanted to go to Paris," I said.

"Paris is wonderful." He came to focus the conversation more on me than on himself. "So," he said innocently, "you seem to spend a heck of a lot of time in the library. I see you going in and out of there all the time."

Again, his focus on me made me blush. He had somehow taken me completely off guard. As if aware of this, Jack admitted to me that he had noticed me from the start of the school year when he saw my parents dropping me off, and that he had wondered and asked about me. "Quite honestly," he said, "and I know this is a weird as hell thing to say, but I admire your self-possession."

A slightly startling and yet somehow comforting feeling came over me—that in all the many hours that I had spent alone that fall, somebody was watching me. Then my thoughts took off in another direction.

"My possessions?" I said.

"No." Jack laughed. "Your self-possession."

"Oh." I laughed. "I'm hardly that. I'm in such a funk about what classes to choose, you wouldn't believe it." This, I believed, would put an end to any misconception he might have, and I thought I might as well get it over with right away. "I've been in and out of the registrar's office so many times that the old ladies in there are ready to have me committed to an institution, or at least transferred to another one. I want to take studio art classes."

"And your parents are dead set against it. I'm just guessing now."

"My dad mostly. My mom is interested in other things."

Jack scratched the fuzz on his chin and contemplated what I'd said. "Very interesting," he said. He took a deep breath and suddenly seemed much older and wiser, like a venerable old shrink who'd been down every wrong road himself a few times. And despite the fact that I knew in my heart that he was probably not so wise and that we were both just barely older than children, I was sure his words would deliver me from my morass of self-doubt. "Maddy, there's a simple cliché that people overlook all the time. It's so simple and repeated so often that people ignore it. Follow your intuitions and your deepest dreams. I can tell you know how to do that—I could tell from the moment you unloaded your things into your dorm. Are you a collector or something?"

"No, I just have a lot of stuff."

"Well, it's not just stuff. You collected it all with your heart, didn't you?" He paused, trying to figure out what he'd just said. "Did you know that there's a whole school of thought that believes that all evil in the world is perpetrated by people who are *afraid* of following their deepest dreams? Think of it. People at the bottom of their hearts are good, but it's their thwarted desires that make them hate and do irrational things to each other. So the real question is what do *you* in your deepest dreams want, not what do they want, your parents, or anybody else for that matter. I'm not just saying that it might be good for you to switch into the arts. It may very well be your *moral obligation*."

At the time this seemed nothing less than profound. I felt clarity about what I should do and I opened up to him. I told him about my crazy obsession with children and babysitting, even though I knew this wasn't exactly attractive to boys my age. Jack seemed to like this and he encouraged me to tell him more. I told him that I was an only child, and that I'd disliked being an only child, and that most of all I'd hated all the silence of our household.

"I feel like I grew up too quickly," I said. "I used to be so jealous of big families that I couldn't even watch sitcoms—

as if all that liveliness represented every other family but mine."

"You know," he said, "I think I grew up a little too fast too. I used to take myself so damn seriously. I think it's the problem of being the oldest of five—it's not all that different from being an only child, you know."

When we walked to my dorm that evening, the square was empty and the shops in the village were closed. It was two a.m., a warm, pleasant night, and I could smell wet bark and rotting leaves. The humidity from a heavy rain the day before was ushering in the rich, muddy smell of the dormant cornfields and the fallow pastures that spread out like a sea around the town. We walked slowly over damp cobblestones and our steps echoed.

"So tell me about these bugs you mentioned."

"*Insects,* not bugs. They demand that title. It's all about respect."

"I only respect the ones that bite me."

"They're found in almost all of Faulkner. I'm trying to figure out why the hell he put them in there—what they mean in context."

Jack thought about this as we walked quietly along. "You would notice something like that, wouldn't you? Well, what did you come up with?"

"Nothing," I said firmly.

"You haven't thought of anything?"

"*Nothing,*" I said, suddenly realizing what I had said. "They mean absolutely *nothing.* I listened to a recording of the bugs and figured out they make a very cool noise. The top-forty all-time greatest hits of bug sounds. Faulkner liked the sound, so he threw them in every once in a while just to remind himself of it."

Jack stopped and stared at me, astonished. I too was astonished at what I was saying.

"That's what they are. No symbolism, nothing profound. Filler. And all they've done is turn me into a miserable wreck for the past two weeks. If I ever come across one I'll squish it, mow it down with Black Flag or DDT or some other godforsaken chemical." I bent down and pretended to spray the pavement. "No katydid shall set foot in this town again!"

Jack thought about this for a minute. "So what does this top-forty all-time greatest hits in bug noises sound like? I mean, could you make the noise for me?"

"God, no."

"Something tells me that you can."

"No way."

"Oh, come on, try it." He stopped and stepped in front of me and smiled at me. I stopped too, and all I could see for that moment was his bright shining face, and his eyes, his bright, beautiful open eyes, inviting me in. It felt like we were the only two people in the world.

"God, I don't know. . . . All right." I closed my eyes, puckered my lips, and blew out.

Jack burst out laughing.

"Don't laugh at me. That's what they sound like."

He kept laughing. "You look a little like a bug when you do that, you know."

"I don't."

"You do. A cricket. I think I'll call you Cricket."

"Don't call me that," I said, walking on ahead of him.

"I won't if you make the noise for me one more time."

"I can't."

"All right, Cricket, do as you please."

I stopped, puckered my lips to make the noise, and then turned around. He was standing right there and I felt his lips press against mine.

*   *   *

We were together so often after that night that all of our friends thought we must have been sleeping together. I felt happy and comfortable around Jack, but for some reason I was sure I would disappoint him if we slept together; he'd see some ridiculously inexperienced side of me that would turn him off of me for good. Sensing my trepidation, he never asked me over to his place or suggested we go to mine. Weeks went by and then a month. We did all the things that lovers do—held hands, went to parties together, but it was like standing at the edge of a cold lake before diving in: The longer I stood there the worse it became. Then one evening after a movie, Jack took my hand without saying a word and led me down a quiet street to the funky old house where I'd seen him sitting on the porch that Sunday morning. We walked through a kitchen, where the refrigerator was shaggy with notices and flyers, to a flight of stairs. His matted futon lay on his bedroom floor, along with most of his other belongings, cotton socks, a wrinkled tie, a deflated football, and a bamboo bong blackened around the bowl. Kneeling down before a phonograph, he placed a needle on a warped record, and as Janis Joplin's passionately sweet and crusty voice began to roll out the lyrics "Sum-mer-time and the living is ea-sy," I decided to make a dash for it. But Jack slipped up behind me and pressed my shoulders gently down until I was seated on his futon. "This isn't going to change a thing. We're just going to sleep next to each other, that's all." I lay down fully dressed and he lay next to me with his arms around me and held me all that night.

I can remember that time as a fragrance more than anything else, something that's both old and new, like skin and dust and beach towels drying in the sun. Before the summer we parted briefly to go to our respective homes. After a week at my house in Connecticut, I gathered up my beach clothes and then met up with Jack and drove to Martha's

Vineyard, where we rented a funky cottage behind a bakery in West Tisbury. Our landlord was an eighty-nine-year-old farmer who once knocked on our door at one in the morning to tell us that he could see two moons in the sky. I was a bit annoyed at being awoken at this hour, but Jack merely put on his bathrobe and stood outside in the wet field behind our house while the old man, who talked loudly because he was going deaf, explained how the moon reproduced by splitting in two, much like an amoeba. "Incredible," I heard Jack say.

For work Jack was a tour guide on one of those crudely painted blue school buses that frighten cyclists off the narrow island roads while the driver barks out the landmarks through tinny speakers—John Belushi's grave, Carly Simon's hideaway, the nude beaches of Gay Head. Meanwhile, I dragged myself out of bed at four every morning to roll dough for croissants in a patisserie in Vineyard Haven. I could not get over what it was like to make dinner with Jack every night, to share the same bed, the same towels, sheets, toothbrushes, to wear his underwear and socks, to not care which was whose and whose was what, and to feel even closer to him.

When we returned to school in the fall, I signed up for studio art classes instead of Chaucer and Shakespeare. I did things I'd never dreamed of before—skinny-dipped at a reservoir with a small crowd of Jack's friends, mostly boys.

We spent the next three summers on the Vineyard, and then after graduating we moved to New York City. I had never even entertained the idea of living in such a vast metropolis—I always considered myself a country person—but it had long been Jack's dream; he still wanted to go into film, so he signed up for night classes at NYU, while I enrolled in the School of Visual Arts and continued painting. Our apartment was on Stanton Street on the Lower East

Side across from the Kettle, a neighborhood bar where we spent many evenings. Jack was a far more social animal than I was. He never tired of meeting new people, and he never limited his friends to people just like himself. He was close to our Armenian superintendent and the Hispanic family who ran the bodega on the corner. He took care of a frail old man in our building, a pack rat who lived among piles of dusty boxes and stacks of magazines, issues of the *Village Voice,* the *New Republic,* and the *Nation* that went back thirty or forty years. Jack called him the oldest living lefty in New York, and he shopped for him, cleaned out his kitchen, and listened to his stories about his life as an activist. It was Jack's magnetism that attracted so many people. He kept in touch with old friends dating back to high school and even grammar school; one had become the local cop in his small town; another was married with a family of four by the time he was in his late twenties. There was never a dull moment in our apartment; people from out of town were always sleeping on our couch and floor and joining us for large dinner parties. Even on quiet weekday nights, somebody would inevitably mention a party in a loft or a band that was playing outside on the street and off we would go. Jack ended up working at the weekly freebie, the *West Side Letter,* and I got a job as a graphic designer.

"I've got it, Maddy. I've got it," he said to me one evening. "I've finally figured out what we are to each other: scrapbooks. When we get older, we're going to be these incredibly detailed scrapbooks for each other. We'll hardly need to say a word, just signal or something and know exactly what the other means. We'll say 'two moons' or 'Scruffy Murph's' and poof! A world will appear before us!" I laughed. " 'Do you take this man to be your lawfully wedded scrapbook?' 'I do.' 'And you, do you take this woman to be your lawfully wedded scrapbook?' "

Four years after moving to the city, we were standing in a field by a lake in upstate New York among hundreds of friends and relatives under a clear blue sky. It was hardly the formal wedding that my parents had in mind, but they seemed happy just the same. A dozen of my relatives and eighty of Jack's attended, and nearly twice as many of our friends. Jack's mother read the vows that we'd written ourselves while my father and mother stood behind me and wept. It was as much a big weekend party as it was a wedding, with people camping out and tents set up along the ridge of the hill above the lake. An R&B band, Johnny Hoy and the Blue Fish, had come all the way from Martha's Vineyard, and there was a beer truck and dancing near a huge bonfire that kept things alive until late into the evening. All of our friends from college and from the city were there. Before the evening was out somebody set off a display of fireworks. The next morning Jack and I drove off in his rusted Fairlane smeared with shaving cream, dragging tin cans, on our way to Nova Scotia. And when the Fairlane broke down that afternoon, we sold it to a gas station mechanic for a dollar and rented a car for the rest of our trip.

Throughout most of our twenties, the intensity of our bond grew even stronger. We made each other laugh constantly. Just the look on his face after not seeing him for a day was often enough to get me going. I could never put my finger on it. There seemed to be a kind of innocent sense of wonder about him, as if he understood nothing about the world except that he loved me. He was famously absent-minded; he was known for locking himself out of our car while it was still running or for leaving big things behind— I don't know how many winter coats he left behind in restaurants. But he always remembered the important things, like the time I came home after a grueling, depressing day in March to a beautiful potted rubber plant that he'd decorated with Kit Kat bars. I loved it most when he would show up unexpectedly at the agency on Eleventh Street where I worked. After my vision was dull from staring at a computer screen, I'd look up and see him coming across the floor to me in his patched jeans and worn brown leather jacket. He always arrived with a gift, something small and often precious. "Here, Cricket," he'd say. "I was just thinking about you."

Holding hands, we'd stroll homeward under the arches of Washington Square, where crowds gathered around the stand-up comics and street musicians, across Bleecker Street with its jazz clubs and repertory cinema and tattoo parlors, to bustling Soho with its glitzy galleries and chic clothing shops. Finally we'd turn east to Orchard Street, where the Old World clothing shops were just pulling down their metal curtains.

For over a decade, this passionate love affair seemed all but indestructible. Jack once called it our own private fairy tale. It wasn't until our early thirties that things finally began to come apart.

I gathered all the contents of the envelope and stuffed them back in, and then I put on my pajamas and sat back down in my chair with a pad and pen.

Dear Jack,

I got your package today. Thank you so much for the pictures. Things are going pretty well here in Georgia. Yes, you did shock me. I too have thought about what it would be like to meet up with you again somewhere, but at the moment I'm not ready for that. I'm still working on my life, if you know what I mean. Not that it wasn't wonderful hearing from you. Right now I

*simply don't know what to say besides that I do miss
you; of course I do. How could I not after our life together? Stay well, and thank you again for the presents.*

Much love,
Maddy

I put it into an envelope, addressed it to him at the *West
Side Letter,* and put it by the door.

After I got ready for bed, I picked up the telephone
again and dialed Andrew's number. This time I hung up the
moment the machine picked up. I couldn't imagine where
he'd gone—and I was actually starting to worry.

Chapter Four

I was hard at work the next morning, toning down the skin of yet another bikini-clad model, when I looked up to see Andrew leaning against the doorjamb, his sports jacket slung over his shoulder with one finger and his famous eyebrows raised ever so slightly. He was one of those rare men whose five-o'clock shadow makes them look handsome rather than homeless.

"Sorry about last night," he said, smirking.

"Where the heck were you? You never called me back," I said, glancing up at him and then back at my screen. I didn't want him to see the rings under my eyes; I lose sleep over the most minor things. "Just for the record, that's really not cool, and unless there's something I don't know about, it's downright rude."

"I really am sorry. I just had to get out of the house. You know, all that stuff on your desk yesterday kind of took me by surprise." I let go of my mouse and looked up at him. He seemed hurt, and I suddenly understood why he hadn't called me back. I might have done the same if I'd come across a similar display of the past on his desk. "You've hardly talked about him, Maddy."

"I didn't know you wanted me to. You never really asked."

"You talked a whole lot more about that guy you met on that bike trip. The herbalist from Russia."

"The herbalist was humorous. He hardly even spoke English. He was an alien—in all senses of the word." I smiled but I could tell he was still thinking about the package. "I took care of things with Jack last night while I was waiting for you to call—wrote him a letter telling him I'm not ready to see him or even talk to him, and I made that clear."

"I don't know if that makes me feel better or worse."

"Well, it should make you feel better."

"Why does he want to see you? He senses something, doesn't he?"

"He's a stubborn fool, that's all. You're not that way, are you?"

Andrew stared at me a moment and then walked away quickly. A few minutes later he leaned into my office. He was smiling.

"All right, I'm ready to play—how about dinner tonight?"

"My place?" I said.

"Sure. I was starting to miss that little circus of yours."

That night my telephone rang two times, once at nine-thirty and once at ten, and each time that it went to the machine, the caller hung up. I was sitting on Andrew's lap watching the last of *Red Rock West,* a thriller about a down-and-out man in a bar who is mistaken for a contract killer and decides to take the job. The film started out with a bang but was ending with an implausible whimper—despite my fondness for Nicolas Cage. Rarely did I receive calls at that time in the evening, let alone hang-ups. I felt in my heart that it was Jack.

At the end of the movie, Andrew and I carried Popeye and Charlie down the stairs for their evening walk; then we came back up and got ready for bed. After sitting down, I took off my shoes and socks and then unbuckled my pants—I was not particularly conscious of what I was doing. Andrew was standing nearby, unbuttoning his shirt and loosening his belt. I noticed something strange then— my fingers were unsteady, my sense of smell heightened, and my skin became prickly and sensitive to the touch, as if I could feel every breath of wind in the room. Suddenly, without thinking, I pulled him on top of me and began kissing him, slipping off his shirt and then his pants. His body was beautiful; he has smooth, olive skin, long limbs, and strong, fine muscles. His hands were strong too. He moaned loudly as I slipped off his underwear and kissed all the way down his chest and over the hair on his belly. Then I lay on top of him, feeling his soft skin against mine, and he held me and slipped inside of me. I was relaxed and aroused and happier to be with him than ever before.

"God, Maddy, I'm crazy about you," he said. I told him I felt the same way about him. We hadn't mentioned the L-word yet, but I thought one of us might be verging on it.

"Don't stop," I whispered, and the night went on into the small hours of the morning.

At seven, while Andrew was shaving, I lay on my back, exhausted and a bit dazed. I was staring through the window at the sunlight that was just then breaking over the roof of the house next door. There were so many birds down here, far more than in New York City, and I could see their silhouettes perched on the crown of the roof against the sky. From down the block I could hear the raucous chattering of children lining up to go inside the elementary school; an occasional shout from a boy or a girl rose above the fray, then several long, rattling bells. Soon it was quiet except for the sound of a teacher yelling at a boy named Ricky or Richard, I couldn't quite tell.

"Now be good, young lady, and don't be late for work or I'll sic Ms. Lavender on you." Andrew stood in the doorway fixing his tie. I threw a pair of my underwear at him.

When I arrived at the office that morning, still aglow from the night, my eyes alighted on another FedEx package on my desk. I walked quickly down the hall to see if Andrew had come in yet. His office was empty, and I remembered he'd said something about a meeting across town, so I returned to my office, closed my door, and opened the package. Beneath bubble wrap and a layer of tissue paper, I uncovered a framed painting, a gouache, and held it up to the light. Slowly I recognized it as my own from years ago, a semiabstract piece, some mix of Mark Rothko and the more playful Paul Klee—I'd never quite let go of that side of myself. The frame and mat made it seem far more polished than I ever remembered my work to be. At the bottom my signature was nearly illegible. I cringed when I recalled how I had purposely altered my signature in order to make people take me more seriously. I had thrown this canvas into a Dumpster on Mercer Street in front of my studio. Jack must have fished it out and kept it without my ever knowing it.

I turned the painting over. Taped to the back a note read:

Dear Maddy,

I found this in my storage unit yesterday and thought I should send it along to you. I wish you believed me back then when I told you how incredible your paintings were. I still wish you hadn't quit.

Love,
Jack

I put the gouache facedown, got up, locked my door, and then came back to my desk. I covered my face with my hands and started to cry. The summer that I had trashed this painting was the same summer that our marriage began to fall apart—and it was uncanny that Jack knew to send this item out of all the things he might have chosen.

At the time I was employed at the small graphic arts company on Eleventh Street and painting during afternoons and evenings. Painting for me was never as easy as writing was for Jack. I liked calling myself an artist—everybody in New York needed an identity—but I hated the scene, and I'm sure it showed on my face at openings and parties, wherever I was supposed to do the civilized chitchat thing to make connections. The *West Side Letter* took up most of Jack's time with late-night deadlines, unpaid bills from printers, complaints from advertisers, and a motley crew of employees that nobody else in the city would have tolerated. Every so often Jack tried to quit, but then a crisis at the paper would draw him back. Half the freakishly eccentric employees would surely get fired if he didn't return. Still, he found time here and there to work like mad on one of his screenplays, and he never seemed to question making it someday—not yet anyway—even after a deluge of harsh rejections.

Shortly after turning thirty, about three years before my relationship with Jack changed, I began suffering from anxiety—more than my fair share of it anyway. All the classic symptoms: insomnia—falling sound asleep at the beginning of the night and then waking three or four hours later; forgetfulness—I kept standing up friends; my sense of humor was at an all-time low. Neither Jack nor I was ever into therapy—it seemed too stereotypically New York. But eventually I decided I didn't have a choice and I answered a flyer on the bulletin board at the School of Visual Arts for a

Dr. Hilary Belheim, a board member of the Institute for Creative Psychotherapy on the Upper West Side.

Dr. Belheim was a large, imposing woman who specialized in helping artists. She was very direct and had the ability to recall the most minute details. I enjoyed our sessions, all the attention rained on me for fifty minutes. She didn't agree with me about everything; she was not a therapist who specializes in head nodding. She challenged me, pointing out inconsistencies in my behavior and encouraging me to think twice about certain things. I liked her approach at first, but gradually she and I went head-to-head on certain issues. She asked what I believed were leading questions that implicated my parents, particularly my mother, and I found myself defending her often. I refused to accept, as Belheim seemed to want me to, that my anxiety was coming from the anger I secretly harbored for her. I loved my mother and felt she was far less judgmental at times than the more educated parents of many of my friends.

"But your tendency is to please certain people in the subtlest ways—and that, in my opinion, came from her," Belheim said to me. "You needed to conform to her wishes."

"I did exactly what I wanted from as far back as I can remember. I made a mess practically everywhere I went in our house, and she didn't care, or at least she didn't do anything about it."

"I think she did care—look at her house now."

"They gave me what I wanted, most of it anyway. I can't imagine I would do much better as a parent. I might do it differently—"

"Differently? How so?"

"Oh, I don't know—Jack and I like chaos. It's half of our bond. And besides, you know, there are aspects of pleasing people that I do enjoy, not with everybody, just with certain people."

"Like who?"

"Him, my husband," I said.

"I don't think anybody wants to merely please another, even a spouse—not unless they're also pleasing themselves on some level. Are you sure you're doing that?"

I thought about this a moment and then mumbled an admission that she might be right.

Later that session, Belheim asked me to describe my happiest moments in order to create a base to work from. I told her about our trip up Mount Lafayette in the snow and about our three summers working on the Vineyard during college.

"And before this relationship—were there any moments?"

"My parents' garage, after I turned it into a place for kids in my neighborhood. I remember walking into it—I felt a kind of rush of satisfaction. I can't even describe it. It was like my real home. I loved the children's imaginations—you know how they live on that border between the real and the imagined?"

Dr. Belheim smiled.

"I'm still so grateful that my parents gave me that space," I said. I smiled, knowing that I was disappointing her.

Around the time of that session, Jack and I decided to take a few days' vacation from the city. It was the dead of winter and we felt the need to see the ocean, so we rented a car, drove up to the Vineyard, and stayed in a guesthouse in West Tisbury. It was a nostalgic trip—long walks on Lucy Vincent Beach, a visit with the old farmer who had rented us the cottage. We ate in the restaurant that I had baked for and then later stood in the back talking to the cook. I started to relax; my insomnia vanished, and I felt lighter and, most of all, closer and even more in love with Jack. We held hands a lot, kissed often, and made love, and I was not as careful as I usually was about protection. I didn't think that much of it—it was the wrong time of the month for something to happen.

But when we returned to the city a few days later, I found myself counting off the days until my period was due, and when I was late by just a few days, my hopes began rising. Then one afternoon at work a few weeks later, I felt differently—my reality seemed to shift ever so slightly. I didn't know if it was psychological; I felt slightly nauseous and full, as if I'd eaten a big lunch even though I'd skipped it. On the way home that evening I bought a pregnancy test and took it in our bathroom before Jack got home. I watched the second pink stripe become brighter and brighter—it was positive. There was another test in the package, so I took that one also just to make sure; then I washed off the two strips and put them in a plastic bag for my scrapbook. I paced back and forth, waiting for Jack to arrive home. I was not used to being afraid of him. I could feel the anxiety mixing with excitement as I wondered what his reaction would be. He and I used to joke constantly about having children. We called them the house apes, which was like our own private code for the future. "We'll move there with the house apes" or "When the house apes grow up, and we retire . . ." It was a given that we would have a family someday, but Jack had also been clear that he wanted to be financially secure before then.

Then I could hear the key in the lock and Jack came in. His cheeks were red with the cold and he held two paper grocery bags in his arms. He put the bags down and then took off his suede jacket and looked through the mail piled on the table while I stood in our bedroom doorway watching him. Unaware of me, he looked through the bills. Then, with that sixth sense, he glanced up at me, registered that I'd been there all along, and then a smile came across his face.

I could feel myself change the moment he laid eyes on me—that's what it was like being in love with him back then; just his gaze was enough to transform me. I was standing there with both hands on the doorjamb about shoulder height. Slowly he walked over to me and stopped, staring at me without a word between us.

"Cricket!" he said, picking me up and swinging me around the room. I had no idea how he knew.

There was no stopping after that; it was as if we had planned this for years. Our excitement only grew—and it remained a secret between us, a precious secret; we told no one, not even our best friends. We bought books on childbirth and child raising, a cradle and baby blankets, a beautiful handmade quilt at a weekend flea market. It was March by then, the drabbest month of the year in New York—buds on the trees but no leaves, cold but no snow, just that chronic gray effluvium that settles over the city for months. But everything came alive for us—every mother, father, and child on the sidewalk caught our eyes. There were happy families everywhere, and we would soon be one of them. At night Jack would come home, drop his bag, and pace around excitedly. He'd get down on his knees and press his head to my stomach, and I'd put my hand in his thick hair.

"Ah, I hear something," he said. "A sound, a little voice, very quiet; now, wait a minute, don't move, hold very still, it's speaking—kitty cat, kitty cat. No, no, wait, wait, what's it saying? It's Kit Kat. What's with you, Mom? Don't you know I like Raisinets?" Usually he'd slip a chocolate bar of some kind into my hand when he said that.

We knew of other couples who had trouble agreeing on a name, but Jack and I seemed perfectly in synch. If it was a boy the name would be Fin, the name of one of Jack's closest friends from grammar school. For a girl we compiled a list of names and then settled on the craziest of them all,

Zuzu. It was my idea; my father once told me he loved that name—it was the name of one of the children in Capra's *It's a Wonderful Life*.

Then one night in early April I woke up to the sensation of water dripping down my legs. I didn't think much of it until I reached under the covers and brought my fingers to my nose. I could smell blood and I began screaming for Jack. He rushed me to St. Vincent's in a taxi. I can remember the look on Jack's face as the doctor explained how miscarriages happen and then without warning he mentioned it was a girl. Jack cried harder than I'd ever heard him cry.

There were no words to describe the devastation that we felt from that night on. All of the things we'd bought for the baby and all the work we'd completed on the apartment were cast in a kind of surreal light. Our apartment was like a funeral parlor; everything reminded us of our loss. I told nobody about it, not even my best friends—I could hardly even think about it, let alone discuss it.

The strangest part about the experience was that we never even spoke about it with each other, and yet it was the most significant thing that had ever happened to us. I tried to get back to normal; I went to my job, saw lots of movies and spent time with friends, but nothing worked. Finally I decided that the best thing to do would be to try again after the three months the doctor had advised us to wait.

When the three months were up I began waiting for Jack to bring it up, but he seemed more interested in his screenwriting than ever before. I was surprised by how timid I was about actually breaking the ice about it. I thought of many ways of approaching it, jokingly, obliquely, or posing it as a direct question. Then one night in bed before turning out the lights, I simply blurted out, "Hey, how about the next house ape?"

Jack rolled over away from me and mumbled something. I didn't hear exactly what he said, but it wasn't the answer I was hoping for.

"Jack, I couldn't hear you," I said.

"I don't know, Maddy. I just don't know if I can deal with that again right away. I mean, you know, it was a big deal."

We stared at each other for a moment. "No kidding," I said.

"Look," he said. "It'll happen again. At the moment, I just want to get somewhere with this script . . ."

I knew then why I'd had such trepidation about bringing up the subject to begin with. It was a sleepless night for me but not for him. Two days later, without mentioning it to him, I returned the cradle to the store where we'd bought it. I even repainted the room where we were planning on keeping the child. I wasn't sure he even noticed. He seemed to become even more remote, lost in his thoughts about his writing—and I became angry with him in a way that I had never been before.

I felt bitter all the time—bitter if I missed a subway, if a taxi cut me off on the crosswalk, if somebody asked me for change at the wrong moment. Everything seemed to boil down to that one feeling, and I hated it and hated myself for feeling it.

A few weeks later I climbed the steep, dusty wooden stairs to my studio on Mercer Street carrying a slide projector under my arm. I set up the projector on a table and pretended I was an art critic.

"This is the period you were imitating Frida Kahlo," I said, pressing the projector button and sinking deeper into despair. "And this was when you were trying to be Paul Klee." My most recent series of drawings were gloomy; I could not believe how far I'd come from the joy I'd felt when

I first started. In a fit I turned and knocked the slide projector off its pedestal. I came to the harsh conclusion that none of it mattered, none of it meant anything. I vowed never to paint again unless it was either with children or for them—I thought about illustrating children's books.

I recounted this incident to Dr. Belheim, but neglected to reveal the most important element, which was that I hadn't mentioned a word of it to Jack. Thoughts about the baby and having children were no longer the only things that we were keeping from each other. For the sake of appearances that month I paid the rent in my studio space, though I went there but twice. Finally I withdrew altogether from paying dues and asked Jack to help me move my canvases into storage. At that time I'd thrown many of them into a Dumpster in front of the building, including the gouache that he'd sent me.

"God, I thought you were . . . you're really giving up your space?" Jack said.

"I'm going to pay off some of our bills."

"It sounds like you're giving up *art* or something. How many times do I have to tell you that it's only a matter of time before—"

"Jack, you don't know enough about the art world to really say that." This sounded harsher than I meant it to. "I mean, how can *you* be objective—we're married."

"And all these art critics are objective? Maddy, would you lighten up? We've been through hell this year already."

"No kidding," I said, and I held my tongue; I had plenty more to tell him.

After finally clearing out my studio, I announced to Dr. Belheim that I was no longer a painter.

"The problem is simple," I said. "I was swept up in a game that I never cared about, not in my heart of hearts. I'm still an artist, but in an entirely different way."

My feelings of bitterness continued—now I had no idea what to do with myself.

A few days later I met a man at a dinner party who told me that he knew of an abandoned garage in Brooklyn, not too far from Atlantic Avenue. He said the owner had offered to rent it to him for a song. The next day I went there, and within an hour of meeting the owner I had the keys. With the help of a few friends, I renovated—soaked up the oil stains on the floor with sawdust and painted the cement block walls bright colors. Then I painted a mural above the metal gate facing the street with colorful letters, *The Puppet Garage,* and put up flyers in hopes of attracting children in need of something like this. Before I knew it, children were trickling in from the nearby neighborhoods, some from as far away as the Fort Greene projects. It was just what I needed to heal my wounds from the spring.

For my first project with the children, we constructed the big masks I'd made in my garage at home; they were six feet tall, a wooden frame wrapped with chicken wire and large strips of papier-mâché—and we kept painting and re-painting them until the layers were thick on their faces. Word got around—a Brooklyn newspaper ran a story on it, and some of the neighborhood businesses pitched in. A restaurant just down the block donated pizzas every Saturday, and a hardware store sent over gallons of paint. I also applied for a number of grants. Meanwhile, on weekday afternoons, I visited thrift shops and tag sales. I was resourceful when it came to finding materials that children could work with. Soon the Garage was filled with sculptures and painted objects, and I had many new friends six years old and up. Even the most hard-core street kids could not hide a little smile on their faces when they entered the Garage, and I too was smiling again, working with my hands as I loved to do. By late in the fall, I thought I was doing pretty well.

But things with Jack did not get better. The night I'd asked him about trying again to have a child kept coming back to haunt me, and I could not seem to get past my anger at him. Finally, around Christmas of that year, we were eating dinner in our apartment when he brought up the fact that a mutual friend of ours was pregnant with her third child. He brought it up incidentally and quickly went on to something else, as if it meant nothing at all.

"I don't know if you realize it," I said to him, dropping my fork to my plate. "But you used to talk all the time about these little things called the house apes. You haven't even mentioned them for how long?"

"I'm really sorry, Maddy. I know how you feel. In fact, I've *known* how you feel, but I don't think we can talk about it much longer. It's just going to get you worked up."

"Oh, like I'm not that already?"

Jack slammed his hand down on the table. "I can't help it that you feel shitty—I feel shitty that you feel shitty. You know that, Maddy. I can't help what happened. I'm not on the same schedule you are right now. I just am not. Don't guilt-trip me about this."

"Like I'm guilt-tripping you, how? By the fact that I've had to start my life without you?"

"Oh, is that what you're doing in Brooklyn?"

"Shut up, you jerk," I yelled, and ran into our bedroom and slammed the door.

Things after that began to change quickly. I spent more time with the children at the Garage and Jack poured most of his energy into scriptwriting. Later in the spring Jack bumped into a friend that he hadn't seen since summer camp, Peter Williams, and the two of them became writing partners. Meanwhile, Peter sold one of his own screenplays for a lot of money—and this fueled Jack's obsession with his writing even more.

In the fall of that year we were spending even less time together; we rarely went out to restaurants, and when we did, it was always with another couple, never as just the two of us. The little gifts that we used to exchange became rarer. We didn't savor returning home after a party and exchanging thoughts about people that we'd met. Compliments about how handsome or beautiful the other looked all but ended, as did the kisses as we departed in the morning and greeted each other at night. One afternoon I realized we had not made love for over three weeks. That seemed like a big deal at first and sent me into a panic, but I did nothing to rectify it, nor did Jack. At one point I looked back over the summer and could not recall the last time we had been intimate.

After drying my eyes, I packed up my belongings at my desk and left a note on the company calendar that I was taking the afternoon off. I had no idea where I was going when I drove out of the parking lot, just that home was not an option. I thought of heading for a Salvation Army, and then suddenly I thought that might remind me of my life with Jack, so I ended up in Nordstrom.

I tried on skirts a hundred dollars or more over my price range, mostly things I'd never before given a second thought to. I stared at myself in dressing room mirrors, backing up, moving forward, turning to the side. I had no idea who I was doing this for. Three hours later I had in my possession two ridiculously pricey skirts, three new bras, a blouse, and a pair of Pradas that I'd been eyeing for months. It was still too early to return home, so I stopped at a dive to cheer myself up—an aluminum trailer with fifties jukeboxes in all of the booths and cigarette-smoking, gum-snapping, no-

nonsense waitresses. I dropped a few quarters in the jukebox and then treated myself to an order of curly fries and a chocolate shake.

I could hear my dogs scrambling against the floor and yelping as I climbed my stairs that evening. As I put my key in my lock, my telephone began ringing. I fumbled with the lock and then nearly fell flat on my face as I clambered over Bella. I thought it would be Jack.

"Hello?" I said.

"Are you okay? Somebody said you weren't feeling well." I was suddenly more relieved than I'd ever been to hear Andrew's voice.

"I'm okay," I said, still out of breath. "I just had an inexplicable need to go shopping. Hey, you wouldn't mind coming over, would you?"

"Like when?"

"Right now."

"Sounds good," he said. "But here's a really stupid joke first—what do you call a nun who gets a sex-change operation?"

"I have no idea."

"Trans-sister."

"That *is* really stupid—now would get your butt over here pronto?"

Chapter Five

Andrew came over that night carrying a bottle of pinot grigio, a quart of mocha chip Häagen-Dazs, and a bouquet of black-eyed Susans. He was still wearing his tie, which I proceeded to unknot as he slipped spoonfuls of ice cream into my mouth. That evening I told him that he was learning all the right moves—and I meant it.

The next evening I invited him over again, and then the night after that, I ended up at his house, along with my dogs. I noticed that I was changing when I was with him. I enjoyed his sense of humor a lot more than I had in the past. I looked forward to his naughty smile and his devilish laugh, which reinforced what he told me about getting kicked out of high school. He teased me often, calling me any one of a list of nicknames, and I told him that he was never going to live down the name the children had given him. Despite carrying the company on his shoulders, he really did have a quirky side, and I began thinking that he was just as creative as my artist friends back in New York.

Doing ridiculous things that neither of us would ever have done on our own was our policy, like our methodical tour of all the miniature golf ranges in the Atlanta area—Andrew's running joke was that I was a miniature golf pro and that he was training to be a miniature golf caddy. "The smaller clubs are much easier to carry around," he'd explain to people. We roller-skated during family night in the suburbs, played bingo at the church on my block, and at a drive-in movie about aliens invading the White House, we made love in the backseat of my station wagon, embarrassing a teenager delivering our dinner. One Saturday we attended a small circus outside the city, and I snapped pictures of Andrew waltzing around the ring with a man in a gorilla suit. Another afternoon I took him to the High Museum to show him the small room of paintings by Paul Klee. Andrew's knowledge of him surprised me. Not only did he understand the subtle relationship between musical theory and space and color that Klee studied, but he was also a fan of another painter I loved—Max Beckman. He even had a small collection of Beckman's art catalogs in his house and professed to own an original sketch of his.

A solid month went by after I'd received Jack's package, and I was beginning to feel like I had things licked. The past was exactly where it belonged.

Then one Saturday morning Andrew picked me up for a drive out into the countryside. He told me to pack a change of clothing in case we ended up back at his house instead of mine. We drove out of Atlanta on the interstate, chatting loudly over the sound of his CD player, when Andrew made a sudden turn for the airport, nearly sideswiping the car next to us. "Forgot to pick something up," he said to me.

The next thing I knew we had driven past the airline terminals and were headed along a smaller road past a sign that said MARQUISE JET CUSTOMERS ONLY. Marquise was the name of the private jets Andrew's company sometimes leased whenever he was trying to impress a client. We came across the hangars and terminal. One of the small jets was already on the runway. Andrew stopped and handed his car keys to a man who appeared to be waiting for us. He then proceeded to lift his bags from the back of his car.

"Come on," he said, and he took my hand. The sound of the jet's engines was deafeningly loud.

"Andrew, what are you doing?"

"I thought you might like to see the world."

"A private jet?" I said. "They get terrible gas mileage."

"Oh, come on, you curmudgeon, you're being offered a ride in a private jet—get over it."

"I'm over it," I said and laughed as he pulled me across the tarmac. The captain smiled at us as Andrew nudged me up the stairs and inside. The interior was smaller than I had imagined these things to be. There were half a dozen lounge chairs and a couch facing each other, like in someone's living room, and a full bar. I sat down in one of the chairs and fastened my seat belt. A few minutes later a woman came on board, a flight attendant. She closed the bar and strapped herself in. Then we were blasting down the runway. Andrew reached over and held my hand.

The jet climbed quickly, my eardrums were popping, and it was far louder than a commercial airplane. I smiled and unfastened my seat belt. Andrew yelled out to me that the ride would be much quieter once we reached elevation. "How does thirty thousand feet sound to you?"

It was a perfect day for flying; there wasn't a cloud in the sky. We circled Atlanta and then headed north.

"Is this what they call a perk?" I said.

"It's called the top of the world," he said, handing me a

drink. Just as I was starting to wonder where we were really going, Andrew said, "How's Martha's Vineyard sound?"

I looked at him. "What do you mean?"

"I've booked a room in Edgartown," he was yelling over the sound.

I stared at him without moving my head, then turned to the window. Of all places on earth to choose to go to—the very epicenter of my past—and I felt caught somehow, unsure what to do, unsure of what it would be like to be on the Vineyard again. I continued staring out the window. I had the feeling that Andrew was looking at me, wondering what was wrong. I was thoroughly shaken, so much so that I wasn't sure I could hide it.

"Andrew," I said, "could we go somewhere else?"

"You're kidding? Why?"

"Lots of reasons," I said. "I'm just not sure I'm so crazy about the Vineyard."

I could tell he was afraid to delve any further into it. He stared at me, and then put his hand on my forehead. "Are you feverish? I thought you loved the place."

I shook my head and tried to smile again, but I was uncomfortable and slightly afraid. Andrew got up and put his head into the cockpit. A moment later he returned.

"The captain knows a great place on the Sea Islands. How's that sound?"

"Thanks."

"Cuts our travel time down. We'll be landing in about twenty-five minutes. He just needs to get the okay."

Soon we reached the ocean, banked, and followed the Georgian coast into North Carolina. The Sea Islands themselves looked like long white fingers sticking out into the water. After landing we taxied over to a small terminal, and then the captain opened the hatch. I was hardly dressed for this; it was windy and cold, and Andrew put his arm around my shoulders to protect me. We crossed the terminal, boarded a taxi, and then drove along a highway between dunes. I sat looking out at the sea grass blowing against the sand. I was glad that we hadn't landed on the Vineyard, but those early years with Jack were still on my mind. It was winter here, and that too reminded me of that time on the Vineyard with Jack when I was pregnant—the winter before everything went to pieces.

Our taxi took us to a huge white Victorian hotel—something akin to the Mt. Washington Hotel in New Hampshire. We climbed the fanning steps and entered a lobby with a striking view of a wide beach and rolling surf with many levels of breaking waves. The interior was a bit drafty, and Andrew gave me his jacket to drape over my shoulders. We checked in and then climbed the wide, carpeted stairs to our room to drop off our luggage.

That afternoon we took a walk along the beach next to the surf that was so high that it felt like walking next to a small mountain of waves. We could hardly talk to each other over the roar and I was glad for that. I wasn't in the mood for conversation. I'd grown sullen in spite of myself. I was thinking of Jack's letters to me and mulling over the mistakes I'd made in the past. In the evening we ate in a dining room with large multipaned windows that reached from floor to ceiling. It was almost empty because of the season. He told me that I seemed distracted, and I told him that I was fine. Later we stepped out on the hotel terrace and I could feel a salty mist in my hair. Clouds had come in, and it started to sprinkle and then pour.

It poured against the windowpanes all night. In the morning we made love and then lay in bed together looking at the drizzle on the glass.

"There's a movie you'd like—*Murmur of the Heart*," Andrew said. "It's French. Louis Malle directed it. Seen it?"

"No."

"It's about a kid who goes on vacation with his mother. He's like eleven or twelve, he's madly in love with her, and he ends up sleeping with her."

"Yikes," I said. "I don't think I'd like that—incest movies are just not my bag."

"This one's different. Honestly, it's the way it's done. It's almost a light comedy, not the least bit depressing, and it's got a certain sensitivity—especially of the way boys really are. I think you'd appreciate it. I'll rent it for you when we get back."

I was put off by this; then suddenly I recalled vaguely that Jack had seen it in one of the revival houses in the city and he had liked it. It was a small thing, this memory, but the fact that Jack had liked it also made me more comfortable with Andrew. I put my hand in his hair and kissed him on the forehead.

We dressed and went down to brunch, where a formal waiter seated us. The dining room was still empty and even lonelier and more desolate than the night before. The sun broke through the clouds briefly, illuminating the misty rain blowing in sheets across the beach, and the brightness in the room fluctuated. I tried to distract myself from this desolate feeling by telling Andrew about my escapades with Penny to estate sales.

"You pull up to some place and see a person's whole life spread out on the lawn. It can be very personal—even touching. It gets your heart beating."

"Isn't that a bit depressing?"

"Oh, no, it's more like the person is alive, right there on the lawn. It's like somebody's soul looking for a new home."

Andrew laughed; he was intrigued by my forays into the world of used goods. I told him about some of the pieces in my apartment. "That hutch of mine? I swear it's possessed."

We chatted on for a while and then we were quiet, watching the misty light outside brighten and then darken. The ghostlike shape of low clouds blew down the beach. Our waiter stood across the room watching us, waiting for us to get up. Suddenly Andrew seemed nervous and distracted. He reached across the table and held my hand.

"Maddy, you know I'm crazy about you." He squeezed.

I nodded my head and mumbled that I felt the same way.

"Are you sure?" he said.

"Of course," I said. I was unsure why his tone had changed.

"I was wondering . . . have you ever thought about, you know . . ." He began stumbling over his words. "I mean, what would you think if we . . . I know you've done it once already and so you probably . . ." Then I realized he was holding something in his hand—a small blue box. He set it on the table near me and opened the lid with his thumb.

It was a ring with a large diamond, probably two or three carats, on a gold band with a four-prong solitaire setting. It was obvious that he'd gotten it at Tiffany's. I was shocked. I laughed a little.

"Are you all right?" he asked.

I lifted it out and fumbled with it. I wasn't sure what I was doing except that I was probably stalling for time. The ring found its way onto my finger and it fit perfectly. I knew he was waiting for my answer as I played with it. When I looked at him, I realized tears were flooding my eyes.

"I made you cry," he said.

"No, no," I said. I thought the tears would go away, but they kept flowing, so I excused myself and went into the bathroom. I was surprised and confused by my own reaction. I was happy—happy that he'd asked me to marry him—but the ring itself was far too flashy for my taste, and it seemed like proof that he didn't know me, not the way Jack had known me.

After drying my eyes with tissues, I gathered myself together and went back to the table, still unsure of my answer. He seemed totally flustered and he kept apologizing. "I jumped the gun, didn't I?" he said.

"No." I took a deep breath and then reached for his hand and squeezed.

"I'm so sorry," he said, and I could tell he meant it.

"Don't be. I'm glad you asked me." I smiled. "I'm not just glad—I'm happy. It took me by surprise, that's all."

I reached over the table and kissed him.

"Do you like it?"

"I love it," I said, though I wasn't telling the truth. "It's beautiful—it's different too." I hardly knew what to say.

That afternoon we boarded the jet again and took off through the showers and sun. I had the ring in my hand, and once we were high above the clouds and the sun was bright in our eyes, I put it on and held my hand out in front of him. I could see how happy it made him feel, and I felt happy too.

"I hope you're okay about this," he said amidst the noise. "I just hope you're okay."

I smiled again and then took his hand and squeezed.

On Sunday evening Andrew left town for four days of meetings in California—he was working out the details for a large order of billboard ads for a soft-drink company. The next few nights I spent alone. I was glad that he was gone, glad to be spending time with my pets and my books. I carried the ring around with me in my pocket, running my fingers over it often. I kept it a secret, still trying to absorb it all, still trying to figure out my real feelings about it. I kept thinking how Jack and I had married after being together for over five years. Though I knew I didn't have that luxury anymore, I'd never imagined it happening this quickly; I'd been feeling truly comfortable with Andrew for only two months at best. The diamond he'd given me was far too large for my taste, too ostentatious, but at least it was put together tastefully. I'd never pictured myself married to a wealthy man—in fact it was just the opposite; the men I liked were the ones who always seemed to just get by. I knew that a therapist might have a field day with that one. The fact was, I felt more on a level with men who had to struggle; maybe I felt they were more vulnerable. Walking into a thrift shop would be different if I were to marry Andrew—the wife of a CEO rummaging through the bargain bin at Goodwill. It was hard to imagine.

On Thursday night I decided to call Jennifer and tell her what had happened.

"Maddy, that's fantastic," she shouted through the phone. "When did this happen?"

"Sunday."

"And you wait until now to tell me? Did you guys talk about a date? Have you thought of what kind of ceremony?"

"It's going to be low-key," I said.

"Maddy, this is a big deal. This is such amazing news!"

"I know," I said. The conversation went on for some time. By the time we were off the phone, Jennifer had asked me so many questions about the details that I was beginning to really picture the occasion.

Later I phoned my parents. My mother answered and I asked that Dad pick up the other line. They too were ecstatic about the news, though they didn't come right out and say it. I'd told my mother about Andrew; she knew I liked him but that I was also still checking things out with him.

She began chattering in a way that she rarely did. She asked me plenty of questions about his parents, his upbringing, his schooling, who were his friends. I was pretty sure she was holding her tongue about the possibility of grandchildren. When I got off the telephone, the wedding was even more of a reality. I felt relieved—as if I'd finally taken care of something that had been hanging over my parents' heads for ages. I was even tempted to phone them back and say to my mother, "Yes, Mom, he does want to have children—he's mentioned it plenty of times."

The next morning, Friday, Andrew walked right in through my office door without knocking, leaned over my desk, and kissed me quickly on the lips. It was the first time he'd done this where somebody might have seen.

"So did you get the contract?" I said.

"Couldn't have gone better," he said. "You look fabulous. Am I going to see you tonight?"

"Of course." I smiled and stared at him and realized he looked great. Just being away from him for a few days made me see him in a fresh light, his black hair, olive skin, and long eyelashes. Now he seemed confident around me in a more personal way, not merely in a business way.

It was a busy day: two deadlines and a department meeting that I was chairing. I was glad that my schedule was full; it made the time go quicker. I was looking forward to seeing Andrew again.

That evening he came over to my place while I was cooking him a welcome-home dinner, a Japanese recipe that I knew he liked. We embraced and kissed and then he paced back and forth in my apartment, telling me the details of his trip to meet the soft-drink executives. They had agreed to nearly twice their initial offer on the contract. He kept coming over to me as I was cooking and kissing the back of my neck.

"I just want you to know, you're a tougher read than my clients," he said. "I'd been thinking of asking you to marry me for about a month now—scared nearly to death of what you'd say. Had it ever crossed your mind?"

"Of course," I said. "I'm just a slowpoke, that's all."

We sat down with chopsticks and drank warm sake and then spent the rest of the evening on the couch, our hands entwined, doing some old-fashioned necking. It was Friday night and we had the weekend together, and I was happier than I'd been in a long time.

By the end of the following week, we had settled some of the details of our wedding—nothing ostentatious, friends and close family. My parents, a half dozen friends. Andrew's friends would be there, his sister, but not his parents, because they didn't talk to each other. "Everything is politics in my family," he said. "The best way to play it is to leave them both out of it, tell them that we eloped. By the way, I've got a great place in mind," he said. We didn't set a date, but it was implied that it would happen sooner rather than later.

The following weekend Andrew drove me to a small French restaurant outside of the city called Olivia's. It was a white Grecian-style building, a former plantation owner's house, located next to a greenish lake with lots of ducks and geese and willow trees. He'd made reservations for an afternoon meal. From the windows I could see park benches and a stone walk leading around the lake under the willow trees. It was a warm, sunny day. The windows of the restaurant were open, the light white curtains billowing in the breeze.

Andrew was wearing a blue short-sleeved shirt that I'd bought him, and he looked relaxed and happy. He'd bought a pair of dark sunglasses during his trip to California. I didn't know what to think of them; they were a bit slick for my taste, but I got used to them as we sat there. After ordering a bottle of wine, Andrew excused himself and got up. A few minutes later he sat back down and took off the sunglasses.

"We've got the place if we want it in three weeks. The owner didn't know how to say no to my offer. You want a Sunday or a Saturday?"

"In three weeks?" I said. I was shocked at how soon that was.

Andrew shrugged his shoulders. "Hey, we can do it in three months if you like."

He put his glasses back on and smiled. I pondered the idea of three weeks—a part of me liked that idea; a part of me wanted to get it over with.

"Well, do you like this place?" he asked.

"Do you?"

"It's you, baby," he said.

"Do you mind if I take a peek around?" I said. I got up and strolled around the place. Andrew knew my taste well; the restaurant was full of delicate touches—some of the paint was peeling on the white exterior, and I liked that. It wasn't perfect, which was good. I kept looking back at Andrew with his dark sunglasses—he looked like an entirely different person with them on. Standing on the terrace I stared out at the lake. I could hear geese and ducks. It was peaceful and beautiful—a great place for a quiet ceremony.

I sat down across from him. "You look sort of Italian in those glasses," I said.

"Ciao, baby," he said, and kissed the tips of his fingers.

"All right, I like it," I said, getting excited at the whole prospect of a wedding. "Three weeks? I mean, people have plans, right? Friends will have to make reservations."

"I'll take care of that," Andrew said.

"Oh?" I said.

"Money simplifies everything, that is, here in America," he said.

"Do you really believe that?"

"I know it. I've been without, Maddy. Life is much simpler with. It eliminates the guesswork. If you want a wedding now—hell, I could charter a jet. Who needs reservations?"

I laughed. "I wasn't thinking of that many people coming. My parents—damn, Andrew, you haven't even met them."

"Well, let's go and meet them."

A week later we landed in Bradley outside Hartford on a commercial airline. Andrew insisted we take a taxi instead of my father picking us up. I didn't quite understand the logic, but I went along with it, and we got in a cab that took us south to Farmington.

When my parents greeted us at the front door, I noticed that both of them were more nervous than I'd seen them in a long time. I was well aware that my getting married was a big deal to them, but their nervousness as they met Andrew, who wore his dark sunglasses into the house, brought it home. I was touched by my father's sudden timidity. He wasted no time taking Andrew's bag and then mine and carrying them upstairs. I didn't have to go upstairs to know that he had put them in separate rooms. Even though I was thirty-seven and divorced, they needed to preserve the illusion that I wouldn't sleep with a boyfriend until I was married. I didn't mind this at all; I even found it a bit comforting.

Andrew and I moved into the living room and sat down on the sofa. The dining room table was already set for dinner— my mother often set it right after lunch whenever we had company over. She offered us something to drink and I said yes and Andrew said no, thank you. Then Andrew did something that took me by surprise: He didn't take his sunglasses off. He was still wearing them even after my father came down from upstairs. I could tell it unnerved my parents, particularly my father, and when I finally reached over to take them off for him, he pulled his head away, then took them off himself. It made me realize that leaving them on was a conscious decision. I didn't know why he'd done this.

Once Andrew's glasses were off, my parents relaxed a little. Andrew cracked a few jokes about Southerners versus New Englanders. "A Southerner will shake your hand warmly and pick your pocket at the same time, if you know what I mean. I'm not like that, am I, Maddy?"

"I don't know, are you?" I said.

"Not at all," he said, and pretended to slip his hand into my back pocket as he talked. Everyone laughed.

As usual, all of the curtains in the house were closed, as was my parents' habit from as far back as I could remember. I got up and opened the drapes in the living room so that Andrew could see our backyard. It was nothing to speak of compared to Andrew's, just a small lot surrounded by a cedar fence so that we couldn't see the neighbors. There were no leaves on the trees yet, and the grass was brown. I'd loved the yard growing up.

"Love the bird feeders, Mrs. Green," Andrew said, standing up.

"They're Ed's," my mother said, referring to my father. My mother had a kind of nervous habit of raising her eyebrows and frowning whenever she met a stranger.

"Are you into ornithology?" Andrew said to my father.

My mother stepped into the kitchen, and I followed her in to help her out with the dinner. I could hear her sighing to herself as she prepared our meal.

"Would you calm down, Mom? He doesn't bite."

She turned and raised her eyebrows at me, as if I'd just made her nervous.

"What's the matter?" I said.

"I think I burned the meat loaf."

"Who cares—just be yourself."

"He's going to think I'm a terrible cook."

"He does lots of things terribly, too, believe me," I said.

"Sorry," she said a little too loudly.

After all the dishes were prepared, I began carrying them out into the dining room. Andrew and my father were already seated at the table. They weren't saying a word to each other. My father was like that—you had to engage him; otherwise he'd sit there as silent as a stone. Jack had always been great at getting him to talk. Sometimes before we'd visit, Jack would look up an old movie and watch it so as to have something to share with him.

My father offered Andrew a beer before the meal began, and Andrew accepted. Toward the end of the meal Andrew went upstairs to use the bathroom. When he came down, we moved into the living room, and my parents went into the kitchen to wash up.

"What's with the bags in separate rooms?" Andrew whispered. "They don't think you're still the Virgin Mary or something, do they?"

"They probably do," I whispered. "It's just one night."

The next morning was uneventful, except that I noticed that neither one of my parents ever really relaxed around us. I wondered what was going through my mother's mind. My dad wanted to drive us to the airport, and Andrew let him, which made me happy. I sat in front next to Dad. For as long as I could remember, he wore a hat, a fedora-style hat that must have reminded him of the movies he loved. There was a certain smell about my dad that I had always imagined came from his hat. I loved his smell.

On the flight back from Bradley, Andrew said nothing about my parents until we were almost ready to land in Atlanta. "So did you like them?" I asked.

"I did," he said, and then looked out the window. He was quiet for a while.

"That doesn't sound too convincing."

"I did like them," he said. "I just wasn't too crazy about the way they live. Like the curtains being closed. Isn't the whole idea of a window to let light in?"

"I'm always going around the house opening them," I said.

"Your dad's very . . . cautious or something. Do you know what I mean?" Andrew said. "What does he do in his free time?"

"He watches a lot of old movies, black-and-white ones." Andrew knew that; he'd seen my dad's basement wallpapered with old movie posters. Andrew looked out the window again and laughed a little.

"What's so funny?" I said.

"I don't know—those old movies, all I can think about is the fact that everybody in them is dead or something."

"Dad's actually pretty cool."

"Well, he's your dad."

"I know, but he's actually a good guy if you get to know him."

"You don't have to defend him. I'm sure he is," he said.

"You're not disappointed, are you?"

"You talked about him as if he's . . . I don't know, some kind of famous mountain climber or adventurer or something."

"I hardly called him that, Andrew. I told you he's set in his ways."

"Well, there you go, we both agree: Your dad's set in his ways."

I realized something then that I had not been aware of in the past: Andrew had a way of twisting words around when he wanted to. I sat next to him without speaking.

After a week had gone by, I'd forgiven Andrew for the way things had gone at my parents' house. Besides, once I was back into my life in Georgia, it didn't seem to matter so much. I was also back into the idea of getting married, and I spent the weekend with Andrew discussing more of the details. Andrew had somehow managed to book a popular band that was usually booked months in advance—he didn't tell me the details of that little feat, but I assumed it had to do with money. We went to a nightclub to hear them play, and I liked their music. Later, backstage, I asked them if they could play some of the songs that my parents liked, and they said they would be happy to. On Sunday, with our wedding less than two weeks away, Andrew took off for another round of meetings with the soft-drink company. I took off from work a day later to spend the day shopping with Jennifer. She'd found a baby-sitter for Max.

All morning Jennifer and I traveled around to dress shops. I wanted something simple, nothing white, something that I could wear again, but beautiful and special nonetheless. After trying on dresses for six hours, I finally found something that I loved—a floor-length strapless dress with folds of organza silk and matching long gloves. I realized that I already had the shoes for this—and a strand of simple pearls from my mom. The dress happened to fit so perfectly that it didn't need to be altered.

Then Jennifer and I headed over to Olivia's, and I showed her the grounds and then took her inside to meet the cook, who let me sample a number of entrées so that I might choose the ones for the ceremony. Finally, exhausted from the day, we sat down to have dinner ourselves.

"You haven't really told me what introducing him to your folks was like," Jennifer said to me.

"It wasn't so great—I don't think he liked them much."

"Well, in-laws . . . it's the fact that people have to get along that makes it so hard to get along—do you know what I mean?"

"I'm past it," I said. I was still imagining the wedding. If the weather was good, we'd hold the ceremony on the terrace. I was picturing the details of the ceremony, the mechanics of it.

It was early evening by the time Jennifer and I got in her car to drive home. We were tired, hardly talking, and I was looking out the passenger window at the houses set back from the road. I was thinking about the honeymoon—Andrew told me that he was working on it and that he wanted to surprise me. I was looking forward to the idea of traveling with him. "Heard a bit of gossip," Jennifer said. "Actually, I heard it a month ago, but I didn't tell you."

I looked at her.

"Jack finally got a Hollywood agent. She's crazy about his screenplay too. She might have sold it by now. She already had interest in it when I heard all this."

"Really?" I said. Jennifer slowed down in front of my building. "That's great." I gathered the box with the dress in it and kept my face turned away.

"Maddy, look at me," Jennifer said as I was getting out of her car. "You're not thinking about him still, are you?"

"Are you kidding?" I said, and tried to smile. "What do you think I am? A sadist?" I held up the box with the dress in it, thanked her again, and closed her door.

As I crossed the lawn to my apartment, I kept thinking how things were working out for Jack after all. Maybe that was what had given him the courage to contact me. I opened my door and put the dress in its box on the table and then sat

down to pet my dogs. I thought I might call Jack to congratu-
late him. It was just an excuse, but it was a good one, considering all that had been sacrificed because of his writing.

I sat down on the couch next to the telephone, dialed his
number, and his answering machine picked up. His voice on
the outgoing message seemed quieter than I remembered it,
more mellow, and most of all lonely. I hung up without leaving a message.

I sat on my old couch looking at the mantelpiece across
the room. Then I realized that Jack's voice on his machine
sounded exactly the way I felt at that moment.

Chapter Six

Two mornings later, nine days before I was to get married, I stepped into my office and shook water off my umbrella. There on my desk were the purple and orange stripes of yet another Federal Express package. I walked over to it cautiously, slipped my jacket over the back of my chair, and picked it up. This one was light. There was no question who it was from, but the timing was peculiar; the overnight package was mailed on Wednesday, the day after my call, and I suddenly wondered if Jack had caller ID. I was sure that it contained something important, even vital, so I stowed it away and didn't open it.

Even later when I got home I merely placed it unopened on the kitchen table. After checking my messages, feeding Cynthia, and walking the dogs, I began to prepare a real dinner, one that required peeling garlic, washing spinach, and opening a half bottle of Chianti. Later at the dining room table, with my wineglass partially empty, Cynthia on my shoulder, and Bella sitting on a chair near me, I finally opened the package.

A brochure for the Caribbean island of St. Marie fell out, and then a JetBlue airline ticket and a reservation confirmation for two single-room cabins.

Dear Maddy,

I probably should have at least called you before asking this, but I didn't, considering your letter. Do you remember that vacation we never took? Tomorrow I'm heading down to this little island—the same place that you mentioned Maggie went to after abandoning the rabbit house. I also know that it's an incredibly beautiful island.

Maddy, I feel ready to let what happened in the past go and to start over, if such a thing is possible. I thought we could at least just go there and see what it's like to be around each other again. It would be my dream come true if you were to meet me there. But only one dream of mine has ever really come true, and that was sharing our lives for all those years. If you do show up, I promise you I will have no expectations and there will be no pressure. If all that's left is a friendship I will take that.

Our flights don't coincide until the airport on St. Ann—from there we'll take a ferry. I'll be looking for you tomorrow afternoon and hoping that you'll be there. If not, I'll understand.

You won't hear from me xxxxx again.

Love,
Jack

I held the letter to the light to try to see what Jack had crossed out before the word *again*. He had blurred it too well, but I was sure that the word *ever* was beneath all the Xs.

Remember that vacation we never took? It was true; we had ever really taken a vacation together—mainly because of our lack of money. Only once did we have savings, which was due to the death of Jack's grandfather; Jack inherited seven thousand dollars. That seemed like a fortune, and we spent one evening after the next dreaming of what to do with it—from a down payment on a cheap apartment to buying a newer car, one that was guaranteed not to break down on the West Side Highway or inside the Lincoln Tunnel. This happened well before I got pregnant, but it occurred to me that it might be a good idea to put it away for starting a family. Jack really wanted to go to Paris. "I'll meet Truffaut and you'll meet Picasso," Jack said.

Jack researched the trip, read Parisian history obsessively. His whole mood lightened and so did mine—I too had wanted to visit Paris for years. Then, a few days before I was to purchase the tickets from a cheap agency in a *Village Voice* ad, I visited our bank and learned that the balance on our account was five thousand dollars short. In a panic I called Jack at work, thinking somebody had surely stolen our checkbook. A few evasive statements later, Jack confessed that he had loaned the money to Michael Boorman, a friend of ours. Michael had been hospitalized for HIV and was about to lose his apartment if he didn't pay six months of back rent. I felt terrible for Michael, but the truth of the matter was that we'd met him in the Kettle and he was a bar friend at best, not so close as to give five thousand dollars to. I slammed the telephone down. I was furious, ready to fight with Jack, scream at him, tell him how I was stuck inside his "Mr. Nice" routine. "Your generosity," I wanted to shout at him, "is a lightly veiled form of narcissism! Your generosity is only to make people admire you—and sometimes, like right now, that's at my expense!"

Jack and I were supposed to meet in the lobby of the

NYU hospital on First Avenue. I waited for him for forty minutes, pacing back and forth between potted plants and slipping in and out of revolving doors. I was so worked up that I could have yelled at anybody—nurse, doctor, or patient—who happened to even walk too close to me.

It was not like Jack to stand me up, so I decided that maybe he had somehow slipped by me. I took the elevator up and peeked into the room. Michael was lying in bed with IV lines in both arms. He caught my eye and I could not back out. He was completely bald, his face had become narrow like an hourglass, and there were stage makeup–like rings around his eyes. I stepped in and said hello. He nodded and said something softly and I realized that he was thanking me for the money. Tears flooded his eyes. He was so beaten down by his disease that it didn't seem possible that his tear ducts were working. I approached him and took his hand. It was then that I understood how much more important this was than a trip to Paris. Veiled narcissism or not, Jack's generosity was both his great weakness and his great strength, and in this instance, it was the latter.

I learned something else too—that no matter how hard Jack tried, no matter how successful he became, he would never allow himself to become rich. He once told me that he was born fifteen years too late. Jack despised all the greed endemic to the eighties and he loved the sixties; most of all he truly believed that one should live one's life as if everybody in the world were a part of one's family. He was a liberal in the truest, most generous and open sense of the word. For everybody else money was a kind of boundary, a way of separating oneself from the rest of the world, but Jack did not seem to care one iota about that boundary except to defy it, and that was both wonderful and terrible at the same time.

*   *   *

The buzzer sounded. I got up from my chair and looked through the window. Andrew's car was idling on the street. I was surprised; I thought he was coming back in the morning, but he must have caught an earlier flight. I skipped down to the vestibule and unlocked the door, and there he stood under the awning holding a large pizza with two chocolate milk shakes balanced on top. In the other hand was another bouquet of black-eyed Susans. "Delivery. You gotta the change for a twenty?"

"Put that stuff down," I said. He did and I threw my arms around him. "Can we go back to your place? Mine's sort of a mess."

"Sure, just bring a bathing suit."

I ran upstairs while Andrew went back to his car to wait for me. I put the flowers in a vase and then shoved Jack's package into a drawer; then I made sure there was food and fresh water down for my pets. I wanted to get out of my place and back to building that wall between the past and myself. No, the eve before this flight would not be a good time to sit around contemplating the possibility of going there to meet him. Jack was right: *Things* had happened between us. Somewhere I'd read that the anger at the end of a relationship is directly proportional to the passion at the beginning of it. There had been anger at the end and there had also been guilt, and if we saw each other again now, there would be tears, bitter tears.

I slipped the engagement ring on my finger and then surveyed the living room. There was nothing in sight, no evidence of what I had been holding in my hand. "Be good, dears," I said as I went out the door. I raced across the lawn and jumped into Andrew's car and we drove across town.

Ten minutes later we entered the front door of his house carrying the pizza; we sat down in the kitchen, and Andrew poured glasses of wine. There were plants and vines everywhere in the kitchen, hanging from the ceiling and on the floor between his appliances. It was amazing how beautiful some of them were, and how carefully Andrew cared for them. After we finished our slices, he put the rest of the pizza away in Tupperware and flattened out the box. "Come here, Mrs. Barnes."

"Mrs. Barnes?" I said. I was stunned that he'd called me that—I blushed.

"Oh, God, Maddy, you take yourself so seriously—I'm just joking. Come here, Ms. Green. I want to show you something." He led me over to three multicolored recycling bins in a closet and placed the folded-up box in the one marked CARDBOARD. "Do you see who's really my boss?" One night I'd told him that it was shameful that his company didn't recycle. A few days later all of the employees received a memo stating that we were recycling everything from paper to the stirrers in the coffee station.

The rain that fell earlier that day let up. It was misty out, a cool sixty degrees. We changed into bathing suits and went out to the edge of the heated pool in our bare feet. Andrew bounced off the board and jackknifed into the water without a splash. I dove in and swam to the bottom, the water pressing against my head and ears. Floating gently to the top, I gasped for air and looked across the glowing surface to him. Swimming was what I needed to do to break those old patterns of thought. He was on the other side, smiling at me. I did the breaststroke over to him, put my hands on his shoulders, and squirted water at him and then kissed him.

That night we made love as passionately as the time after Jack's first package arrived, and then I lay next to him, holding his hand, our naked bodies covered with a slick coating of sweat as we dozed off.

I woke up and looked over at the red numbers of his digital clock. It was 2:14 A.M. I sat up a little and suddenly felt like I might be getting sick, perhaps a stomachache. Then I realized it was not that at all—it was an ache deep inside my chest. It was coming from a dream I'd just had—I was in a foreign airport waiting for Jack, pacing, biting my nails; I'd been waiting for days and I was haggard and exhausted, but all the while I knew in the back of my mind that he would never show.

Now I was so awake that I knew sleep was far off, and I decided that the best thing to do was to get out of bed. Andrew was sleeping soundly. I put on his bathrobe and slipped out of his door. With my hands in his warm robe, I walked through his house, imagining what it would be like to live here as his wife. Standing in the annex, I looked out through the glass doors. The mist had lifted and there was a yellowish half-moon and faint stars. I could see the silver glittering of his pool and the half dozen Japanese maples on the grassy hill that was his backyard. It was so quiet that I could hear his refrigerator go on in the next room. I walked through the kitchen and down the hall, peering into the rooms. I thought of things I might do to each one—most of his curtains would have to go, and I'd lighten up the walls and replace some of the carpets with subtler patterns and colors. I'd feel much better once I made at least part of this house mine. Then I came to his study, with its dark leather swivel chair and wood paneling and large-screen TV built into the wall facing the couch. I thought how glad I was that the television was in here rather than in the living room. The room smelled faintly of cigar smoke. I sat down at his desk and fiddled with his three paperweights and then a letter opener. Suddenly I had an idea; I would do a funny little drawing and leave it for him under the paperweight. Perhaps I would draw Ms. Lavender in a cowboy hat with her hands on her six-shooters and then a little gravestone with

Andrew's name on it in reference to what he had said about her burying him.

I opened the desk drawer, looking for a pen, and found myself staring at a small photograph of a woman in a clear plastic sheath, the kind used for wallets. I picked it up, struck by her appearance—she seemed familiar at first, and then I realized that she was nobody I knew; it was just that she and I looked alike—straight brown shoulder-length hair, a long neck, and large green eyes. We might have been mistaken for sisters. Turning it over, I saw the name on the back, Martha Barnes, and I knew immediately that it was Andrew's second ex-wife. I held the picture closer to the light. I could not believe the similarities between us.

I put the photo back and closed the desk drawer; then I walked quickly back through the house into Andrew's bedroom. I dropped his robe on the dresser and slipped under the covers. Andrew was breathing deeply still. It was dark in the room except for moonlight coming through the venetian blinds. I stared at the patterns on the ceiling, thinking about what I'd just seen. I had never asked him about his marriages because I had been afraid he would start asking me about mine. Martha Barnes looked like she was in her early to mid-thirties. Andrew had never mentioned exactly how long they were married or when they were divorced.

"Trouble sleeping?" Andrew whispered.

I was so startled he was awake that for a moment I was afraid he'd overheard my thoughts.

"I'm always a light sleeper," I said.

"A lot on your mind?" he said.

"Nothing in particular," I said. Then I was silent a moment. "Hey, you know, I was just kind of wondering . . . about New York—what were you doing there?"

"Well," he said, and rolled over onto his back. He lay there looking at the ceiling for quite some time. "I didn't always want to be a businessman. I got an MFA from Columbia—in fiction, writing fiction."

"That's why you were there? You never mentioned you had aspirations like that."

"Well, there you are—I do have another side to me," he said. The last thing I had ever associated him with was pursuing one of the arts. His "nonartist" status made him seem in some strange way exotic, since everyone I knew in New York had at least a closeted fame drive.

"So what happened?" I asked.

"I had some fun, I mean writing stories and everything. But I never seemed to be able to make a dime doing it. Hell, I was in the right program, rubbed elbows with the right people, even started seeing an editor at the *Paris Review* who swore she was going to run one of my stories. First I got frustrated. Then I got pissed off. Then I just up and quit. I decided that getting an MBA was a much better way to make money."

"Did you meet your first wife then—in New York?"

"Around that time," he said. "She was a writer too. We were in the same place, at least mentally, at the time."

"Oh?"

"It's all a game," he said. "Some people think if they just don't play the game, then everything will fall into their laps. But you have to play the game—everyone does."

"What kind of games are you talking about?"

"Well, take the literary establishment, for example. Now there's a game, a system really, with its own set of rules— secret rules, but they're there nonetheless. Idealists think they can break into publishing naïvely, write the greatest stories ever written, and have editors eating out of their hands or some nonsense like that. But the game is rigged. It's as hermetically sealed as the caste system in India. Oh, sure, one or two get through here and there, but they're the chosen ones from the other class or race or whatever, the lottery winners—but most writers need to either be born into the American upper crust or work the perfect PC angle or master what I call the basic system first. I've got nothing in my past that would make me PC, just working-class parents, so I decided to go with the latter."

"The basic system?"

"Ever meet somebody who manages his own money for a living?"

"I don't know, have I? What's it mean?"

"It means your portfolio is large enough so that managing it becomes your actual job."

"You mean you're so rich you don't have to work?"

"Absolutely," he said confidently. "And I wouldn't be the least bit ashamed of it."

I lay there as if I'd been hit by lightning despite the fact that what he had said was the most obvious thing in the world. Andrew did not merely want to get rich; he wanted to *be* rich. And yet somehow I had avoided considering how different that was from what I cared about—and what Jack believed in. Jack's idealism, his naïveté, his refusal to play the game on so many levels was exactly the thing that I loved most about him. And that's what struck me about the packages he had sent. There was no gamesmanship about those—he had laid his heart out on the table, shown his cards and taken a risk. I knew he wouldn't chicken out; he'd fly all the way down there and wait for me in the airport. My flight would come and he'd watch the passengers unload and then he would be crushed.

"Haven't you ever thought you were just afraid of failure?" I said.

"I've thought of a lot of things, but don't you see, Maddy, the myth about the starving writer who finally made it big-time? Never met the fellow."

"Where did you meet your second wife, down here?" I asked.

"Yeah."

"How long ago did that end?"

"Three years."

He was silent for a while. I was trying to figure out why I'd had the impression that it was so much longer ago.

"Andrew?" I said, quietly. "Why do you like me? I mean, what attracted you to me the first time?"

He thought for a moment. "You're beautiful—that's part of it. I'm not going to deny that," he said. "What's the matter? Is the wedding scaring you?"

"No," I said. "I don't frighten easily—but it's a big thing, you know, getting married. It's a really big thing."

"I know it is," he said, changing his tone. "Don't worry about me. I just get on my high horse occasionally." He kissed my cheek, then ran his hand through my hair. "Sorry. Maybe you're right about the writing. Maybe I just chickened out."

Chapter Seven

Early the next morning, we took a swim, showered, and then sat down to a breakfast of waffles and fresh fruit. Andrew told me funny stories about run-ins Ms. Lavender kept having with some of his clients. "She costs me an arm and a leg at times, but she's worth it because she makes me laugh."

"But she only makes *you* laugh," I said.

"That's part of her charm," he said and smiled.

I was starting to feel comfortable with him again. Then we got in his car and he drove me back over to my house so I could walk and feed my animals and then take my own car to work. We sat in his car outside my building for a few minutes before saying good-bye. It was a warm day; a fog was already starting to burn off and it smelled like spring. I could hear the children in the schoolyard nearby.

"You know, I wanted to talk to you about something," I said. "When I was awake last night, I walked around your place and ended up in your study. I opened your desk drawer by accident—I was going to draw you a funny picture—but I found a photograph. It was of Martha." I laughed a little and looked over at him.

He stared at me as if he were at a sudden loss for words. Then he sort of smirked.

"I mean, is that a coincidence?" I said.

"Is what?"

"You know what I mean," I said.

He took a deep breath. "You mean that you guys have a similar look?"

"It's more than that, Andrew."

His hands were on the steering wheel. "You're wondering if that's a coincidence—I mean, that you look alike?" he repeated, as if to play for time. I could tell the question had taken him completely by surprise and he was nervous, tapping the steering wheel with his fingers. Suddenly he turned to face me and he put on that look of his, the one he used to show his authority at work.

"Not at all. Of course it's not a coincidence," he said, raising his voice a little. "I mean, I found her attractive when I first met her, and so I found you attractive too. Makes sense, doesn't it?"

"But you never told me about this."

"Never crossed my mind."

"Come on, it did. You haven't really told me how it ended with her."

"In a mess, that's how it ended," he said. "It got ugly, but I haven't looked back since."

He took a deep breath and looked over at me. I suddenly realized how little I really knew about him.

"Well, what do you think about the fact that we look alike?" I said. "Isn't that sort of disturbing?"

"You're a very different woman."

"That's not the point."

He continued tapping the steering wheel. "All right,

Maddy, what did you want me to do? Not go out with you because you looked like somebody I knew? I mean, I didn't jump all over you the minute I met you, did I?"

"You haven't gotten involved with anybody else since ending it with her, have you?"

"What's this, an interrogation?"

"Just a question."

"I'll take the Fifth."

I stared at him. "I just wish you had told me about her."

He continued holding the steering wheel as if he wanted to drive away. "Well, it was a mistake," he said. "Everybody makes them—haven't you?"

"A few," I said. I opened my door and slid down off the seat so that I was standing. Just before closing the door, I said, "I'll talk to you at work, okay?"

He stared at me and I stared at him for one of those moments that seem longer than they actually are. I wondered what was on his mind, and I'm sure he wondered what was on mine. Then I turned and walked across the lawn to the door of my building. I did not know what to think about what he'd just told me. I just knew that I was shaken. As soon I got inside, I took the ticket out of the drawer and checked the time. The flight left in less than two hours. I put the ticket away again and picked up both dogs and carried them downstairs. Children playing in the schoolyard next door came over to the chain-link fence to pet them. I was thinking about what Andrew had said about life being a game, every bit of it, and I wondered how I fit into that. I thought about what it would be like at our wedding, the guests murmuring about how similar I looked to his ex-wife. Suddenly I remembered the look on Ms. Lavender's face when she first laid eyes on me before the interview—and I had thought my makeup was a mess. No wonder she had hated me. Then I laughed to myself,

thinking what a fool I was for caring about what somebody who had a life-size statue of John Wayne in her living room thought of me. I walked back to my building, put
my two dogs under my arms, and carried them up the stairs
to my apartment.

Cynthia was making a loud racket, so I changed her
water dish and fed her; then I took Jack's packages out of
the drawer and dumped out the contents on the kitchen
table. I was planning on putting everything into one large
package and then putting that into storage somewhere,
someplace that wasn't easily accessible; instead I began examining the contents as if they would offer me some clue
about him or about my life.

I laid out on the table the photograph of the two of us
covered with snow on the top of Mount Lafayette, Jack
holding me in his arms. His curly hair was crested white
and my cheeks were bright red from blushing and the
cold—everything we'd been feeling that day was right on
our faces; I could practically reach out and touch it. I put it
back into the package.

I picked up the photograph of my mother and me on my
summer camp's dock. She was about the same age in the
picture as I was now. I still loved her and still talked to her
on the phone every Sunday after she and my father returned from Mass. The same church was still there, but they
no longer went to the IHOP afterward. If I was glad of one
thing it was that I'd never said an unkind word to either of
them. I put that one away too.

Then I had a third photograph in my hand. I was surprised; it was the first time I'd seen it, and I wasn't even
sure which package it had arrived in. I was about fifteen
years old in the picture, facing the camera; my hair was
parted in the middle—two braids resting on my shoulders. I
was wearing a smock with six or seven children busy at ta-

bles around me. The huge papier-mâché masks were hanging from the walls of my parents' garage. I could see scraps of paper and yarn and wood on the floor. We'd been finger painting and so everyone, myself included, was covered with colors, spots of paint in my hair, on my hands and face. There was a look on my face of utter joy—not unlike the look on my face in the picture of us on Lafayette in the snow. Turning it over I noticed faint writing penciled on the back. It had been erased, leaving behind the indentations of the lead. I brought it up to the light and read:

Dear Maddy,

There's something I've been meaning to tell you since our fateful spring, something that I wish I had been more honest with you about . . .

I stared at it, thinking about this. I wondered when he had written it—recently or sometime after the spring of my miscarriage. There was so much going on in our lives that year that we hadn't shared with each other.

Suddenly I had an idea; it was a crazy idea. I would go to the island and ask him. It was hardly a viable reason to go all the way there to see him; nevertheless, I could go and resolve things with him right there in the airport. Maybe I wouldn't even have to stay overnight. I'd take a return flight that evening and be back with plenty of time for the wedding.

I looked at my watch. To catch my flight I would have to leave right away. I began packing, tossing things into my two carry bags, slipping out of my work clothes.

Then I lost steam and flopped down in my great big antique armchair. Bella jumped on my lap and I stroked her back. It was crazy—I was getting married in eight days.

Here I was traveling across half the hemisphere to ask some-body a question that could be asked on the phone. I took a deep breath and continued petting Bella. I kept thinking how I needed to see clearly—I needed to take responsibility.

Then something small came to mind, ridiculously small, and yet somehow it seemed important, hugely important—Andrew referring to me as Mrs. Barnes the night before. He was just being cute, but Jack had always told me that he loved my name; he never assumed that I would change mine to his. After we were married I made the decision on my own. I picked up the photograph again.

All right, I thought, *I will go, but only to ask this one question.*

I finished packing my bags and then went downstairs and asked Penny if she could take care of my animals for a few days, that I had a flight to catch. I told her I was off to the Caribbean. She was glad to take care of things for me; she'd offered many times before.

I hadn't even thought of how I would handle telling Andrew that I would be gone for the weekend. I picked up the phone and dialed his number at work. Ms. Lavender answered and said he wasn't in yet. I asked her to put me through to his voice mail.

"Andrew—hey, I'm not going to be at work today. I'll be out of town—back either tonight or tomorrow. I just have to straighten some things out. All right, I'll call you as soon as I get back."

I was late, so I drove as quickly as I could to the airport, parking my car in the pricey short-term lot and then running inside and down the corridors. At the gate I studied the monitor and realized my flight was delayed. I bought a mag-azine and then sat down to read.

There was a news program on the television above me and I could see Fifth Avenue in New York. It was raining and windy and everyone on the street looked cold and miserable. A vivid picture came to mind of Jack in a taxi sloshing through the rain on Eastern Parkway, making his way to JFK this minute. It was warm here, and I thought of how different our worlds were now. I looked up at the monitor and saw that my flight was delayed for another ten minutes. I couldn't concentrate very well as I flipped through the magazine. After twenty more minutes my flight was finally called for boarding—the row of seats in the rear; mine were in the middle, so I knew I had a little time. I continued flipping through my magazine as the other passengers gathered at the gate to enter the plane.

Suddenly I felt the presence of somebody sitting right next to me. I looked up.

It was Andrew. He was dressed in his business suit. He had a look on his face, the same one he'd had when he first walked into the room to interview me. He lowered his eyebrows. "Where are you going, Maddy?" he said.

"Andrew," I said, surprised. "What are you doing here?"

"I called your landlady when I got your message. She said you were here." He nodded, as if he'd just caught me in the act of a crime. "I happen to know where you're going, but I thought I should come here and ask you first." Then he stared at me with an intense look in his eyes. He was waiting for an answer, and suddenly he seemed creepy.

"Andrew . . . I know how this is going to sound, but—"

"You're going to see your ex-husband, aren't you?"

"I am—I'm actually just going to ask him something—"

"Going to the Caribbean to ask him?"

"Yes, I know how it sounds. I just need to straighten something out," I said. "And I was going to call you and let you know what I was up to, but I didn't have time. It's hard to explain—but I just need to talk with him face-to-face, not over the phone. You once told me that everyone our age has lots of baggage. Well, I do have a lot, and last night I found something out—you do too. I just thought I should try to get rid of a little of mine."

He continued staring at me intently. "You don't really expect me to believe this cock-and-bull story, do you?"

"It's not bull," I said. "I'm sorry. I know how it must sound to you, but I was planning on talking to you about this. Look, Andrew, if we are going to get married, I need to clear the air."

"Clear the air?" he interrupted.

"You need to too."

"I do? What kind of bullshit are you saying?"

"I'll give you the benefit of the doubt, but you should give it to me too. Just be patient with me. Let me go do this and I'll be back—"

"You'll be back? Give me a fucking break, Maddy. Do you take me for a sucker or something? He calls and you come? What are you, his lapdog?"

"I'm not anybody's lapdog." I was suddenly standing and almost shouting at him.

"You are too."

"I am not—and I am certainly not yours," I shouted. I grabbed my bags and started across the floor.

"You get on that plane and we're finished. Do you understand that? Finished!"

I continued walking. At the door, I gave the woman my ticket and then walked down the ramp, passing the captain and flight attendant as I boarded the plane. The airplane was nearly full; everyone was already settled in their seats. I found my seat number next to a teenage girl reading a magazine. As I fumbled with my bag in the overhead compartment, I could feel a pain in my chest, as if I were being pulled in ten directions at once. I buckled my seat belt and stared out the window. A torn red-and-white wind sock flapped near a stand of pine trees. A jetliner touched down, bounced a little, and puffs of smoke rose from the tires before making the connection. Everything seemed like it was in slow motion. Then I realized there were tears in my eyes.

Chapter Eight

As the plane taxied down the runway, I sank deep into my seat. The young girl sitting next to me closed her magazine as the flight attendant began going through her preflight routine. Then we were cleared for takeoff and I could feel the thrust of the engines as the plane lifted off the ground. Atlanta grew smaller under the wing. I could see the rows of hangars and warehouses and the many cars on the crowded interstate. I knew that Andrew was in one of them. Things had changed between us so quickly that it hardly seemed possible; I still could not believe he had called me a lapdog. We passed through the clouds and came out in bright sunlight. Suddenly I felt totally reckless and foolish. I was thirty-seven years old, in no position to limit my options like this. The plane hit turbulence, my ears kept popping, and then it was smooth again. I glanced over at the girl's magazine. There was a photograph of a young model in a bright yellow spring jacket—at work we were already into the summer season. I tried to think what I should do with the ring that Andrew had given me—

send it in along with my work resignation? *Lapdog* . . . He must have known what that word meant to me. The mere fact that he had used it said more about him than about me.

The plane began banking and I stared out the window at a carpet of white clouds stretching out as far as I could see. The clouds were the exact picture of heaven that I had imagined as a child. I recalled all those early years in church when I had taken every word of our priest literally. Suddenly I had this idea that I should call my mother and tell her what had just happened. It was a crazy idea; I loved her but I never felt the need to fill her in about the details of my life. Still, I thought it might be comforting to hear her voice. A flight attendant leaned over and asked me if I wanted something to drink. I shook my head and then closed my eyes again, still thinking about my mother. Both my parents adored Jack, and Jack loved them too, despite their limitations. He knew that there was nothing outstanding about them—two people who went through life questioning little but trying hard to be good parents—but he had a certain way of bringing out the best in them; every time we visited them Jack reached out to them and charmed them. My father's mood would brighten the minute Jack walked in the door. It was subtle—my father never said anything to me about it—but I knew how much he admired the way Jack was living out his dreams. I can still remember the tears on my father's face at our wedding; the ceremony meant more to him because of who I was marrying, I was sure of it.

After our separation, I immediately went home for the weekend. I suppose it's anybody's instinct to run back to what you know after something like that. On Sunday we went to Mass and my mother held my hand for the entire sermon—as much for her own sake as for mine. She was totally shaken by our decision. All that day I noticed her silently going over her life. I knew what was on her mind—she was blaming it all on herself, wondering where she went wrong raising me. Then, that evening as I lay in bed about to turn out the light, she came into my room and sat on the covers. She was wearing her white bathrobe and she looked very neat and tidy, but I could sense the turmoil that was going on inside of her.

"Maddy," she said quietly. "I've been meaning to ask you something—was it hard on you being an only child? I mean, did it affect you adversely?"

I smiled. I was right about what she was thinking. "Mom, I loved my childhood—you know that." I propped myself up against the headboard. My mother was looking down at her knees. I thought she was going to speak, but she didn't. "Why do you ask?"

"Well, I want you to know that I knew that our household really was too, too . . . I don't know, closed?"

"No, Mom, I loved our life—I still do. I love the fact that you guys still live here. I wish you'd open the curtains more often—but that's about it."

"I think you should know that your father and I did want to have a bigger family—for you, I mean." She drew her breath in steadily and then raised her head and looked me in the eyes. "We tried, but it never quite worked out. Not the way we wanted it to."

I studied her, trying to figure out what she was talking about. I'd always assumed that they had decided against having more children when they realized what cleaning up after me was like; I was always onto a new project and I was not very good at putting things away.

"What didn't work out, Mom?" I said finally. She reached over and held my hand. Suddenly I could see the wrinkles and pain in her face and I knew exactly where that pain came from. I slipped out of the covers and put my arm around her shoulder. "I'm so sorry, Mom," I said. She nodded her head.

I sat there holding her, squeezing her hand. I thought she was about to get up, but she turned to me.

"You know, Maddy, I never saw you two unhappy—not once." She continued looking at me, and I was starting to wonder if she was asking me a question. "But you two must have had your troubles."

"Of course," I said. I tried to smile.

"I never pictured you without kids."

"I never did either." My mother continued to study me, and I knew I would have to say something. "We tried, Mom, once . . . and I guess, as you can see, it didn't work out either."

My mother took a deep breath, and then leaned over the covers to hug me. At first I drew back a bit. I didn't want to go over this territory, considering everything else that was going on in my life—then I realized how much I appreciated being touched by her.

We exchanged some of the details of what had happened to both of us—the child she lost was a boy. I was two years old at the time. "Your father and I . . . well, it was the hardest time in our marriage," she said.

I told her how hard it was on my marriage. Finally she squeezed my leg warmly and told me to have a good night's sleep. At the door she turned to me. "Do you want me to turn off the light?"

"Sure," I said.

She put her hand on the switch, but hesitated. "You know, there's an old saying—nothing is ever really over until it's over. It's a bit of a cliché, but it's true," she said.

"I don't think I should be thinking that way, Mom."

"Well, you two with your big hearts, I don't know . . . I doubt there's much you can't forgive each other for."

She turned out the light and I lay there in the dark, staring at the ceiling. My mind was reeling with everything— my mother's miscarriage, my own, my new life ahead of me, and most of all, what she'd said about our hearts being big. Jack did have a big heart, but I was not sure it was big enough to forgive me for things I had done.

As I stared out the plane window, we were beyond the white surface of clouds and traveling along the coastline. I was thinking about forgiveness again and about Jack and about something that I had never been able to face up to— involving Jack's writing partner, Peter Williams. I began thinking about Peter—I too had become friends with him. Then there was something else, something about him and Andrew that connected, but I wasn't quite sure what that was.

Chapter Nine

Jack and Peter first met when they were assigned to the same cabin in summer camp. They were both fourteen years old with birthdays that happened to be two days apart—Jack was born on the nineteenth of May and Peter was born on the twenty-second. The two boys immediately formed a friendship that was so close that counselors and some of the other campers referred to them jokingly as "the shadows"—it was nearly symbiotic. Two months later the friendship ended as abruptly as it began in a fight—not just an argument, but an actual physical wrestling match. Peter came out of it the loser, with a bloodied lip and two black eyes. It was difficult for me to imagine Jack injuring anybody, let alone a friend, let alone punching somebody in the face, but he once described the match in such vivid detail that I knew it was true. After that summer the two boys lost touch and did not see each other until years later.

I was with Jack when he first bumped into Peter after all those years—in the spring, almost exactly a year after the miscarriage. We were passing a crowded fish market when a tall young man in sunglasses and a leather jacket stepped out between bins of squid and sea bass.

"Jack," he said, taking off his glasses.

I had never seen a picture of Peter, but something about Jack's descriptions of him clued me in that this was him. His light blond hair hung so neatly down the sides of his face that it might have looked feminine had his cheekbones not been so high. He sported a clean, summery, Californian look—the appearance of somebody who has stared at too many blue horizons. Hanging from his fingers in a clear plastic bag was a speckled green eel.

Jack laughed, surprised. "What are you doing here?"

"What am I doing here? What are *you* doing here?"

They were both glued to the spots where they'd just met each other, and they continued to stare.

"Well, you look the same, just about seventeen years older," Jack said.

"Is that how long it's been?"

"What's that?" Jack said, pointing to the eel.

"I've never tried one of these, have you? That guy in there just talked me into it. I bought it because I didn't want to hurt his feelings."

"The guy's or the eel's?"

Peter lifted the bag that was smeared with blood. He seemed suddenly taken aback by what he was carrying around. The eel's mouth was cracked open, its razorlike teeth showing. "Damn, this poor guy's had a bad day, I guess."

Jack and Peter began talking about some of their old friends from summer camp. We were standing among the throngs of Chinatown, and I had to keep stepping out of the way of shoppers and clerks pushing boxes of fish and vegetables on hand trucks. I could smell hot pretzels and roasting chestnuts. Jack seemed to forget about me. Then he stepped aside. "Oh, sorry. Peter, this is my wife, Maddy."

"I've heard about you," I said.

"Nothing true, I hope," Peter said.

Peter made a fist and tapped Jack's arm. "Hey, New York is strange, huh? A lot of fish, and the pond's not exactly what you'd call small."

"I just love it here," Jack said.

"You're one of the few," he said. He seemed rather nervous around Jack, as if he still remembered their fight.

The two men chatted a little longer, just enough to learn that as far apart as they had been in camp, they were now on similar career paths—writing screenplays as a means to directing films. To pay the bills, Peter was a freelance journalist; he'd had some success—a piece he'd written on professional gambling recently ran in *Esquire*. Jack was running the *West Side Letter*. "I'll look you up soon," Peter said and disappeared into the crowd.

"Don't bother," Jack said quietly as soon as he was out of earshot. He took my arm.

"I thought he was sort of nice. He bought the eel to make that guy feel good."

"I thought you'd feel sorrier for the eel," Jack said.

It was strange having finally met the person whom Jack had spoken about so frequently. There had definitely been a kind of energy between the two of them that was difficult to put your finger on. The rest of that day Jack seemed unnerved and even a bit upset.

A week later Peter did call Jack as he promised, and they met in the afternoon at Dean & DeLuca for coffee, and a few days later he showed up at the Kettle and was soon a regular there. It was hard to avoid him, and slowly Peter worked his way into our lives, but not without some dismay on Jack's part. "We're like oil and water," Jack said. "And yet I don't have what it takes to tell him to beat it." I didn't believe him. Jack was gentle but stubborn and perfectly capable of telling somebody to beat it if he wanted to. Maybe he still felt guilty about the fight; whatever it was, he did not tell me.

Meanwhile, at every opportunity, Peter did favors for Jack, introducing him to editors, throwing him extra magazine assignments that he didn't have time for himself, and inviting us to parties, mostly among New York's literati but sometimes to wrap parties for film crews where Jack could make connections. Though most men who knew Peter didn't particularly care for him—perhaps they didn't trust him—I was amused to note how many women like myself found him attractive. It was a combination of his athleticism, his rather serious intellectual demeanor, and a trait that was hard to put your finger on, but could be seen as either shyness or loneliness or both. His shyness was a kind of weapon, and it was impossible to tell whether he was aware of its power.

I made it a point to hide my feelings about him from Jack. "A guy who spends too much time in front of the mirror is a guy with a problem," I said to Jack once. Part of me believed what I was saying. His hair did seem to fall a little too perfectly across one eye, so that he had to shake his head to get it out of the way.

When Jack read Peter's first screenplay, he told me that he hated it—he actually used the word *loathed*—but he also admitted that the story had an edge missing from his own writing. "It's commercial as hell," he said, "but it lacks an 'inner self.' That's because Peter doesn't really have one, despite all his bravura." The remark struck me at the time, and I thought about it often.

In July of that summer an agent took on Peter's first script, the one that Jack had said was without an inner self, and within a week the script went to auction among the studios. At the end of the three-day auction, Peter was sitting on a sum of money that rapidly changed his life. Within a week of the deal, Peter bought a new car, rented a house for the rest of the summer on Martha's Vineyard, and drove up there with his girlfriend, Micha.

Once Peter was out of the city, Jack seemed to understand what had really happened. He didn't admit that he was jealous, but there was no question that it had thrown him off balance. Stuck in the miserably hot and dirty city for the summer with little money, Jack became even more dogged about his work. I felt even more ignored by him.

Around this time, it so happened that two friends of ours backed out of a weekend workshop about relationships and gave us their spots for free. I asked Jack if he would attend. He was reluctant but eventually he agreed. The workshop was led by a well-known marriage counselor and was conducted with eight other couples in an apartment in Tribeca.

Sometime during that weekend, the workshop leader asked everyone to make a list of the traits that originally attracted us to our partners as well as a list of the ones that we now found problematic. Our leader told us that she believed that everyone carries childhood wounds no matter how loving their parents have been, and that people are often unconsciously attracted to others who they believe can heal them. "But unfortunately," the leader said, "after the honeymoon period passes, the qualities in the other that seemed so attractive actually end up reopening the old wounds. We find ourselves angered by the very thing that we loved before. It is not easy to save a marriage when a couple reaches this point—two out of three fail within seven years. Divorce is one of the most traumatic experiences that people go through in this society, so if you're experiencing problems of any sort, it's time to get to work."

As we went around the room, her point was clearly demonstrated in one couple after the next. The qualities that attracted people to each other were the same ones that became troublesome later on.

Then it came to our turn, and Jack went first. "I fell in love with Maddy not only because I was attracted to her physically, but because she seemed to have this incredible quality of self-possession. Back at college I felt like I was floating from one person and one idea to the next and that I needed an anchor, somebody who would ground me. But the thing is," he said, looking at the leader, "I have no complaints about her. I love her as much as I ever did, and I love spending time with her. It's just that I want to be an accomplished scriptwriter. I don't want to be one of these people whose kids know them as someone with tons of regrets." I found it interesting that he was able to say this in front of a group, but not in front of me.

Then the attention of the group was turned on me. "Jack is very gregarious. I'm not." I was nervous. "I remember seeing him around campus. He was so much freer than I ever was. I still remember the night I met him. Merely being around him felt like a kind of release. He seemed capable of talking about any subject in the world. But now I do find some of these things problematic. Not that I don't love it that he knows so many people. I just find myself wanting to be alone with him more. There are things he and I have always wanted that I still want. I don't quite understand it." I laughed nervously and tried to smile at everyone. "It's all very complicated, because I too want Jack to do well as a scriptwriter—he's so passionate about it. It's so much a part of him and what I love about him."

At the end of the weekend most of the other couples signed up for the intensive workshop that met twice a week for six months. I encouraged Jack to do it with me, but in the end he told me that he needed every moment of his time to work on his script.

It was around this time that I was pouring a great deal of energy into the Puppet Garage. I was there both weekend days all through July and August and at least one or two evenings after work. I paid several visits to the public grant library on Twenty-third Street to apply for funding. I was excited about what I was doing. I felt like I had a lot to talk about, and I told Jack stories about the children and the many art projects, but he seemed withdrawn, hardly capable of focusing on conversation. I knew what he was doing; he was trying to counter his unhappiness by throwing himself into his writing.

Then, one day in August, I came home to a letter in our mailbox addressed to me from a law firm in Soho. We were often behind on our bills, and I feared somebody was looking for money. It even crossed my mind that we were being evicted from our apartment. I unfolded a letter.

Dear Ms. Green,

Enclosed please find a check in the sum of five thousand dollars to be used toward your Brooklyn art project, the Puppet Garage. Please cash this check only with the agreement that you will never attempt to find out the source of this money.

Sincerely,
John Greer, Esq.

I pulled the check out of the envelope—a bank check for the amount the letter had stated. I was stunned. I had no idea who could have sent such a wonderful gift. I tried to call Jack at work, but he wasn't there. Then I sat down on our couch and thought about all of our friends. A few of them were rich enough to do this. Then I began thinking about my parents. Jack and I had visited them that summer and I told them about the Puppet Garage; I even mentioned applying for a grant. Suddenly I thought it was my father who had sent the money. I was thrilled by the thought that it must be him.

I couldn't wait until Jack got home to tell him. The minute he opened the door, I held the check up to him. He was elated.

"Jack, I think it's Dad—you once said he's a mystery. You were right. He is. He really is."

Jack thought about it a minute. "But why wouldn't he have just given it to you? Why go through a lawyer?"

"I don't know—there must be a whole side of him that I don't know about. He's a romantic at heart—that's why I fell for you. You guys are both romantics. It all makes sense."

I had trouble sleeping that night, thinking about my father in this new light and about my plans for the Puppet Garage. I had this idea of buying bicycles for many of the children, making each one of them unique with paintings and fancy handlebars. I was glad I had quit taking myself so seriously as a painter, and now I felt like I had the subtle approval of my father. I considered calling him, but then I thought it better to leave things the way they were.

A month later, in mid-September, we left New York to visit Peter at his house on the Vineyard. Jack and I had not been speaking much, but the next thing I knew we were standing next to each other on the ferry from Woods Hole, looking across the sound. I felt hopeful again. We had conceived here over a year ago and now we were back. I thought perhaps it would trigger a change in Jack; we'd go back to the way we were before then.

Peter met us at the ferry and then walked us across the

parking lot to his car. I noticed how his sudden success had changed him. He was unusually relaxed, confident, and tan. I also noticed that the car he led us to was a brand-new Volvo station wagon. It struck me that a station wagon was an odd car to choose to buy for a couple without children. I'd always pictured him driving around in a sports car, a convertible of some kind. A Volvo was just the car I would have bought had I been able to afford it. Then I began wondering what his plans with Micha were; I'd heard they were getting serious. He drove us to Gay Head, which was now called Aquinnah, and then turned down a long dirt road. The house we came to was an unpretentious, salt-gray Cape off the spectacularly beautiful Squibnocket Pond, not far from the Kennedy estate. He helped us unload our bags and told us to make ourselves at home; then he left to pick up Micha, who was painting outside. She was a short, pretty, meticulous woman who always knew exactly what she wanted. She was a painter of landscapes, miniature landscapes.

While Peter was gone, I walked through his house. I had to admit that I too was jealous of Peter for getting to spend two months in this light, airy Cape with a view of the ocean and a saltwater pond. From the top floor I could see wild swans crossing the huge pond toward the sea. The pond was calm and a sweet shade of soft blue and separated from the surf of the ocean by dunes. As I stepped out the door I noticed two garbage cans lying on their sides; Peter had mentioned that there were skunks all over the island. Garbage had spilled on the grass right near the cans. I went down the porch steps, bent over, and picked one up. There were lobster shells and steamers. Securing the lid on the can, I noticed a piece of cream-colored paper that had blown into the short bushes at the edge of the lawn. As I picked it up, I saw that it was the same stationery as that of the law firm from

Soho that had sent me the check. My breath caught in my throat. He was the one who had sent it.

I rushed back to the house to tell Jack. He was in the bathroom taking a shower, and that was just enough time to give me pause. I felt as if I had done exactly what the letter that accompanied the check instructed me not to and I knew I'd feel even worse if I told Jack, so I went back outside and put the stationery in the trash. I said nothing to Jack. I was amazed but I was also disappointed. I had so wanted it to be my father.

When Peter returned with Micha, I watched him in this new light. He was happy that we were here, and he seemed warm and suddenly very generous. Now that I knew about his secret, it was also as if he were playing a part just for me. I had to admit that I felt mildly irritated at him at first for making me think so differently about my father and then letting me down. But then I was thankful. It was a warm feeling to know that he'd shared some of his wealth with me in this selfless way. I was no longer jealous of him, just happy to be in his house.

Over the next few days we rode bicycles into the village of Menemsha, lay on the beach in Gay Head under the clay cliffs in nothing more than suntan oil, and swam in the late-summer water. I began to relax. I felt like what had happened in New York was behind me. I was happy about myself, especially the success of the Garage in Brooklyn, which I'd left with a friend. The four of us stayed up nights drinking wine and playing poker and Monopoly. On a rainy day we chartered a boat to fish in the sound, and later we grilled striped bass over a driftwood fire in the sand.

Late one afternoon on the beach, due to a rising wind, Jack and Micha returned to the house while Peter and I stayed on our towels. It was the first time I'd been alone with him after knowing he'd given me the money. He casually asked me how things were going at the Puppet Garage.

"Somebody sent me a check for a lot of money," I said, knowing it was he. "An anonymous donor."

"You're kidding," Peter said. He was really good—he seemed truly astonished.

"It's made my life a whole lot easier. What a wonderful, generous gift somebody has given me." I wanted to sound grateful. It was my one chance to thank him in this way.

"Do you have any idea who it was?"

"My dad—I'm pretty sure it was him."

"Would he do something like that?"

"Oh, yeah. I love my dad. He's a romantic at heart."

We got onto other subjects. Peter told me about his family. He grew up in New Jersey with three brothers. He was into sports growing up; his high school soccer team had won the national championship, and he had been chosen as an all-American athlete. "All of my brothers are married with kids; can you believe it? They think I'm the weirdo."

I told him about growing up in my quiet family. "My parents used to worry about me—I think they still do."

"You're married and they're worried about you? My parents would kill to see me at the altar."

"Everything is about security with them."

We began talking about Paris. Peter had spent several months there, and he described it in vivid detail. His attitude about New York was exactly the same as mine. We both disliked the gridlike pattern of the streets, the lack of public courtesy, and the presence of money or the lack of it that infected almost every place in the city.

Then we began talking about Jack. Jack had been warmer to me the past few days, but the Vineyard hadn't ignited the spark that I had hoped it would on the ferry over. In so many words, I admitted to Peter that I was having a hard summer. I didn't mention what it was really about, just that we'd participated in a marriage workshop in August.

Peter was sitting on his towel with his arms around his knees. The wind was whipping past our ears. "Jack's an incredible person—everybody knows it—but sometimes incredible people can be hard to deal with—I mean in a way."

"How so?" I asked.

"Charismatic people can act differently with the people they're closest to. They're often sort of split—do you know what I mean?"

"I'm curious," I said. "You guys got in a fight in summer camp?" I posed it as a question.

"Oh, that," Peter said. "Well, you know, we became very close friends back then—I mean, at least I thought we were. Suddenly at the end of the summer Jack started avoiding me like the plague—it seemed like he couldn't stand the sight of me. When I confronted him about it, he called me a sycophant. I didn't even know what it meant, just that it was hurtful. Then when he got invited to a party across camp with a bunch of older kids, he told me he was going alone. I was really hurt, but as kids will do, I decided to follow him there along a path in the woods. When he realized I was behind him, he turned around, ran directly at me, and knocked me flat on my back. I fought back but he was stronger than me and he really hurt me. Anyway, it's not much of a story, except that I went home pretty bruised up—and Jack was asked not to come back to camp the next year. A counselor had seen the incident."

His tone of voice made me realize he was still in pain over what had happened. I wanted to say something to comfort him, but nothing came out of my mouth. I was thinking how Jack told me that he had chosen not to go back to camp the next summer because of Peter. I was also thinking how I sometimes felt like Peter did when I was with Jack.

"You and Micha are pretty serious, aren't you?" I said.

"Sure, but just between you and me, she doesn't want to have kids."

"Really? She seems like she'd be great with them." I wasn't being totally genuine. I liked Micha, but she had a need for perfect order in the house that went against the idea of children. "So the station wagon was your idea?"

"We had a bit of an argument about that," he said and laughed.

"If I had the money, I'd get one of those—or a minivan. I don't care what kind of symbol it is."

"Hey, minivans are sexy," he said.

"Are they?" I said, taking him seriously. Then I realized he was joking and I laughed.

As we talked, the sea became choppy and the waves grew bigger and broke farther out. Peter got up and asked me if I wanted to go for one last swim and I followed him in. The water had cooled down considerably. Frightened of the undertow, I swam next to him, diving under the big breakers and then checking for him when I came up.

We climbed out, wrapped ourselves in towels, and then started back to the car. Fingers of dark clouds ripped in off the water; a sharp gust nearly knocked us down, sand pelting our faces. Peter lent me his Windbreaker and then took me by the sleeve and tugged me inland. The next thing I knew I was walking in the cover of tall dunes in a kind of wind-protected pocket that was much warmer and quiet. We climbed partway up a dune and sat down together, Peter just above me on the slope of sand.

"Isn't it fantastic?" he said. I thought he was talking about the patterns the wind made on the sand below us and so I nodded. "I've come to appreciate you and Jack on a whole new level this trip."

"I appreciate you too, Peter." I had meant to say *we* but instead said *I*.

There was a moment between us. Neither of us spoke. I felt content and happy to be sitting with him.

"You know, I've wanted to ask you something for a long time," Peter said. I detected a tremor of some sort in his voice, turned, and noticed his chest was moving up and down quickly. With a kind of shy uncertainty he glanced away, and I caught a fleeting glimpse of what I believed at the time was my own shyness. He and I seemed a lot more similar to each other than Jack and I were. I zipped his Windbreaker up to my chin. It smelled of him, subtly.

"Just a question," he said in his shaky voice. "Did you ever . . . ?" He stopped speaking.

"Did I ever what?"

"Forget it." There was silence, except for the wind moving high over the dunes. I turned to him again; this time he smiled quickly, and again I saw my own fear reflected on his face.

"All right," he said, lifting sand and letting it sift between his fingers. "Well, I guess I should just tell you something that I've been meaning to. A little secret of mine."

He paused. I thought for sure he was going to tell me about giving me the five thousand dollars. "What's on your mind?" I wanted it to be out in the open so that I could truly thank him.

"No, it wouldn't be right."

"That's silly," I said.

"I can't."

"God—what are you trying to do, torture me?"

He hesitated. "All right, against my own better judgment. You've got really nice lips."

I laughed a little and then fell silent. If I hadn't been expecting him to say something else, I might have taken offense, but instead I sat there motionless, feeling a warm chill race up my spine; he had disarmed me.

"I mean, you have the nicest lips I've ever seen." I smiled and noticed how Peter's words seemed to ease a pain that had been building up in my chest since the first time that Jack had turned away from me in bed. "Sorry," he said. "I shouldn't have said a thing, but it's done, and what's done is done, so there." I knew he was looking at my back and I felt violated—gently violated, and yet I could still feel that warm chill throughout my body.

"Is that all you wanted to say?" I asked.

"Well, yeah, sort of. I have more but . . ."

"But what?"

There was another long silence.

"I saw the way you were with those kids in Brooklyn. I got a real kick out of that. I think you'd make an incredible mother."

The strong wind brought in clouds with hard, marble gray edges. Between dunes a slice of sea was visible; whitecaps lifted brilliantly against the darkening water.

The warmth I felt moving up my back became so real that I believed he was touching me. I turned and realized that he was sitting too far back for that to be true; then I got up and walked down the dune, sand sliding under my feet, while Peter continued to sit there. When I turned again, Peter looked small far up on the slope of sand and I felt relieved, as if the intensity of what I was feeling were merely a kind of playful joke. Peter turned a somersault, landed on his feet, and ran down to me in his baggy blue shorts and faded red T-shirt.

We walked into the wind, the clouds racing from the churning sea to the land, and the breakers growing ever louder. Finally we turned off on a sandy trail that led up to the road and opened the car doors and they banged closed as we got inside. The wind stopped whistling in our ears and, in silence, we watched the storm clouds in the dark purple-gray light coming low over the sea. Then the rain splashed down on the windshield as Peter started the car. "Sorry about all that back there," he whispered.

We drove along the wet road toward the rented house. I thought how I had dreaded the possibility of rain on our one-week vacation. I was afraid of yet another thing bringing me down. Now I felt happy, almost relieved; my legs tingled as if I were anticipating something momentous. Then I realized that there was so much going on inside my head that I had neglected to respond to Peter's apology.

"Well," I said, unsure of what I would say next, "I'm glad you told me that."

He reached over and took my hand, which I had balled into a fist, and squeezed tightly.

From the beach we went to Larsen's on the Menemsha pier and bought lobsters and steamers and then stopped at Sewards, the small grocery store on the other side of the harbor. When we arrived home, Micha and Jack were taking showers in the two bathrooms off their bedrooms. Once again, I felt nervous being alone with Peter.

That night at dinner, I was afraid that the little exchange with Peter, the spark that he'd ignited in me, would somehow reveal itself to Jack or to Micha. The sadness I'd felt since the spring had all but vanished; I could not stop myself from laughing a little too hard at the jokes and good cheer around the table. We played Scrabble before going to bed as the rain continued to come down, and every once in a while I stole a glance at Peter to see if he was looking at me. He kept pulling his turtleneck up over his fine, delicate nose like a bank robber. He had all the classic features of the American boy, a pretty boy, as my girlfriends liked to call him.

Later, after I got into bed with Jack, my eyes remained open. I listened to the rain on the roof and the water pattering down from the eaves. I attempted to look at my situation rationally. I hardly knew Peter. I believed that whatever I was feeling must be less about him than the fact that I was away from my normal routine in the city.

We drove back on Interstate 95, which took us through Rhode Island and Connecticut. Micha was chatting with me in the backseat. She belonged to the National Arts Club in the city, and she was telling me about the perpetual battles among its wealthy members. They liked her work there, she said, and there were few other places in New York that cared for landscape painters. I was distracted, amused at what had happened with Peter. I didn't believe I should take it seriously; I was sure my sudden fondness for him would vanish just as suddenly as the wind had come up that afternoon on the beach, that is, once we were far enough away from the Vineyard.

We got out of the car on Stanton Street in the city and said our good-byes, and then Jack and I dragged our bags up the three flights to our apartment. In bed that night I kept thinking about Peter on the other side of the city, wondering what was on his mind, whether he too felt the subtle ache in his chest. The next afternoon I checked out of the office early to head over to the Garage and see what the children had made while I was gone. It was a cool day and the air suddenly smelled of fall; some of the leaves had already fallen to the sidewalk and they were crisp underfoot. I noticed things on my way to Brooklyn: billboards of sexy couples in the subway, punks with neon yellow hair and crudely stitched-together outfits, old men and women who walked with such similar gaits that they must have been in love. I wasn't admitting it to myself, but I was also keeping an eye out for Peter on the street. I hadn't the slightest idea what I'd say to him if we did meet up. Seeing him had to be by accident, a moment of sudden, unexpected recognition.

On the Vineyard I had assumed my feelings about Peter were shallow and would suddenly vanish on their own. But the opposite was true. I kept thinking about the money he had sent me, how he never took credit for it. I also kept thinking about what he'd said about my making a great mother. I wanted to be thought of that way. The more I thought about him the stronger my desire to see him became.

Suddenly I envisioned a disaster looming on the horizon of my marriage if I didn't do something quickly, so I drew up a plan. I would tell Jack about what was going on in my mind, bring my feelings into the open and divest them of their power over me. It would hurt Jack, but I thought it also might spur him into at least discussing my desire to have a family.

But telling Jack about my feelings for Peter was harder than bringing up the subject of the house apes. "You know Peter?" I imagined myself saying. "Isn't he weird? Doesn't he bring out weird feelings in you? I mean, he's just so different from us." But I could never get that far with Jack in the room.

Then one evening I had plans to pick Jack up outside the Film Forum and walk home with him. Before that, I spent an hour in a bar on Seventh Avenue, drinking scotches and contemplating what I was going to tell him. Finally I met him and we began walking east on Houston toward our apartment.

"Jack, there's something I've been meaning to ask you about," I interrupted him. He stopped and looked at me.

"Sounds important," he said.

"It *isn't,* at all. It's just something shallow and stupid."

"Well," Jack cut in front of me, raising his arm to flag a passing taxi. The taxi shifted three quick lanes and stopped abruptly in front of us. Opening the door, he put his hand out for me to get in.

"What's this?" I said, surprised.

"Go on," he said, taking my arm and nudging me inside. "You can tell me over dinner." As Jack slid in next to me, he gave the driver an address uptown; then he put his hand on my leg and gently squeezed.

"What on earth are you doing?" I said.

We arrived at a French restaurant on Fifty-fourth Street called La Cité. At the front desk it became apparent that Jack had called to make reservations earlier that day. It was a very formal restaurant with marble pillars and professional waiters with long white aprons taking long strides back and forth, the kind of place we never went to. After we were seated, Jack glanced around. He was a bit uncomfortable in here, but he seemed very happy.

"What in the world gave you the idea to do this? I thought you said we're broke."

He put his napkin in his lap. "I got a fortune cookie the other day that said, 'Do something special with the one you love.'"

"Are you serious?"

"No. But I do love you and I know how I've treated you this summer. I'm sorry, Maddy. I don't want to blame it all on what happened with Zuzu, but I think I was sort of reeling from that. It's one of those things that can affect you even though you're not aware of it."

Suddenly I understood what his hesitation had been about, and my anger at him turned to compassion. I felt relieved that he finally brought up the subject. There was an awkward pause as he tried to come up with something to say. He looked down, almost as if he were ashamed.

"Sometimes big dreams can be devastating," he said. He

tried to smile. It hardly masked his pain. I reached across the table and held his hand.

We drank two bottles of wine during the meal and spared no expense when it came to ordering; then we returned by cab to our apartment. Jack went into the bathroom and came out carrying a lit candle and a bottle of massage oil. I was already in bed. He lifted my nightshirt and massaged my back. Then he turned me over and began kissing my stomach.

It was the first of many nights to come when Jack attempted to put the romance back into our marriage. There were more dinners and more back rubs and sweet words that hadn't been said for quite a while. And it worked. I felt closer to him for weeks.

Then things began to slow down and return to the way they had been before. One evening in bed before falling asleep, I turned to him and said, "You know that five thousand dollars? I haven't spent but a thousand of it."

"Really?" Jack said.

"I've been saving it. I mean if money's an issue, I think we've got enough. I really do want to try again, Jack."

Jack lay there thinking about it for a long time. "Maddy, I have to be honest with you. I'm still not quite ready."

"Why? Please tell me."

"A lot of reasons."

"Tell me just one."

"I feel like a failure," he said. "I don't want to have children while feeling this way."

"You're hardly a failure."

"Honestly, I'm just not ready yet. I need a year, at least."

"A year?" I got out of bed and went into the other room. I felt like there was nothing left to say.

Chapter Ten

In early November Jack took off for a weekend at the Vermont Studio Center, an artist and writer's colony in Johnson, Vermont. He thought time away was just what he needed to finish his script. For me, time apart from each other was exactly what I didn't need.

The night Jack left, I came back to our apartment to a message on my machine from a friend, Gina, inviting me to a large party in a Soho loft. Gina was a tall, slender blonde with lots of gay male friends. She was also married and rumored to be having an affair. I was not that close to her, but I was always amused by the coterie of people around her. The thought of staying home that night alone was just too much, so I dressed and headed over to Spring Street. It was a cold and windy night; winter seemed like it was on its way early, too early. I was thinking as I walked that I didn't want it to be cold again; I was afraid that it would remind me of what had happened two years before.

The effect of stepping into a lively crowd didn't help matters at all. I slipped from the bar to the hors d'oeuvres table alone. Then right next to me I listened to a scene that might have been from my own past. A confident boy just out of college awkwardly broke the ice with a not-so-confident girl. There was something pathetic about the girl's reaction, as if she were following a hackneyed script, lots of stuttering and laughing at the wrong moments at trite, not-so-funny things. And yet as I listened, I became jealous of her and decided to get my coat and leave.

Then somebody tapped me on the shoulder, and I turned around to see Peter holding two glasses of scotch. I was surprised, to say the least. Just as I was about to accept his offer of a drink, a man stepped between us and asked me to dance. This too was surprising, considering the state I was in; I'd forgotten that other people might find me attractive. The young man led me away—I was pretty sure he was somebody Jack knew. His big ears made him look a little like a leprechaun, though he was tall and his hair was blond. I turned in the crowd and smiled back at Peter as if I had so many men after me that I didn't know what to do.

On the second song Peter cut in. "Excuse me, sir. I'd like a dance with my wife."

I didn't know why he'd said that, and yet I laughed a little too hard and nervously to keep my composure. The dance was slow, and whether it was Peter's unconscious suggestion or not, I found myself pressed against him.

"That was crazy—he knows Jack. I'm sure of it."

"How's everything? How are things at the Garage? What kind of projects are you up to?"

"We're into fish—everyone is painting these metal fish and hanging them from the ceiling. It's the season for them or something. How are you?" I asked, attempting to deflect the attention.

"So-so," Peter said, and looked down at me with his hard blue eyes as if to say that was a loaded question. "Actually, things have been going pretty well. I've been hoping to bump into you."

"Really?" I said, remembering how I had hoped to bump into him.

"Yeah, I never seem to see you guys. I feel like Jack isn't the same toward me these days—he suddenly hates me, doesn't he?"

"He's really into this screenplay. He went to Vermont to work on it," I said. It was true that Jack had completely lost touch with him.

"You know, Maddy, there's something that I've really, really wanted to tell you. But I don't know if it's appropriate right now."

I pushed back from him and looked at his face. He was blushing and I was suddenly afraid of what he would say. The music quickened, and we danced without touching for a while; then it slowed and Peter took both my arms and waltzed with me. Sweat was rolling down the side of his neck; his shirt was wet.

"You know I broke up with Micha right after the trip to the Vineyard, don't you?" he asked, nervously.

"I heard," I said.

"Do you know why it ended—I mean, can you guess why?" I was beginning to be afraid of the real answer.

"I remember you mentioned something about—"

"You." He pointed at my chest. "I'll be honest with you. At first I didn't think it was anything. But it is. I haven't been able to think of much else. I'm crazy about you, Maddy."

Suddenly his words felt as much like a kind of threat as they did something that I had wanted to hear. I let go of him and stood still on the dance floor as other couples slipped around us. Then I turned and walked over to my coat. Peter followed. "Hey," he called.

I didn't know what to do except run away. I pushed through the crowd, buttoning my coat, and shouted to Gina over the music that I was going home.

"What's wrong?" Gina stood among her many male friends. She had a great big smile on her face, as if she were aware of what had happened. "Oh, I know what it is—it's him. He's a lady-killer. I wish he were after me."

"It's not that at all," I said.

The freight elevator rattled its way to the bottom level and I opened the door to the street. Suddenly I saw Peter leaning against a sports car in front of the building. I had no idea how he'd gotten down here ahead of me. "I just screwed up, didn't I?" he said. I turned away from him and started walking quickly down the street. "I'm sorry, but sometimes you just have to tell somebody how you really feel," he called. I did not turn as I raised my hand for a taxi.

The taxi let me out at my stoop and I raced up the flights of stairs to my door and began cleaning up our apartment. It took me a moment to understand what had happened. It wasn't just that he'd been inappropriate. I had always believed that I would rather have killed myself than to hurt Jack. The fact that I had fallen so deeply in love with him when I was young was wonderful, but now I wanted a family. It wasn't necessarily his fault that he didn't want what I did; it was just the way it was, and now I was afraid I was going to do something to hurt him.

As I lay in bed, I reached for one of his T-shirts and put it to my nose. I missed him already, though I didn't have a concrete plan about leaving him. It was merely the feeling that I was open to the possibility of leaving after being so sure for so long that that could never happen.

The weekend went by. I went to the Puppet Garage in the daytime and continued painting the metal fish with the children and hanging them from the ceiling. At night I met with friends across the street at the Kettle. By Sunday afternoon, when Jack returned from his trip, I felt like an entirely different person inside. I was hiding something from him, and for the first time in our marriage I was aware that it was something I might not be able to control.

I told nobody about these feelings: not Gina, who had called me to find out what had transpired between Peter and me that night, nor Jennifer, who was too busy talking about her own problems with men. Jack and I spent Thanksgiving at his parents' house in Massachusetts. I had always loved spending time with his big family. It had the perfect mix of chaos and intellectualism—the two qualities that I had so missed growing up. Jack's father taught American Literature at Williams College, and his mother was a part-time nurse. There were always people from the community at dinner, people who had nowhere else to go, and it was a festive occasion. But my mood was subdued; I could not help but feel like a bit of a traitor.

On Sunday afternoon Jack drove back up to the Studio Center in Vermont to write, while I took a bus back to the city. That evening I took a walk alone, thinking about what I should do. As I passed a bodega, I saw a copy of the *New York Post* on a metal rack. The headline read: "Batten Down the Hatches . . . Snow Is on the Way". I stopped and read the weather report. They were predicting eighteen inches. It didn't seem possible. It was a cool, overcast evening. The many dried leaves still clinging to the trees were more redolent of fall than winter.

I stopped into a bar called Scorpions, a little-known hole-in-the-wall on Avenue A. Peter had mentioned offhandedly that it was his new hangout. I ordered a beer and began to read at a table. Many young men who might have been Peter came in that evening. When I finally caught sight of him—I recognized him from his legs down, his motorcycle boots and jeans—I merely stared back at my book and waited for him to pass by before glancing up. He hadn't seen me; his arm was around a woman, an "East Village mannequin," as Jack might have called her, in a tight black-and-white dress with two-inch heels and a kind of retro fifties haircut. Peter glanced over his shoulder and caught sight of me. His intense eyes widened. Then he settled his friend at the bar and strode over to my booth near the pool table.

"Maddy, you came," he said, as if he knew right away why I was there. "Stick around for a minute, would you?"

"Why?"

"Give me ten. I'll be back."

"Where are you going?"

He went up to the bar and began whispering in the ear of the woman. She laughed aloud, spilling some of the martini in her hand. Then she put her arm around him and the two went out. I slipped change in the jukebox and then bought another beer. When Peter returned, he was alone, dazed and red in the face. His worn leather jacket was open and his blond hair was pushed behind his ears. "Got a cab waiting," he said.

"What? I just bought this," I said, holding up my mug of beer. I didn't want to seem too malleable. The song that I'd chosen had just come on. "Plus, my round is finally coming up on the jukebox."

"I'll get in trouble if I hang around in here."

He slipped my beer between the zippers of his leather jacket and then took me by the elbow and took me out to the cab. Leaning forward from the seat, he told the driver to go up to Central Park South and Sixth Avenue. "Where the carriages wait," he said.

"Hey," I said as the taxi jerked forward. "What is this?"

"You told me you were crazy about animals, not just

kids." He slipped the mug out from under his jacket and gave it to me.

"We're not really taking a ride in one of those tourist-trap things, are we?" I laughed.

"Didn't you admit that you're a romantic at heart?" Peter's leg was pressed against mine.

"I am, but I feel sorry for the horses," I said.

"Well"—Peter smiled—"I feel *sorrier* for romantics who feel sorry for horses." He looked away.

The cab arrived at the line of carriages waiting for fares. Peter found one with a driver wearing a top hat and a full tuxedo; some of the other drivers were pretty shabby. The driver snapped a short whip, the horse jerked forward, and we were off into the park, the sound of horns and traffic growing quieter.

Peter pulled a blanket over our legs and looked around at the soft yellow lights against the trees. I was nervous about sitting so close to him, but the rocking of the carriage began to settle me. It had never occurred to me, Jack, or anyone I knew to climb into one of these prohibitively expensive carriages. They were for the kind of tourists who came to town from the Midwest to see *Cats* or *Phantom of the Opera* or some other corny musical.

My leg was pressed up against Peter's. I could smell the horse's coat, the leather harnesses and wooden seats of the buggy. There was something wonderful about this smell in the city. It was so unexpected here and yet reassuringly old, like the hand of a grandfather. Taking in everything around me, I felt like I was in a foreign city, one that I had ventured into unaware. Through the trees we could see the softly lit rows of windows of the towering buildings of Central Park West and hear distant sirens, horns, the squeal of taxi brakes.

"Any new developments at the Garage?" he said. "How are the kids?"

"There's always something new going on there."

"Finished with the fish?"

"They sort of morphed into Christmas ornaments. One kid's been doing these crazy naked Santa Clauses."

Under the streetlamps the carriage moved from dark to light to dark, and there were lanterns glimmering on the far shore of the boating lake. Then we passed a fountain lit from below in a circular square of cobblestones.

Peter laughed. "Tell me if you think this is true," he said. "Kids have no sense of time, really."

"It's different from ours."

"They're naturally disorganized. I've noticed that about them. They leave a mess everywhere they go. They have no sense of an hour or a day. But that's exactly why they're able to experience life in ways we can't. They're more in tune with life, more sensitive to it because life—and forgive me for sounding so philosophical—is nothing more than a series of random events. There's no real order to it. To experience life, a person has to kind of be part of it, like a random little thing himself, and that's what kids do naturally."

I laughed silently. I thought of my life and marriage and how planned out it was. Maybe that was why I felt so bad. Something in my chest let go. "You're right," I said.

"You like getting close to that, don't you?" he asked.

"Being around them is the next best thing to being one," I said.

Peter stared directly into my eyes, and just as I was about to turn away he said, "Forgive me, Maddy." Then he bent over and put his lips to mine.

At first his mouth felt rough, his jaw and lips were so different from Jack's, and my jaw tensed. I thought, *He's not gentle at all*. Then I realized how curious I was about this new way of being kissed; I liked the taste of him and the smell of him and the feel of his thin nose against mine. His features were finer than Jack's.

Once we were back on Fifty-ninth Street, we climbed out of the carriage and Peter paid the driver. I stood there dazed, staring at everything around me as if for the first time—the tall buildings of Central Park South, the yellow cabs waiting in front of the Excelsior across the street. A city bus was making its way toward Columbus Circle, its blue interior illuminated in the windows. Suddenly I seemed to understand the line I had crossed by kissing Peter, and I became terrified.

Peter caught a taxi that took us to a private club, where he paid the bouncer a ridiculous sum to let us in. We danced for one song and then realized the music was too loud, and so we went to a café where we could talk. He told me the plot of one of his scripts and I was surprised at how coherent it was, and I was even more surprised that it had an ending. I wouldn't say it was the most original story I'd ever heard, but it was different enough to set it apart from other stuff out there. He was so much more adept at screenwriting than Jack; *savvy* might be the word for it.

"Jack's really good at dialogue, you know," he said suddenly, as if reading my thoughts. "I gave him a title back on the Vineyard. Did he ever tell you that?"

I shook my head.

"*Kissing Your Ex.* He's got a good idea for a script. If he plays his cards right, that and the title could take him a long way."

At one in the morning, as I sat with Peter in the back of a cab outside the apartment on Stanton Street, snowflakes began falling on the windshield and the cabby put on his wipers. Peter pointed to a streetlight. The snow was coming down hard; it looked yellow in the light.

"Good night," I said.

He held my hand. "Are you free tomorrow?"

"Peter, not so soon." His face was covered with red blotches, as if he were blushing. "It was kind of an accident that we met tonight," I said, turning to him. "Please don't tell anyone that we saw each other tonight, please, and don't ever call me at our apartment. I'll call you, okay?"

I dashed upstairs to my apartment, locked the door, and lay down on our unmade bed. I could not believe what I had done. I wondered if I'd already ruined things with Jack. I had no idea how he'd ever get over it if he found out I had kissed somebody else. It was a terrible feeling.

At eleven the next morning, the telephone woke me up. It had been ringing in my dreams for a long time before I rose and answered it.

"Hey, were you just sleeping?" Jack said. He was calling from a pay phone in the Studio Center in Vermont.

"Yes, I was," I said, disoriented. Suddenly I said, "I'm sick—I mean, I feel sick." It was the first time I had ever directly lied to him. I noticed that I could not hear my own voice as I said it.

"A headache?" he said.

"No—my stomach. I threw up last night."

"Oh, no, are you okay?"

"I'm better," I said. "I'll be all right."

"I'm sorry you're feeling so bad," Jack said. We talked for a little while and then he asked me if there were any messages.

I looked over at the machine. I could see it blinking—how I had neglected to get the messages earlier I could not say. "I think so. I can't remember. Do you want me to play them?"

As I reached over to the machine, I thought, *These are the kinds of things I must think about now*. It was a voice inside my head that said this, a separate voice. There were two messages for me and none for Jack; usually it was the other way around. "Boy, you must be feeling really bad. I wish I were there."

"That's all right. You need a break."

"I heard you guys are getting slammed," Jack said.

For a moment I had no idea what he was talking about. Then I looked to the window and saw that the fire escape was piled high with snow and it was still coming down.

"Yeah—we are," I said.

"Are you okay? Are you sure you shouldn't call the doctor?"

"It was just something I ate. I'm feeling much better. I might even go out later."

After hanging up, I went to the window; a snowball fight had started at the door to the Kettle. It was strange to see snow so soon in the season. I thought of going out and playing too, but decided to stay inside, read a novel, and try to reclaim my life as I had known it. If I stayed inside all weekend, if I stayed away from Peter, if I kept to myself and read or watched television, Jack would come back and then everything would eventually return to normal. There would not be that strange feeling that all that was innocent and precious in our life together was vanishing.

Chapter Eleven

It snowed the rest of that day and all night. It was just starting to let up when I awoke on Sunday morning. Three stories down I could see that the cars were completely buried and people were walking down the middle of the street, wearing colorful mittens and carrying snow shovels. The telephone began ringing and I went over to it and picked it up.

"Hey, would you and Jack care to go to a tobogganing party?" my friend Margie said. "It's upstate, an overnighter, a great big mansion or something. Supposed to be amazing. You guys have got to come."

"Jack's out of town."

"Can he meet us there?"

"He's writing."

"Oh, you poor thing. You married a writer, didn't you?"

"I'm staying in—snowflakes make me feel like a homebody."

"All sorts of cool folks are going, Maddy."

"You know me, always a bit of a party pooper, Margie."

It was not easy getting her off the telephone. When I hung up, I realized one of the reasons I had said no to going was because leaving the city would actually take me farther away from Peter. I didn't want to see him right away, and yet I didn't want to be too far from him either. Then the telephone began ringing again, and for some reason, I had the feeling it must be Peter.

It was Jack. He'd forgotten to pay our Con Edison bill and thought I should write a check and drop it into a mailbox soon. He asked me how I was feeling and I told him I was fine now. Before we got off the telephone, I mentioned the invitation from Margie.

"If you feel better, you should go," Jack said. "You love the snow. All you've talked about is spending time in the country. You've got to go. Besides, someday snow is going to be a distant memory, the greenhouse effect, you know."

By midafternoon I felt like days had passed. I was lonely. On the street below me I could hear another snowball fight starting—everyone else in New York was out on the street having fun.

Then my doorbell rang and I looked out the window to see a bright red Jeep with two toboggans strapped to the roof parked in the middle of the snow-covered street.

"Who is it?" I said.

"Maddy, it's Margie—you're coming."

"I'm in my pajamas."

"Well take *off* your pajamas, girl, and let's go," she said, and I could hear laughter in the background. "Or keep them on and put on a coat. But please let's go."

"You'll wait for me?"

I dressed quickly, packed a bag, and ran down the stairs and out onto the street. The car was packed with people my age and I slid into the backseat.

Fifteen blocks later we slowed down to make another

stop. Suddenly I saw Peter standing on the street corner wearing a tight ski jacket, a racer-style ski hat, and thick gloves. He looked like Jean-Claude Killy with his bright red cheeks. He pretended not to notice me, got in on the other side, and then leaned over the laps of the others and grinned at me.

We stopped at a rest area with a Burger King just north of the city, and everyone got out to examine the tall piles of snow at the edges of the parking lot. I turned to Peter, who was packing a snowball. "Why didn't you tell Margie to say you were going too?"

"Because I knew you would come only if there was a slight chance I might not be there."

His insight into my thoughts surprised me.

We got back on the highway. Soon all but one lane was closed down and the banks of snow were so high that it was like driving down the corridors of a maze. At the town of Cold Spring, we stopped at a package store and then followed a country road to a private drive flanked with snowbanks so high that we could barely see the meadows and forests around us, and it wound along for almost a mile.

"The guy who lives here is serving nine months in Danbury. Insider trading," Peter announced to everyone. It was the sort of scoop he always seemed to have.

"You're kidding," somebody said.

"No judge could fine him enough to put a dent in his assets, and so he's just waiting until he's free to enjoy it all. He once told me crime pays—even if you get caught—provided you go all the way with it. I guess he meant it."

"You're friends with him?" I said.

"We're pretty close," he said, and I thought how different this was from Jack's friends. "He's got style, you'll see. His wife doesn't seem to care. She's still throwing parties like there's no tomorrow. Most people would be ashamed, but she told me once that she married him for the money. She fools around behind his back all the time and he doesn't seem to care. The guy actually comes home wearing an ankle bracelet on the weekdays, but he's got to go back to his cell on the weekends. White-collar crime, you know— they put you up in a suite with room service for a few months. The last time I talked to him, I asked him how he liked prison. 'Great,' he said. 'Just as long as they don't turn off HBO.' "

Everyone laughed.

"How do you know this guy?" I whispered to him.

"High-stakes poker."

"Oh, really?" I said, smiling. "You've done that?"

"At times."

"Isn't it . . . isn't it"—I stared over at him and his eyes caught mine—"expensive?" I had been thinking of saying *immoral*.

"Only if you lose."

"And I take it you don't."

"It's happened—but I usually have a backer."

"God, you're one of those. What on earth do you get out of it?"

"I love gambling because"—he thought for a moment, and I almost told him how much Jack hated it—"because it's meaningless. I mean yes, you might make or lose some money—but in the end it's neither profound nor spiritual, neither good nor bad. It's nothing."

"I don't get it."

He thought about this some more. "Sometimes you need something in your life that means nothing because it makes the rest of your life meaningful."

It occurred to me that maybe he was right.

The Jeep stopped under a portico and everyone unloaded their bags and stomped their feet clean of snow in the lobby in front of a wide, fanning staircase where three hired men in orange snowmobile suits showed us to our rooms. Cars and vans of guests converged on the house that weekend, but there was enough space so that everyone had their own bedroom.

At least five toboggans were in play on the long, steep field behind the estate. A snowmobile was towing one up the hill while the others were gliding down the slippery course, snow spraying high from their bows. Smiles on the red faces of the riders were visible across the bright white field.

As I settled into my room, somebody knocked on the door and I opened it. It was the young man who had asked me to dance just after Peter tapped me on the shoulder at the party in the city, the man who looked a little like a leprechaun.

"You're here too?" I said.

"Across the hall. I'll wait for you?"

I was dismayed that he was here. I was still unsure whether he knew Jack. I pulled on my mittens and knit hat that I never wore in the city and followed the young man outside and down the front steps. We crossed the snowfield to the hill, and I saw Peter up high under the line of trees ready to make a run down. The young man and I joined a party and climbed the hill. The sun was bright in my eyes. As I lost myself in laughter, I thought that maybe flirting was what I needed to learn how to do—maybe women got through the rough spots in their relationships by simply flirting without letting any one man take hold of them. At the top I climbed onto a toboggan with four others and we flew down the hill, all of us pressed against each other, our hearts in our throats.

That night after dinner a group of close to two dozen people sat around the stone fireplace that crackled with fresh logs. Most of us were drinking eggnog. It was delicious and strong and people were talking loudly, as if they were drunk. Peter was on the other side from me on the carpet on his knees, wearing a flannel shirt, the red light flickering across his face. I didn't know how many people here might end up meeting Jack and me later, and so I was playing it cool. But then my longing for Peter overcame me and I went over next to him and tugged on his shirtsleeve. Without looking at me, he took my wrist and brought my hand onto his lap and began rubbing my palm with his thumb.

People got up one or two at a time and went to bed. Then we were alone on the couch and the fire had turned to red embers. Peter stepped outside in his woolen socks and returned with a large unsplit log under his arms. He dumped it over the andirons, and sparks flew high against the black soot-covered brick. It was very late and I was feeling drunk from the eggnog. Sitting next to me on the sofa, he turned and pressed me back against the armrest. I closed my eyes tightly and kissed him. It was the second time I had kissed him, and it was easier to slip into and somehow more serious, as if I were aware this time of its implications. I loved the feel of his lips and tongue. I ran my hand through his silklike blond hair and pulled at his ears. He squeezed my whole body against him and I began breathing hard and moaning quietly. I felt his hand climb along my ribs and against the underside of my bra. I hadn't expected this, but nor could I muster what it would take to stop him. Gently he caressed my breasts and I could feel it all over my body and between my legs. Then he lifted my shirt and kissed down my neck. Finally, he put his mouth over my nipple.

Then we heard a door open and the sound of voices in a back room. I rose to my feet quickly and tried to straighten out my hair. A group came in from a midnight walk. Red in the face, I passed them, went down the hall, and opened the door to my room. My heart was beating quickly. As I got into bed, I heard a knock at my door. I opened it just enough to see Peter's face.

"No," I said quietly. "Too many people here."

I kissed him quickly and then closed the door. I could tell he was disappointed. I got back into bed. I was relieved that we hadn't gone further. It was one thing to fall in love with Peter—I couldn't control that—but it was another thing to sleep with him.

Chapter Twelve

We returned to the city in the Jeep, driving between high banks of melting snow. Peter got out with me near my apartment and I stood there with him, keeping my eyes down so as not to appear connected to him.

"Okay," he said quietly. "Now I know I'm not crazy." I could see my breath and smell the pavement sweating under the snow. A truck went by with chains that sounded like tiny bells on its tires. "I knew what I felt for you on the Vineyard had to be real," he said.

I raised my head and kissed him quickly, as if we were just friends, and then I started walking away.

"I'll go crazy if you don't phone me tomorrow," Peter called.

I thought I should tell him that tomorrow was too soon, but I kept walking, thinking that I might have to call him. I had grown used to being with him over the weekend, the way one is with a lover. I thought how I might be deeper into things than I knew.

At a green market near our apartment, I picked up dinner for Jack, who was coming home in the evening. I would keep to my normal routine—make the sort of meal that I would usually make and do other things that I usually did. In the apartment I changed and washed the clothes I'd worn with Peter in the machine in the basement. Then I took a long shower.

I began making one of Jack's favorite dishes, all the while listening for the door.

"Hey, stranger," Jack said when he came in. His cheeks were rosy from being out in the cold. I kissed him and then turned back to the cutting board, where I was cutting garlic. I could tell just by his tone of voice that he had been looking forward to seeing me. It was quite a change from the way he'd been all summer. "Have fun?" he said, referring to my trip upstate.

"It was okay," I said, crushing the garlic's thin shell. "How was Vermont?"

"I got a heck of a lot done," he said. "Anybody upstate that we know?"

"A few," I said quietly. I put the garlic in the press and began to squeeze it into a small jar of olive oil. "Peter was there."

"Really?"

"He was there with somebody—some new girlfriend, I think," I said.

Jack thought about this a moment. "What an odd duck." He put a paper shopping bag on the kitchen table and took out a large wrapped present. I wiped my hands on a dish cloth, sat down, and looked at it.

"What's this?" I said.

"Open the card first," he said.

I opened it and read:

Dear Maddy,

> *There are still no words for the amount I love you,*

Jack.

He put the present in my hand and I began unwrapping it slowly. A seal carved by Eskimos from soapstone, a book on knitting, and a box of maple syrup candies in erotic shapes.

Jack put his arms around my waist the way he used to do and kissed the nape of my neck. "I know I've been acting like an idiot the last few months," he whispered. "I really am sorry."

I had no idea what to say. I only knew that I wasn't ready to suddenly switch and become physical with him again. I thanked him for the presents. Then I put my hand to my temple and told him that a headache was coming on and I needed to lie down.

Jack sat next to me as I lay down on my stomach on our bed. He began rubbing my back gently, his fingers kneading my spine. He did this for a long time until I finally began to relax. Then he helped me slip my shirt off and continued rubbing my back some more. Finally he put his head down against me and slipped his hand under my chest, massaging along the base of my breasts and then slipping his hand closer to my nipples. I thought I had separated myself from him—at least mentally—but I was becoming very aroused. Jack continued caressing me; then suddenly I flipped onto my back and pressed my lips tightly against his. He slipped my underwear over my thighs and kissed my belly all the way down to my waist. A sudden shiver rushed through my body as he moved farther down. Then we were making love in a way we hadn't for a long time. It was so intense that I suddenly burst into tears.

Afterward, as I lay next to him, an idea occurred to me—that our marriage must still be alive as long as I could feel this attracted to Jack; maybe there was some way things could work out. I was thinking this despite the fact that I didn't have any idea how to break things off with Peter.

Chapter Thirteen

Jack and I made love every night that week. In the daytime, I decided that I should avoid Peter with the hope that my feelings for him would go away. Meanwhile the snow from the early storm melted and blackened in the piles under the parking meters. The holidays were coming up quickly. Santas were standing on street corners ringing their bells, and I was busy at the Garage. I had put up a large Christmas tree and a menorah and I was organizing a grab bag for the children. The prospect of presents had brought in more children than ever before, sometimes as many as thirty at any given time.

One night at around ten, when Jack was still at work, I picked up a ringing telephone in our apartment. On the other end, I heard a soft voice amid loud music and voices. It was Peter, calling from a pay phone. He apologized twice for having phoned me at the apartment and promised he wouldn't do it again. "I just have to talk to you. Just a few words. Please. I'm right down the street at Angel's Pub."

I was struck by both the strangeness of his voice and yet

its familiarity, as if I'd been conversing with him inside my head all along.

"I can't," I said.

"Oh, Maddy, please." He had lost a little of his poise. There was an urgency in his tone. "As a friend, please." I could hear the noisy bar behind him. I didn't know what to do. "Listen to me. I know you must be feeling the way I do. You can't just end something like this. I certainly am not going to forget about you, and I don't think you will about me. Not seeing each other at all is just going to make it worse."

He was right. I had been thinking about him a lot despite what had been going on with Jack. I thought I should at least touch base with him, so I dressed and went downstairs to Angel's. Peter was sitting at a booth, his hands tapping the table nervously. He got up and tried to hug me, but I sat down across from him without reciprocating. He slid a drink across the table for me.

"Things between you and Jack are working out, aren't they?" he said.

I stared at him, unable to speak—it was uncanny that he knew this.

"They are. They have to be," he said, and a nervous smile flashed across his lips. I wrapped my hand around the cold drink and brought it to my lips, sipping from the stirrer. I was searching the tabletop for something to say to him. "I just need to know where I stand," he said. A voice in my head nearly as loud as the bar's television was saying, *It's over.* But I continued to look down at the table, caught, unsure of where to turn. He put his hand out and took mine. I knew that I should get up and leave, but I could not even pull my hand away.

"I don't know what to do," Peter said. "I just know that I feel like I'm in limbo. I'm miserable. Please tell me what I should do—should I try to move on?"

I looked up at him as he leaned back against the vinyl seat. I wanted to nod and say yes, but I was unable to do that. I didn't know how I would really feel if I couldn't see him again.

"Tell me the truth. Do you feel what I do?" he said.

I looked down at the table and nodded.

"Then what should we do about it? It's not like we can control it," he said.

"I don't know, Peter."

He sat there holding my hand across the table and looking at me.

"I don't see how it's going to work out like this," he said.

I closed my eyes. "I'm so sorry. I never meant to make you miserable. I just don't know what to do."

"Well, maybe we should just kind of act like it's over. I know it won't work, but maybe that's what we should do. Do you know what I mean?"

I looked at him, unsure of what he meant.

"Maybe you're a stronger person than I am," he said. "Maybe you can get back into your life. Just so you know, if you do make things really work out with Jack—I mean without me in the picture—I won't ever tell anybody what has happened—that I promise you."

"But I'm not sure things are going to work out with Jack," I said suddenly.

"Then you can call me."

"But what if you're—"

"We'll just let the cards fall where they may. Who knows where I'll be in my life? I can only tell you that I won't forget you."

Peter stood up and I got up and hugged him. "Well, you let me know if you've had a change of heart," he said. He kissed me for a long moment, then turned and walked out of the bar. I ran out after him, then stopped, afraid that Jack might be on the street. I was beside myself as I walked back to the apartment. Opening the door, I knelt down to pet Bella. Jack was still not home. I thought it best that I fall asleep right away in order to get back into my life as usual. But once the light was out, I began thinking how easy it would be for Peter to meet another woman. He was one of those handsome men one sees walking out of a music shop or a downtown bar with a certain gait, neither too awkward nor too smooth, his long legs and broad shoulders always complementing his slacks and jacket. His choice of clothes always seemed casual, never careless nor self-conscious, and yet somehow stylish, and I noticed there was a smell about him that I loved.

Chapter Fourteen

ater that evening Jack came home and got
into bed. He kissed me and began rubbing
my back and I knew that he wanted to make love. I put my
face into my pillow. Suddenly my desire for him was gone
again. I didn't want to make love to him, not tonight.
Through the pillow in a muffled voice, I asked him not to
touch me. He drew his hand away.

"Are you okay?" he asked.

I started to answer him. I lifted my head and was going
to say I was fine, but instead I broke into tears. He tried to
comfort me, to get me to roll over, but I clung hard to my pillow and said I couldn't tell him what the matter was because I didn't know.

"Maddy, I know there are things on your mind. Please,
you must be honest with me," he said.

I thought maybe he was right; maybe I should tell him
the truth—the chasm between us had become even wider
than before. Turning over onto my back, I stared up into his
eyes. He was looking at me compassionately, as if he were

ready to accept whatever I told him. He also seemed tired, and something about him was sad. Suddenly I had the feeling that what happened with Zuzu had taken an even greater toll on him than on me.

"It's nothing, Jack. I'm just getting my period, that's all."

I slept in his arms that night, but I kept waking up, thinking about having cut things off with Peter.

The next day I got off work early and spent the afternoon walking around to thrift stores, gathering small presents for the Christmas party at the Garage. I wanted to keep myself busy; the conversation with Peter was having an even stronger effect on me than I had anticipated. I could sense that things with Jack had already gone cold again. By the end of the week I had wrapped nearly forty secondhand presents and put them around the tree and menorah in the Garage. I had avoided making love with Jack all week, and I was still thinking about Peter.

In the middle of the following week, I threw the party for the children, with the help of several of my girlfriends. A Santa Claus was on hand, and there was pizza and the grab bag. More children showed up than ever before. It was a wonderful feeling, seeing the Garage packed full of screaming children and mothers. I felt like what I was doing was truly a success. In the midst of the fracas, while I was pouring soda for the children, I looked up to see Peter standing in line. His face was bright red and he was smiling.

"What a zoo!" he said over the noise. "I can't believe this; it's wonderful."

I was happy to see him, but I was afraid my friends would see, and so I simply poured him a cup of root beer and handed it to him.

"How many of these little two-legged creatures have you attracted? Seems like half of Brooklyn."

"They like it here," I said.

He walked around the space, looking over all of our projects, and then came back to me. "You wouldn't be free later, would you?"

I hesitated, not knowing what to say.

"Couldn't we just sort of call this separation thing off?" he asked. "I mean, what do you say we just pretend we're friends and grab a drink?" He slipped me a pack of matches with the address of a bar on it. "I'm sorry, Maddy. I'm not as strong as I thought I was. I'd love to at least talk to you, really, just as a friend."

"I don't know," I said and suddenly remembered that Jack was supposed to meet me here.

"Well, if you do decide, I'll be there."

It took me close to an hour to clean up after the party. I called our machine at home—Jack had left a message that he wasn't going to make it to the party, but that he would have a late dinner ready. He apologized, but didn't say why he couldn't make it. After bidding my friends good-bye, I headed over to the bar. Peter was already seated at a booth when I stepped in the door. I sat down across from him.

"I admire you. In this city that's so . . . I don't know . . . career-oriented, you've just broken free."

"Hardly," I said. "I'm full of worries."

"You don't show it. You look like you're proud of what you're doing. That place is like a . . . It's another world."

"It's an escape," I said. "And I don't have to worry about art critics, except the ones who are twelve years old."

"They can be pretty tough, can't they?" He laughed and so did I. "Where did you get the idea for those heads?"

"You mean the masks? I don't know. I like things that are bigger than life."

"So," he said, "what else has been happening?"

I picked up my drink and shrugged my shoulders. "I'm glad you came by," I said suddenly.

He smiled, reached across the table, and held my hand. "Your cheeks are all bright red," he said. "You look like you just came down from the North Pole."

We began chatting, and right away I remembered how much I liked our conversations. He did not mention what he was doing in his free time, but he did not seem desperate, like the last time I'd seen him. I wondered if he didn't have somebody else to keep him company. It was a difficult notion to grapple with.

I filled him in about everything that I had done in the past two weeks, and he told me about his writing projects. His career was taking off, and it was fun to hear about some of the celebrities he was dealing with. By the time I looked up at the clock, two hours had vanished and it was late. I dashed into the bathroom and tried to fix my hair and wipe away the trace of smudged makeup. My eyes were puffy, my skin whiter than usual. I thought how I looked as desperate as I felt.

In the taxi as we headed home, I told Peter that I didn't know what to say to Jack. He sat there staring out the window trying to come up with a line. "You bumped into one of your girlfriends after the party. . . . How about Gina?"

"She's not a girlfriend."

"You guys bumped into each other, okay, and she asked you for a drink. Tell him you kind of like her now. And come up with a few crazy details to make it real—she was wearing these black-and-white saddle shoes and she stepped on your foot or something. A good lie needs petty details."

Before getting out of the cab, Peter asked me if I would mind if he came by the Garage the next day. I told him that I would like that.

"Are you doing anything for Christmas?" he asked.

"Going away," I said.

"Where to?"

"To see some friends upstate," I said.

"With Jack?"

"Sorry," I said, nodding and seeing how disappointed he was. "He planned this trip a long time ago."

Then I raced up the stairs to our apartment. My dinner was sitting on our dining room table, cold. Jack had eaten his, had left his dirty plate there, and was now sitting on our bed watching the ten o'clock news. I stepped inside the bedroom. "Jack, I can't believe the time. I am so sorry, darling. I bumped into Gina; I thought it was eight. Oh, boy . . ."

Jack continued watching the television. "Well, I was getting worried—it seemed weird."

"*You* think it's weird? How about *me*? I mean, I'm the one who went into the time warp. Maybe it was just in the air . . . Gina stepped on my—"

"I thought you didn't like her?"

"Actually I do like her. I was just so shocked to like her." I wasn't hungry, but I picked up my plate and brought it over to him. "By the way, the party was amazing," I said. "At least forty kids showed up. I wish you had been there, Jack."

Chapter Fifteen

The next afternoon I went to the Garage and worked with the children. Then around five Peter showed up, as he had promised, and we headed over to the bar. It was a cozy neighborhood bar with sawdust on the floor and Christmas lights on the walls and ceilings. We talked about our day, and at the end of the night we kissed and made plans to see each other the next afternoon.

Over a period of but a few days this became a regular thing, and I found myself more deeply attached to Peter than ever before. Every day at work I looked forward to seeing him, to sitting next to him at the booth table, holding hands and kissing. Jack was in his own world. He believed that I was working on the bicycle project and that it was keeping me there late. One afternoon I took off early from work and spent the rest of the day with Peter. We went out to Brighton Beach and had lunch at a Russian restaurant and then walked along the boardwalk to Coney Island.

As the holidays approached, Peter became more anxious about the prospect of spending Christmas day without me. I wanted to find a way to reassure Peter, but there was no excuse that could possibly get me out of going away with Jack for the holidays. We had plans to spend the weekend with friends in upstate New York.

"You know," Peter said, "I hate to bring it up again, but I do think we need a game plan."

I knew that he was right, though I didn't have the slightest idea how to make the first move in his direction. I told him that I would think about it over the weekend and that we could talk about it the next time I saw him. "But I'll call you from up there if I get a chance."

Peter gave me the number to his parents' house in New Jersey, where he would be staying.

On Christmas Eve Jack and I drove out of the city on our way to Woodstock. I was far more nervous than I thought I would be. I wasn't sure what it would be like to be far away from Peter physically. I felt distant from Jack as I sat next to him. I was keeping a secret from him—my liaison with Peter—but I felt like he was keeping secrets from me too, though I didn't know what they were. As we were nearing the town of Woodstock, Jack turned into the driveway of a real estate office and parked the car. "What are you doing?" I asked him.

"I asked Dave if there was anything for sale up here in our price range. He said there was something he was pretty sure we'd like. He wouldn't tell me the details, just told me to speak to a guy in this agency."

"Jack, I don't know about looking at houses."

"We don't have to buy one."

Jack stepped into the office without me. I thought how not long ago he would never have done something like this without consulting me. A few moments later he came out with a real estate agent who waved for me to follow him. We got into his car, and the agent introduced himself and began driving us through the countryside.

"Dave thought you two might be interested in this place—admittedly it's not for everybody. What do you two think about rabbits?"

"Rabbits?" I looked at Jack. He smiled and nodded. He already seemed to know about the place.

"Two old women lived in this one—eccentrics, nobody knew them, but they had a thing for white rabbits—and *Alice in Wonderland.*"

Jack watched my reaction from the front seat.

"Put it this way," the agent said. "There were close to five hundred of the creatures when the last of the two sisters suddenly took off on a trip and never came back. The rabbits had full run of many rooms in the house—and they weren't exactly housebroken."

"What do you mean?" I said.

"Some of the rooms have rabbit dung in them—not all, and it's not as bad as it sounds. If you could hire somebody to clean the place out, you'd have yourself an amazing deal. It's set up on a hill far away from the road—most of the old gems are alongside a busy road—and it's got a view to please the Prince of Wales."

The agent turned off the road and drove up a hill bordered by pastures of brown grass and patches of melting snow. The weather had been mild the past few days. Rusted barbed wire etched a crooked line from post to post next to the rutted road. Thistles teetered in the fields, and a deeply trodden cow path zigzagged down the steep hill between cedar trees.

We came to the driveway with a view of the house resting high up on the hill. No yard, just pasture. At the bottom of the hill the agent got out to open the gate, and then we drove on. We got out near the porch and looked around. The view included a valley of two large working farms with tall white silos, tobacco barns, and a tractor far away plowing a muddy field. Behind the two farms rose a dark mountain of fir trees that the agent said was part of the Catskill National Forest. The land behind the house was part of a trust and would not be developed, save for two new houses out of view. Jack took my hand and we climbed up onto the sagging porch and did our best to imagine that we could afford this place together. The agent had not yet told us the price.

The agent opened the door and began giving us a tour. He opened the door to one of the rooms for rabbits. It had obviously been cleaned up, but there were still bits of straw and the boards were stained.

"You'd have to yank up the floorboards, that's all. It's got a feeling about it, doesn't it?" the agent said.

I held tightly to Jack's hand as we moved from room to room. The agent was right; it did have a splendid feeling about it, something warm and beautiful. There was an old wood stove that the sisters had used for cooking, and yellow electrical wires taped here and there, and hanging light-bulbs, antique multipaned windows with uneven, bubble-filled glass. The sort of place I'd always dreamed about owning someday.

"Here's what's odd," the agent said through his hand-kerchief. "This place is cheaper than if it had just been an empty lot. This structure can't be knocked down. It's a land-mark."

"All the way up here?" Jack said.

"You can't knock it down without violating the law."

"But why a landmark?"

"Some famous architect who used to design bridges and parks. It's one of the only houses that he did. I could find out the whole story for you."

Upstairs he showed us the bed that the sisters had slept in. Fortunately there was no sign of rabbits. Framed archi-tectural blueprints of bridges hung from the walls of flaking paint. The agent pointed at warped, moldy paperbacks of *Alice in Wonderland* on the bookshelves. "You thought I was kidding, didn't you? I don't know what came first, the books or the rabbits."

"Did you ever meet these two?" Jack said.

"Nobody did. One of them, Gwen, died—rumor has it she's buried on the property. The other one, Maggie, is the one who let the rabbits go in here. Then she suddenly pulled up stakes and left. We discovered the rabbits when somebody notified the Humane Society. They occupied at least five rooms. People in town didn't want to kill the poor creatures, but what could anybody do?"

"What *did* they do with them?" Jack asked.

I turned around and walked out of the room to avoid the story. I felt strongly that I didn't want to hear it if it was bad. In this other room I opened a moldy copy of *Alice in Wonderland* and discovered that the margins of the book had served as a diary. The writing was almost illegibly small. There were dates that went back twenty years. I put it back and returned to the room with Jack, who glanced over at me, knowing why I'd stepped out.

Outside we looked back at the discolored siding of the house. "It takes a little imagination to make this work, but it's definitely doable," the agent said.

"What do you think?" Jack said to me.

"They didn't kill the rabbits in here, did they?" I said under my breath.

"Everything that happened here was cool."

The question had been an important one, a kind of hurdle. "It's a beautiful place." There was an ocean of feeling in these words. It really was a beautiful place, the sort of house I had dreamed of owning with Jack. Maybe it would be a chance for a new beginning, but it would certainly mean giving up what I had started in New York.

"Could you give us some time alone up here?" Jack said to the agent.

We climbed the hill behind the house, following a path through the trees that came out on a kind of overlook where we could see the house's patched roof and decrepit chimney and, far below, a fenced-in rectangle of tall weeds that must have been a vegetable garden. Jack grabbed me and pulled me against him. He held me firmly. I could sense passion and perhaps a bit of desperation in his grip, though I wasn't sure.

"At least if we had some place we were fixing up, working toward, a kind of goal, what a difference it would make," Jack said.

Only an hour before this I was unsure if anything could possibly save our marriage. Yet now, staring at this beautiful funky house with its cupolas and cornices and its strange history, I was beginning to see things in a different light.

"Maybe you're right," I said.

I was envisioning all the rabbit-filled rooms in the house and this woman, Maggie, whoever she was, with her mad obsession with *Alice in Wonderland*. Feelings for Jack came rushing back to me.

"This is it, Maddy. We've got to get the money for this place."

"It would be an awful lot of work."

"We'll come up here every weekend, do it bit by bit. We'll turn this place into a haven. God, we're going to be happy here. I know we will. We'll have friends parading in and out from the city. . . . We'll tell our kids about all the rabbits that lived here before us. Can you imagine what that would be like for them? Living in a place like this that you knew had been the home of hundreds of rabbits and two crazy old dames? Maybe we'll go crazy and have a few thousand offspring ourselves!" Jack was almost yelling. I couldn't believe that he'd said this. Despite everything that was happening to me at the time, I became swept up in the dream.

We ran down the hill past the house. I stopped and called that I wanted to get something inside, then ran back up the stairs to the second floor and pocketed the copy of *Alice in Wonderland* that had been scribbled in.

We got back in the car with the real estate agent and returned to his office. Then we drove on to our friends' house in Lake Hill, just outside of Woodstock.

That evening we drank eggnog and decorated a Christmas tree while Jack talked to his friend about the rabbit house and renovating houses in general and what it would be like to move up here. I retired early to bed to read the diary. I felt sure that it contained something important, that this woman who lived with the rabbits would impart some wisdom, even if she were totally insane.

The very first thing I noticed was that our handwriting was similar, and right away I jumped to the conclusion that we had things in common. Though her description of meeting Gwen bore no resemblance to how I had met Jack—Maggie had pursued Gwen—there were other similarities. They had met at Radcliffe, where Gwen was a popular figure, a wild actress who was in plays all over Boston. She was also incredibly wealthy and seemed to have an attitude about money that was similar to Jack's—she gave it away whenever she could. I pored over Maggie's writings, looking for guidance to my own life. When she wrote in her diary that Gwen had died of a heart attack, I became even more eager to read the subsequent entries. Just as I feared, Maggie began a descent into a hellish madness. At least three times she attempted to take her own life, and each time she was revived. According to her, the mere fact that somebody happened upon the house and rescued her, despite her extreme isolation, was evidence of some sort of supernatural presence, perhaps a ghost on the premises. *Somebody called an ambulance,* she wrote; *it certainly wasn't me.* During her third stay in the hospital, Maggie drew an image that she said appeared to her on the brink of death. It was a heart with an eye in the center. Below it, she wrote out a poem that that she ascribed to the troubadours in the eleventh century.

> *So, through the eyes love attains the heart:*
> *For the eyes are the scouts of the heart,*
> *And the eyes go reconnoitering*
> *For what it would please the heart to possess.*
> *And when they are in full accord*
> *And firm, all three, in one resolve,*
> *At that time, perfect love is born.*

To her the image of the eye in the heart symbolized her first and only love, which was Gwen. She seemed convinced, at least in this part of her diary, that a first love was one's only true love. *Everything thereafter is near-beer.* Evidently her musings were a struggle to save her own life after the loss of that first love. I found questions everywhere in the diary. *How can you survive when the meaning of your life has not? Is it ever possible to recover from such a loss?*

Later that night Jack crawled into bed with me.

"I was just talking to Dave about something," he said. "We could camp out at the house tomorrow after Christmas dinner, you know, just to get a feel for it. It's supposed to be something like fifty-five degrees tomorrow. Dave's got the equipment and he knows the Realtor. He also knows a house inspector. What do you say to that?"

"Sounds great," I said, and I meant it. I was really starting to get into the idea of buying this.

The next morning I was able to slip off to town on an errand so that I could call Peter, as I had promised him I would do. I had been having second thoughts about calling him, but I had promised, and I didn't want to break yet another promise with anyone. Besides, I felt sorry for him spending Christmas alone.

I was nervous making the call; the last person in the world I wanted to talk to was his mother. I had the feeling that she was like my mother, though I didn't know why. I had the feeling that she'd see right through me the moment she got me on the line. Fortunately Peter answered, and I was reminded of what I liked about talking to him. I was comforted by him. We talked for a while, and then suddenly I began describing Maggie's diary to him. I told him how much I was identifying with her, despite her madness.

"You just found a copy of this book in a house, whose house?" Peter said.

I ended up describing the rabbit house to him.

"There's no way you guys are looking at houses together, are you?" I could tell how upset he was.

"It was Jack's idea," I said. "Don't worry about it. It's pretty outlandish." I told him that some of the rooms were full of straw and rabbit droppings.

"Yuck," he said. "What are you two thinking? Do you realize what it would mean if you bought the place? It would be the end of us—and you just tell me this as if I should be happy for you."

"I'm sorry—I don't know what got into me."

When I walked away from the pay phone, I felt bad for having told him about the house. Already it seemed like something private between Jack and me.

Chapter Sixteen

We had a festive dinner that afternoon with our friends, and Jack seemed like a different person, telling stories and cracking jokes. The very idea of buying the house was working on him like a drug. I was laughing too. Late that afternoon Jack and Dave filled the back of our car with enough equipment for a small expedition—a tent, sleeping bags, a backpack full of pots, a gas stove, and a cooler of leftovers for dinner—and we set off for the night.

"Wow, we're two nuts—camping out in December at this old house full of rabbit poop," Jack said. He stopped at the base of the driveway, and I got out to open the metal gate. It was nearly fifty degrees out, and all of the snow had melted, leaving brown grass and mud on the hillside. I could see up the long dirt driveway to the house on the hill. The place reminded me of the run-down mansion in *It's a Wonderful Life* before Jimmy Stewart and Donna Reed fixed it up. We drove right up to the front steps, parked, and climbed onto the porch. Taking a deep breath, Jack turned and looked over the valley and I could feel his joy. The door was unlocked and I began walking through the rooms. Many of the windows had been left open, and now the smell had dissipated somewhat. Maggie had drawn a floor plan in her diary with names for each room: the Den, the Warren, the Carrot Pantry, the Kitchen Hole; the smaller bedrooms were the Burrows. At the top of the stairs to the second floor I stepped into the master bedroom, the Hutch. There were broken lamps in here, a night table with only two legs. Plaster had fallen from the wall above the headboard.

Stepping over to the bay window, I looked out at the dramatic view of the valley. Other than the few telephone poles in the distance, the vista was probably no different than it had been a hundred and fifty years ago. I heard Jack coming up the stairs.

"Can you imagine waking up to this view?" he said, pacing around. He came over and hugged me, and then he went back downstairs to set up the tent.

I walked through the upstairs rooms with my hands behind my back. I could definitely see his point—we would be different people here, with different goals. Suddenly I spotted an old photograph in a frame at the top of a bookcase. I pushed a chair over to reach it and dusted it off. It was of a woman with curly hair heaped high on her head, powder-white skin, and lips so thin they were ready to disappear into her face. She had that stately look of old portraits, a real matriarch, and she held the curved end of a cane in her hand. I found the picture a bit spooky, so I put it back on its shelf and then went downstairs to help out.

We finished staking the tent and laying out our sleeping bags. From the house we carried a small table out onto the porch, spread a cloth over it, and set up two chairs. We heated up Christmas-dinner leftovers on a camp stove, and when all was ready, we sat back in our chairs and opened a bottle of wine. We were bundled up in our coats. Not a word passed between us as we ate dinner. The sun went down behind the mountain, and fiery red light illuminated a haystack of clouds. It was spectacularly beautiful. As darkness fell, the smells of the winter earth kept changing. In the distance a cow was calling. I didn't realize how much wine I had sipped until I heard Jack uncork another bottle. The stars were out by then and we'd finished most of our food.

"Hey, what are you doing?" I said.

"Oh, come on. Let's be ourselves again." He raised his glass to toast. I took another sip; then I got up and went around the back of the house to a corner of the lawn to pee. When I pulled my pants back up, I felt dizzy and quite drunk. I climbed back onto the porch. Jack was sitting there in the dark, starlight reflecting off his eyes.

"It's so warm out, I think there are actually bugs out. Something bit my butt," I said.

"Lucky bug," Jack said, and I laughed and looked out over the valley. A blinking radio tower and the windows of two farmhouses cast the only light in the shadow of the mountain.

"Jack," I said suddenly. "Do you believe in ghosts?"

He looked at me and smiled. "Do you?"

"The lady who used to live here believed there was a ghost here. She wrote about it—in the *Alice in Wonderland* book."

"A good or bad ghost?"

"She thinks it saved her."

"It must be a good one." Suddenly he got to his feet, cupped his hands around his mouth, and yelled at the top of his lungs, "Hey, ghost, are you good or bad?" A moment later we heard the faintest echo: . . . *good or bad*.

"Somebody's going to call the police."

"Nobody can hear us up here. Try it, Maddy."

I stood up, cupped my hands around my mouth, and yelled, "Ghost, are you there? Let us know how you stand."

The faintest echo came back from the hills: . . . *how you stand.*

"Maddy, do you realize this is our fourteenth year together? Isn't that incredible? How many people have been together that long?"

I shook my head. "We're getting to be a couple of old fogies."

"You think so? I think it's an amazing accomplishment. I think we should do something about it, become marriage counselors or something—a husband-and-wife team. Think of all the wisdom about human relationships that we've gathered," Jack joked.

I laughed.

"If anybody comes to us with a problem, we'll just tell them to sublimate. We'll solve everyone's problems." He took another sip. "Men are good at it. Cigars, big cars, golf, football, and writing, of course—all in the name of sublimation. But what do women do? Knit?" He looked at me.

"We knit our eyebrows, silly."

"Come to think of it, the common wisdom is that it's the man who has the affairs—but that's not the case at all, from what I can see. Maybe women don't sublimate. Maybe they just go and do it." He was trying to be funny, but I wondered why he was saying this and I became terrified. "I swear, Maddy, every time I hear about an affair—it's a woman doing it, not a man. I'm sure plenty of men do it, but it doesn't seem that way, at least in New York." He thought about this a moment. "It must be strange. I mean, to lie to the person you love. Wouldn't that be strange?"

I looked over at him cautiously and realized he was staring at me. My heart was pounding.

"Ever think of what it would really be like?"

I saw that he was expecting me to say something about this. "It would be crazy, Jack."

"It's the sort of thing that could break somebody's heart," he said. "The person doing the lying as much as the other." Now I was sure that he knew something.

I spoke so quietly that he might not have heard. "It definitely would."

I waited for the subject to pass. He seemed tense, and then he sighed and I could hear him pouring himself another glass of wine. It was too dark to see his face, but I could sense that a change had come over him. He went over to our tent and began fixing our sleeping bags. I turned on my flashlight and went back inside the house. I could feel blood racing through my body. My legs felt weak; I wanted to cry or run away. I climbed to the second floor, went into the master bedroom, and pointed the flashlight at the picture. The woman's thin lips were curled up ambiguously—either frowning or smiling.

Then I heard a voice from behind me: "Ridiculous!"

I was sure it had come from the hallway. I flashed the beam against the walls and then turned it off again. I was too drunk and too unsettled to know whether it was my imagination or something real.

I went back downstairs and outside. Jack was sitting on the porch steps, watching the stars. I sat next to him.

"I heard a noise; there really is something in there, Jack," I said.

"You don't really believe that, do you?" He took my hand and squeezed. He could feel me trembling. "You don't really believe that?" he asked again.

I shook my head.

"Are you okay?" he asked, continuing to squeeze my hand.

"Things are so complicated, Jack, aren't they?"

"Maddy," he said quietly. "They don't have to be, I promise you."

"Why do you say so?"

"Because I love you."

I looked at him in the darkness. "You do?" I whispered.

"More than ever," he said.

"I love you, too," I whispered.

He led me down the steps and around the back in the damp grass to the tent. We slipped into our sleeping bags.

I woke up at first light and lay there looking at the tent roof. Birds were just starting to sing. A vivid memory came to me of a dream: Jack and I bought the house, began renovations, and then moved in. Some weeks later I heard a horrible morbid hacklike cough coming from upstairs, and when I climbed the stairs I saw an old woman lying in our bed, a rail of a woman, pale and extremely sick. As I looked at her I had this feeling that she was too obstinate and stubborn to move. She would have to die in the house, and her death would be prolonged and tortured and would take a huge toll on me. I couldn't remember the rest of the dream, but I had a haunting feeling that I had done something to hasten her demise—I'd stuffed a sock down her throat and left her alone.

The feeling continued to haunt me as I lay awake next to Jack. It was the knowledge that I was a murderer and my life would always be poisoned by the secret guilt of my crime. Unzipping the tent, I slipped out and put on my clothes as I stood in the cold, wet grass. The clouds were thin and high and the earth still. I walked over to the porch and began cleaning up our dinner dishes from the night before.

An hour later I was sitting on the porch when I saw a

pickup truck coming up the driveway slowly. The truck seemed like an ominous intrusion—an investigator perhaps, or even a policeman coming up to arrest me for my crime. Then I remembered that Jack and Dave had called a house inspector to check the place over for us this morning. I woke Jack up and he dressed quickly and came around the front to greet the inspector. I took Maggie's diary into the field below the porch and sat down to read while the two men went through the house. I read:

I've finally figured out what is necessary, 1) To find my dream—not Gwen's dream, but mine. 2) To believe in it as mine and not anybody else's. 3) To step into it and live in it.

An hour later Jack sat next to me with the report in his hand. "The guy couldn't believe this place. I mean, he said if I didn't buy it, he would. He called it a gold mine, said it will be worth a ton of dough if it's fixed up. There are problems like water damage from the leaky roof, but these are minor compared to what the resale value would be worth. Maddy, this is our next big step. I really think we should make an offer. He said we can't go wrong."

In the afternoon we returned the camping equipment and bade farewell to our friends, then we got on the highway back to New York City. The vague guilty feeling from the dream still lingered, and I could no longer separate that sense of guilt from what I was feeling with Jack. I kept thinking how fragile people are, how important trust is, and yet how easy it is to lie and break that trust.

Chapter Seventeen

Early Monday morning Jack made the offer by telephone. The house was owned by a foundation that had been set up on a Caribbean island, and it would take time to hear back if the offer was accepted. Jack quickly went to work raising money for the down payment from everyone he knew—friends, family members. By late afternoon his own generosity over the years had paid off; almost everyone had pledged enough money for the down payment if the deal went through. That night Jack and I went to a dinner party at a friend's apartment, and he showed everyone pictures of the house, and his enthusiasm grew. I was as excited about it as he was. I had completely forgotten about my troubles. On the way home Jack was holding my hand tightly. He stopped a few blocks from our building, turned, and looked at me.

"You know, I've decided this is no ordinary house," he said. "It's actually us. It's the incarnation of us—do you know what I mean?"

He was staring at me and smiling.

"Let me explain," he said, pushing hair out of his eyes. "It's like a big collection of everything that makes up life— craziness, love, passion, mystery, obsession, madness and . . . rabbits. Yes, rabbits. Rabbits are far more important to life than anyone ever knew. Rabbits rule! They really do, you know; people just don't realize it." He was getting so excited that pedestrians were walking far around us on the sidewalk. "See these people around us?" he said excitedly. "Nobody has the slightest idea that the world around them is ruled by rabbits. They're the kings and queens of the world. I bet those two women up there were so full of life that they didn't know what to do with themselves. I bet they lived it up in there."

We began walking again.

"I don't know, Jack; it looks more like a ship to me, the way it sits up on that hill, a ship that's ready to sail," I said, strolling along, my hands in my pockets. "Once it's ours, it's going to take us to far-off lands where we never dreamed of going, wonderful places that no other couple has ever been before." I took his hand and pulled him against me, kissing him. It felt like the first time we had ever kissed.

All the next day at work, I was feeling giddy about the prospect of getting the house. Late in the afternoon, just as I was leaving, I got a phone call and it was Peter.

"Hey, where you been? I thought you were going to call when you got back."

I apologized. "I've been busy," I said.

"How about this evening?"

I stumbled for a moment. "I'm busy for the next couple of nights. How about the day after tomorrow?" I said. "I've got a lot of little things to take care of tonight."

"Two days—after work? I can't meet for long that day, but I do want to see you so badly."

I liked the idea of seeing him for a short time. We agreed

to meet in Tompkins Square and then stop at his apartment, which he had wanted to show me for weeks. After I got off the phone with him, I drew up a plan for our meeting. I would muster up the courage to break things off with him. I would tell him that I'd had a change of heart; I was going to try to make things work out with Jack. I wouldn't tell him the rest of my plan: Every time I thought about him in the future, I would block it out by focusing on some aspect of the house, even if I became obsessed with the house. That night Jack and I went out to eat together and we began talking about all the things we were going to do to the place. We were sitting at a booth table, and halfway through dinner Jack moved over to my side and put his arm around me.

The next morning I got to work early and began thinking some more about my meeting with Peter the next day. It would take a lot of strength to simply cut things off, but I was sure I could do it, and the firmer I was about it, the better off we would both be in the end.

Around midmorning my mind was ablaze about the house, and I left the office to run a quick errand on Sixth Avenue. Suddenly I spotted Jack coming down the sidewalk toward me. He was walking slowly, with his hands in his pockets. I was about to yell for him but held back. There was something different about him; all the inspiration that had been on his face for the past few days was gone. I stopped to watch him. He hadn't seen me yet, and I was wondering if I were seeing a side of him that he had always kept hidden from me.

Then I called his name and he suddenly looked up. He was bewildered, so lost in thought that he didn't recognize me at first. He started shaking his head angrily, as if I had done something wrong. I thought that he must have found out about Peter and me. Unable to move, I stared straight into his ashen face as he came right up to me.

"Jack, what is it—what's the matter?"

"We lost it. It sold." I was so astonished that this was why he felt bad that I hardly registered its implications. "That fucking inspector—he's the one," he said. "He was so damn pumped up about the place when he gave me the report. He kept telling me there was a profit to be made. He must have cut a deal with the agent."

"But he can't do that. We could sue him."

"No, Maddy, it's a small town. I already talked to Dave about it. Dave knows him—he only called him because it was such short notice. The guy's corrupt as hell and so is the real estate agent. Remember what the inspector said about buying it himself? I guess he just thought, 'Fuck it, what can a guy from New York do about it?' He couldn't resist." I thought he was going to cry. "He had no idea what that place meant to us, Maddy. None. That place was crucial."

"Oh, come on, Jack. There will be others."

"Oh, no, Maddy, not like that." He kept shaking his head despairingly. "Well," he said, taking a deep breath and attempting a smile, "I've got to get to work." I hugged him hard, pressing my face against the side of his. It felt like the life had gone out of him completely.

I returned to work. Slowly, the rest of the day, the loss of the house sank in. I tried not to think about it, but I felt like one of those cartoon characters that has just run off a cliff but won't fall until she looks down. That afternoon I took off early and did what I usually did in times like these: I headed to Atlantic Avenue, opened the Garage early, and began working on a huge collage that the children had begun with me. Part of what was so upsetting was knowing how Jack was going to continue to react. I had the feeling he would cut me off again. I didn't know why I thought this; maybe I was just shy from the way it had happened before. I dreaded going home that evening.

When I did get home, there was a message on the machine from Jack saying he was going to be at work late. His tone of voice confirmed what I had suspected—he sounded cold. I stayed up late to wait for him, and sure enough when he came in the door he simply went into the bathroom without saying a word to me. Then he came out, slipped into bed, and turned out the light.

"Jack, aren't you even going to say good night?"

There was a pause. "Good night," he said quietly.

The next afternoon I met with Peter in Tompkins Square, and we walked east together toward his apartment on Avenue D. Right away I was surprised at how happy and upbeat he seemed as he talked to me about the things that were going on in his life. It was a great relief from what I had been experiencing all day. I'd woken with the cold, alienated feeling I'd suffered through all summer around Jack. It was windy and cold, and Peter kept telling me how much he missed me over the weekend. He talked about his family. They drove him crazy, he said. "They're so damn normal, Maddy, they make your parents seem like rock stars. And here I am in love with a married woman." Then he stopped and told me that it was worth all the pain just to be able to be with me again. "Are you okay? You seem upset."

"Jack lost the house," I said.

"What house—the one you guys were looking at?"

I told him what had happened—Jack calling everyone for money and then making the bid on it. "The inspector bought it," I said. "A real bastard."

He put his hands on my shoulders. "Damn, Maddy, I can't believe that you guys almost went through with that."

I tried to smile as if it were nothing.

"That doesn't make me feel good. I mean, heck—why did you do that?"

"It happened fast—but it's over now. It's really over."

We came to his building on Avenue B. It was one of those newly renovated buildings with large, tinted plate-glass windows and bright red brick, the sort of modern façade that never really fits into the poor neighborhood around it. He unlocked the lobby door and we took the elevator up to the eleventh floor. His apartment was a one-bedroom with hardwood floors and a small fireplace and mantel. I was surprised how barren it was; there was hardly anything on the walls and nothing on the mantel. In one room there were cardboard boxes, as if he'd never really unpacked. Peter's laptop was set up facing the window that looked west over the tops of the buildings. There were papers spread across his desk. We sat down on his couch. My hands were cold, and he rubbed them together for me. Then he turned to me and said, "Maddy, I missed you like crazy. You know, the fact that you didn't call me when you got back hurt me."

I apologized.

"But I have to say, the minute I am with you, I know why I like you so much. I love you," he said, and then he kissed me.

I suddenly realized how glad I was to be with him now. I did not want to go back and face Jack.

"Do you love me?" he said.

"Yes," I said. He seemed relieved and began kissing me. I knew I should stop him, but I couldn't bring myself to do it. We lay back on the couch and he rolled on top of me and began unbuttoning my coat and then my blouse. After feeling so alienated, I needed to be touched like this, and I could feel the pleasure rippling through my body. I told him to be careful, but those words were quickly lost as his hands caressed my skin. He kissed both sides of my neck and then worked his way down to my chest. Then he began kissing my breast and I began moaning. I could feel his tongue against my nipples. I closed my eyes, holding his hair in my hands. Then I realized he had unbuttoned my pants and was slipping off my underwear.

"No," I said, my heart beating hard. I was so turned on I could hardly move. I managed to sit up and drag my pants up to my waist. "I'm sorry—I can't do this. Not until Jack and I are separated."

Peter rolled onto his back. He seemed deeply distraught.

"You're right," he said. "I can't believe I just did that. I'm sorry."

I sat down on a separate chair. I was still turned on; I could feel the moisture between my thighs. I was afraid that things would start up again. Peter finally got up also and apologized again.

"You know, I've been dreading telling you something. I'm moving out of this place—that's what all the boxes are about. I'm half-packed. I found an apartment on the Internet." He smiled weakly. "It's in Paris."

"Paris?" I said.

"It's a beautiful place. It's on the Left Bank near Boulevard St. Michel—it's got a view of the Jardin du Luxembourg. It's plenty big, tons of sunlight. One room would make a great studio. The pictures of it made me think of you. I'm moving there."

"What?" I said, shocked.

"I can't stay in New York any longer, Maddy. I just can't stand this situation. I don't think it's healthy either. I'm going to wait for you there."

"Wait a minute—"

"I couldn't take another week like the one I just went through—and New Year's is coming up in a few days. It will be the best thing for both of us. You don't even realize the pain you're in too, Maddy. You'll feel so much better once you're there." He reached over to his desk for an envelope and handed it to me. I became very frightened about what might be inside of it. "Go on," he said. "Open it."

I opened it and took out an airline ticket: DESTINATION: ORLY, PARIS, FRANCE.

"It's an open round-trip and it's yours. All you have to do is check it out for a few days, see what living there would be like."

I looked into his eyes. I could not say a word. "And here," he said. "There's something else I wanted to give you." I looked down and realized he was slipping a ring on my finger, an ornate silver ring with rubies and sapphires and horses engraved in the silver. I lifted my hand and looked at it in the window light. I wondered where he had gotten it, and yet I didn't even want to pretend it was mine. It was obviously old and must have been expensive. It was one of the most beautiful silver rings I had ever seen.

"Look inside it," he said. I took it off. An inscription read: TO MY LOVE, M.G.

"Where did you get this?"

"It used to be my grandmother's."

"You can't give me something like this," I said.

"Please, I've already inscribed it. It's yours." Then as if reading my mind, he said, "If he sees it, tell him you found it." Glancing at his watch, he got up and kissed me on the cheek. "Now I've got to get to a meeting downtown. It's about the new script."

We dressed and went downstairs. It was starting to sleet outside. Peter hailed a cab and told me he would drop me off near my apartment. We held hands in silence. I was trying to imagine what it would be like not to see him at all. The cab stopped on Delancey Street four blocks from my building to let me out, and Peter still held my hand. "I'm not going to make this good-bye a big deal, because I know I'm going to see you soon, right? I'll call you at work as soon as

I have a number. Then you can call me back on this." He stuck a cell phone in my bag. "Maddy, if you don't come soon, I don't know what I'll do."

I dashed through the freezing rain all the way to our apartment building. Jack wasn't home. Just inside the door I took the ring out and examined it again. It truly was the most beautiful ring I'd ever seen. I started walking around the apartment looking for a place to hide it. Soon I was panicked, imagining a crazy scenario whereby Jack would walk in and find me with the ring in my hand, distraught, still desperately looking for a place to conceal it from him. I first tried putting it in a jar of pennies that dated back to college, and then I taped it to the underside of my dresser drawer. Finally I settled on the underside of a loose parquet floorboard, assuming that upon its discovery I could claim the former tenants had left it there.

At around ten o'clock, Jack came in soaking wet and went into the bathroom to dry his hair with a towel. I got up slowly from our bed and met him at the bathroom door, where he kissed me briefly. Sitting down on his desk chair, he began pulling off his wet sneakers, his pants clinging to his legs. He slipped into a pair of long underwear and an undershirt and then came to bed. His hair was all messed up, Einstein fashion.

"Look what I had to buy," he said. It was a book about renovating old houses. "I ordered it on Monday."

Then he rolled over in bed and turned off the light. He lay there silently.

"Jack," I said, "are you okay?"

"I'm okay, Maddy. I'll recover. It will just take some time."

I lay there in the dark.

"It was just a house, Jack."

"Yeah," he said, and sighed. "I know."

Chapter Eighteen

When I woke up the following morning, a Thursday, I was aware that Peter's flight had already departed. He'd left so quickly I hardly had time to register it. I couldn't figure out whether he'd done this to shock me or simply because he was so insecure that I might never leave Jack. One minute he seemed manipulative; the next he seemed frightened. I couldn't imagine what I would do if I was in his position.

Later, as I walked up Broadway to work, I was feeling vaguely relieved that he was gone. But the relief diminished quickly that morning, and by the afternoon I was waiting for him to call.

When the call finally came, Peter sounded as excited as I'd ever heard him. He was phoning from the street and I could hear the traffic behind him, the whining of mopeds and a French police siren. "The place is a gem. On one side, you can see the dome of the Pantheon. On the other, the trees of the Jardin du Luxembourg. It's a bit noisy but it's wonderful." He described the surrounding neighborhood so well that I felt as if I were there. There were moments in the conversation when he was waiting for me to say something definitive about my going. "Maddy, come here for a few days—or even a night—and see what it's like."

"I'll have to lie to Jack—how will I explain the ticket?"

"Make it vague."

"He's not going to believe I just found a ticket or something."

"Come on, you're good at this. Just tell him a friend had an extra ticket. Things will work out. We'll make plans about how you can move out without him knowing about us. It will be the best thing that ever happened to both of you."

"Does he know you moved to Paris?"

"Everyone thinks I'm in Hollywood—I don't want Jack to find out about us any more than you do."

The idea of creating a whole new life for myself was more than just appealing. After I got off, I went into a room where I could use a telephone privately, sat down a moment, and thought of a story to tell Jack about how I'd gotten a ticket to Paris. I couldn't come up with one, but I called him anyway and we chatted for a while. "Jack, you know Ray?" I said without knowing exactly where I was going with this. "He called to say his firm bought him a round-trip ticket to Europe for tomorrow that he can't redeem. He wants to give it to me. I told him forget about it."

"Where in Europe?"

"I think he said Paris."

"Are you serious, Maddy? Paris? You've got to go." He knew that Ray had a crush on me and that I didn't like him, so it all fit together.

"I just don't think I'll be up for a six-hour flight," I said.

"You can't be serious. We're talking Paris, France—not Netcong, New Jersey. I mean, come on. I'd be out of here in a flash if I could."

"I know, but things—"

"It's been your dream." It was a combination of Jack's encouragement and the fact that he used the words *your dream* that made me sad.

I called the airline and made arrangements to fly out the following evening, then I called Peter on the cell phone and told him what I had done.

When I got home that evening, Jack's spirits seemed to have lifted a little. He had bought me a present. I opened it on the kitchen table—a Michelin map of Paris and a guidebook.

The next morning I brought my packed bags to work with the intention of leaving for the airport in the afternoon. My flight was at seven. At noon Peter called me, and when I mentioned that I'd brought my bags with me, he was elated. At five o'clock I left work and flagged a taxi. The taxi crossed town at Fourteenth Street and then headed up First Avenue for the Midtown Tunnel. As I stared out the dusty windows, I started thinking that all of this must have happened for a reason. Maybe the gods really did want me to be with Peter. The more I thought of this, the more convinced I was that I was doing the right thing.

My cab encountered none of the expected traffic on the way, and so I arrived at JFK with time to spare. After checking in at the gate, I paced back and forth to gather my thoughts; then I took out Peter's cell phone and dialed the number he'd given me. Somehow merely making the connection on the phone again would seal my destiny with him. It was eleven o'clock in Paris.

Peter answered. "Maddy!" he said excitedly, and then breathed a sigh of relief. He began talking about what an incredible time we were going to have once I arrived. He had the day planned out for us already. He would pick me up at Orly in the morning and we'd tour the city in a taxi. "I want you to see the Champs Élysée at dawn, and then all the bridges along the Seine. We'll end up at Nôtre-Dame. Remember what you said that nothing man-made will ever match the beauty of nature? That theory will be history soon." I tried to muster enthusiasm that would match his, but I couldn't quite let go.

"Is everything all right?" he said finally.

I was silent.

"What's wrong, darling? Are you afraid?"

"I'm worried about Jack."

"He'll be all right. He's a survivor."

"I just wish that he hadn't gotten his hopes up about that house. It's going to make breaking his heart even harder."

"Sorry," Peter said. He sounded genuinely sympathetic. I was silent; then he said, "But I do think it's better this way. Getting into something like that when things aren't going well . . . it's just not the way to go. It will never be any easier."

"Maybe you're right," I said.

"I mean, after all, that place sounded like a quagmire. I mean, rabbit shit? Come on—who would want something like that?" He laughed a little. "You wouldn't believe what I saw this afternoon—you said you love little circuses? Well, I saw one on the street, just a few acts, a tightrope act, a contortionist—and a . . . a guy who swallowed himself." Peter continued laughing and talking but I wasn't listening. When I got off the phone, I went over to my seat to wait for the flight. I felt uneasy about something. I started thinking about the house again. I was angry. I was thinking how this house inspector had changed our destiny in one fell swoop. I called information and retrieved the phone number to the real estate agency. I couldn't remember the inspector's last name, but I thought I would at least tell the real estate agent what I really thought of him. I let the phone ring a dozen times before finally hanging up. Then I stood there looking at the wall. For some reason I started thinking of how Peter had mentioned seeing a circus. He knew that Jack and I liked small circuses; in fact, we often made trips outside of the city just to see the sort of run-down old show that nobody paid any attention to. It seemed too perfect that he had seen one too. I certainly did not believe he had seen a man who had swallowed himself. Passengers were lining up at the desk to check in; announcements were coming over the loudspeakers. I dialed Peter back.

"Hey, Maddy," he said cheerily.

"Peter," I said quietly. "I need to ask you something, but first I want you to know that you can be honest with me. I mean, I'm open to anything."

"What's on your mind?"

"You don't happen to know who bought that house, do you?"

"What? How would I know that?"

"You can be honest with me," I said.

He hesitated. "Of course I don't know. How would I know?"

"Peter," I said, surprising myself, "I called the real estate agent just now."

He hesitated. "Real estate agent?" he said.

"The one handling the house." I was silent. I wanted him to register what I had said. "Peter, the agent told me you bought it."

Peter laughed nervously. "Why would he say that?"

"I don't know. That's what he said."

There was a long pause. "Look, Maddy—whatever I did, I did for us."

I suddenly felt something well up in my throat, a knot

of anger. I could hardly speak. "So you did, didn't you?" I said.

"What?"

"You bought it."

"Maddy, let's talk—"

"No, let's not. How the fuck could you do that to Jack? I mean, he's your friend—he's done all sorts of things for you. You just buy the house out from under him, just because you can and he can't!" I shouted. "You betrayed him."

"*I* did?"

"Yes, you!" I shouted. "You betrayed him!"

"Maddy, you're his wife. You married him. I'm hardly his friend anymore anyway," Peter said.

There was a long silence between us, and in that silence, I began to understand something. Jack was right: That house was us. I couldn't explain it then or even now. Time and history had given the place its true value, and the value of our marriage was partially based on the same. Peter was interested in the house as an outsider, and he was also interested in what Jack and I had as an outsider. He did not understand what our marriage meant and probably never would. He only understood enough to know that he wanted it for himself.

"Now come on, Maddy. I don't want you to miss your flight."

I turned off the phone, staggered back over to my chair, and fell into it. I was in such shock that I couldn't move. I felt as if I were getting heavier, sinking sadly into my seat, unable to bend forward or backward. My flight was called again—another row of seats. I could see myself getting up but I still didn't move. Passengers lined up at the gate, and one by one they disappeared until no one was left in the room but me.

I felt as though I had swallowed poison and I could feel it seeping into every molecule of my body.

That evening I climbed the stairs to our apartment. Jack had fallen asleep in bed in front of the television. I went into the bathroom to undress and then turned off the television and slipped under the covers next to him. He was breathing quietly and I lay next to him for a while and then put my hand on his chest.

Chapter Nineteen

I went to work the next day and did my best to lose myself in my old routines. I could hardly think about what had nearly happened. Peter called late that afternoon at work, but I didn't take the call, nor return his subsequent ones the following day. A few days later I received an e-mail from him. He wrote that I was a cold-hearted person, that I'd broken his heart.

I thought you were special, but now I know there are plenty of you out there. You seemed like a strong person when I met you, but now I see you're not capable of making a decision for yourself. Thank you for helping me learn how to avoid the type.

It went on for almost a page, but I deleted the rest before reading it. I knew I'd made this decision on my own and that it had been the right one. I had made a terrible mistake by getting involved with Peter to begin with.

My marriage resumed, but it was changed in a fundamental way; I definitely wanted things to work out. Some-how the underhanded thing that Peter had done made me see more clearly the value of Jack's way of looking at the world. Jack would never have undermined my own chance to make a decision the way Peter had done by buying the house. Jack was anything but manipulative, and that was probably why he was not very good at playing the game; he respected people in a way that few people do.

I still wanted children, but I felt like I was willing to wait longer for that. Maybe I would have to have a smaller family than I wanted, but at least the child or children would have a father whom I admired.

My biggest problem was that I had no idea how to get our relationship back on track. That winter Jack seemed far unhappier than he had in the past, as if he had never recovered from that moment of discovery about the loss of the house. I wanted to get him to talk about it, but I quickly became plagued by this sneaking suspicion that he knew about what had gone on between Peter and me. A few times Jack mentioned how much he still disliked Peter, and this seemed more than mere jealousy over Peter's success. I wasn't sure how Jack would have found out, but I wouldn't have put it past Peter to have discovered a way to let Jack know. Peter felt like he'd lost the game, and tipping Jack off to what had happened would be his parting shot, maybe his parting shot to me as well as to Jack.

I continued spending time at the Garage. I'd developed a close relationship with a twelve-year-old black girl named Sally Neil. Every afternoon, she took the train down from Eastern Parkway, where she lived with her grandmother. We were fond of each other; I wasn't quite sure where the chemistry came from. I became a sister to her, perhaps a mother. I took this very seriously and even ended up visiting her school during parent-teacher conferences, knowing that her grandmother wouldn't be there for her. Unlike me, she was very meticulous. She was working on a replica of the Brooklyn Bridge made out of tiny pieces of balsa wood.

I would see Jack mostly in the evenings in our apartment. I never knew what to expect from myself when I was with him: Sometimes I wanted to confront him about what was really on his mind; other times I was overwhelmed with guilt and the fear that he would confront me about what I had done. I thought about confessing to him what had almost happened, but I had the feeling that would instantly end our marriage.

Three months after I broke things off with Peter, Jack and I had a date to meet some friends in a restaurant in the East Village for dinner. It was March, and the date when I had lost Zuzu two years earlier was approaching. After waiting for our friends for over half an hour, we sat down to a meal ourselves. It was a little odd; we hadn't eaten out alone for a long time. The restaurant was poorly heated and I kept rubbing my bare shoulders to keep warm. Toward the end of our dinner, a serious look came over Jack's face and he stopped the conversation. "Maddy, I've got to talk to you about something, something serious," he said. I picked up my napkin and prepared myself; I was absolutely sure that he was finally going to confront me about Peter. "You've changed in some fundamental way, haven't you?"

"Have I?" I said after a hesitation.

"I've got this sneaking suspicion I've done something wrong—I mean something other than all of our other issues."

I laughed nervously. "Like what?"

"I don't know. I feel like I said something or did something to hurt you."

I shook my head. "I don't feel like you've hurt me, not anymore," I said, and sipped my wine.

He watched me, staring into my eyes, a penetrating gaze that sent a wave of grief through me. I felt guilt about the house, of course, but the irony that *he* believed that he had hurt *me* was too much for words. Then he sort of laughed nervously and waved at the waiter for our check. We went home together that evening and watched television in bed. Jack turned and began to kiss me, and I kissed him and held him, but I felt like he was drifting even farther away than before. In the morning we went out to brunch at a café on Avenue A and then later strolled through the park. The park was packed—that unsettling mix of the indigent and the hip of the East Village. I put my arm around his waist as we walked, hoping to get closer to him. We found a seat in the sun next to a man quietly strumming a guitar, singing out of tune. Jack grinned at me as if to say we'd chosen the wrong spot, but then he grinned again and I realized that something else was on his mind.

"I'm thinking of moving out," Jack said, hesitating. "I mean, just for a little while."

I could feel something move deep in my chest, like the shifting of tectonic plates. I wondered how serious he was about this. Jack watched me carefully, and then he took my hand and squeezed hard, harder than usual.

"Somebody at work wants to sublet her place. Just for a month. It's cheap. I'll still pay my half of the rent."

"Are you serious?" I said. "For what?"

"It could make things stronger between us."

"How?" I said. "Don't you think that's the last thing in the world we need?"

"I've made up my mind about it, Maddy," Jack said. "It's for both of us."

"For both of us—for you, not for me. You haven't even consulted me."

"I'm sorry, Maddy. I can't consult you about this one."

He rose to his feet and stared at me. "At the very least, if we do decide to move back in with each other, it will be more like a decision to be together rather than something we're simply accepting."

Jack left the next day with a duffel bag and two suitcases of his belongings. As soon as he was gone I began mulling over his saying, "If we do decide to move back in . . ." The *if* was so troubling that I was unsure he'd actually said it, but it was too late to ask him.

For the first few weeks, he and I talked on the telephone two or three times a day, but didn't see each other. At first living alone was a novelty—cooking for myself, deciding which friends or what movie to see. But soon I could feel how difficult this new life was.

I spent more and more time at the Puppet Garage. I continued to help Sally with her model of the Brooklyn Bridge. Many of the other children were working on the used bicycles I'd bought them. A welder visited us and made the children crazy handlebars to their liking. Sometimes, after I closed up, I took Sally out to dinner at a restaurant down the street called the Fountain and helped her with her homework.

Meanwhile, a kind of desperation crept into the other aspects of my life. I began dreading certain times of the week, especially Sunday evenings. There were many parts of the city that I didn't go to because they reminded me of something I had done with Jack.

I kept thinking of how Jack always had a soft spot in his heart for single people. I remembered him once saying, "Never underestimate the difficulties of coming home to an empty apartment every night." He was always understanding of his single friends whenever they let him down, and so in a strange way I couldn't understand why he wasn't more understanding of me now that I was single.

After over a month apart we made plans to meet for dinner in a few days' time, and I began looking forward to this, counting off the days. Jack suggested a restaurant in Little India that we had frequented when we first came to the city. It was just another inexpensive little place on Sixth Street, but I took this to be a good sign; I remembered how in love we'd been when we first went there. I could hardly concentrate at work the day of the dinner, wondering what it would be like to see his face again.

He was already seated when I arrived, a bottle of wine open on the table. Standing up, he hugged me for a long time, and I hugged him. I spent over an hour telling him things that had happened to me while we were apart. I wanted his approval for everything, and he said all the right things. It felt wonderful. After finishing our main course, Jack lifted a beautiful pair of handmade earrings out of his shirt pocket and gave them to me. It was typical of him to give me presents, but the fact that he had done this now made me particularly happy. I tried them on, turning my head so he could see both ears.

"You look fabulous," he said, and I felt that rush of happiness from being looked at by him again. I felt like my old self.

Then he reached across the table and took my hand. He told me he had something important to tell me. "Maddy, I found an apartment in Fort Greene and signed a lease, but I could always get out of it if need be. You can have our apartment."

For a second I thought I would argue with him, stand up for myself. Then suddenly I realized that would only make things worse. I stared at his face for the longest time. It was the face that I had loved for so many years that I could hardly remember my life before it. I didn't know what to say. I put my napkin over my eyes and began to cry.

A few weeks later, Jack moved into the apartment in Fort Greene and I found a sublet on the Upper West Side. By the time I moved out, I realized I could not have stayed in our old apartment another day. After dividing our possessions, I stood on the street looking at him. "I need to ask something of you," I said. "That we cut off communication until we're both back on our feet. It's got to do with the position I'm in and the fact that I still love you."

He kissed me and there were tears in both of our eyes. Then I turned and left him standing there.

Chapter Twenty

During this time I didn't see or hear any-thing from Jack. I still wondered what had really inspired the move, whether he knew of the affair or whether he believed that our love had atrophied. I thought of him almost any moment of the day—buying toothpaste, I bought his brand, or fruit—he bought the white grapefruits rather than the red. On my way to work every morning, I read the entire op-ed page of the *New York Times* because I knew he did. After dinner I sometimes turned on C-SPAN because he was the only person I'd ever met besides my fa-ther who watched it. One night I rented Fellini's *La Strada*. I had cried at the end of it when I saw it with Jack the first time, and he had comforted me.

I kept an eye out for him on the street, hoping to bump into him while being terrified of it at the same time. When-ever I was at the Garage, I walked over to Flatbush and took the subway from there, knowing that this was the line that he would use to get to Fort Greene. I had a crazy scenario in mind if I did see him in the subway or on the street. We'd stop and stare at each other without saying a word and then rush back to an apartment, his or mine. We'd tear each other's clothes off and make love like two forlorn teenagers. Afterward, we'd confess the emotional pain that we were in and realize that the separation was pointless. Everywhere I went in the city I watched for him, scanning sidewalks, groups of pedestrians waiting at the crosswalks. I couldn't help it. Even outside the city when I visited my parents, I remained on the lookout for him.

Then something small happened that had an effect on me. Sally Neil moved to Chicago to be with her real mother. It happened quickly—I never saw her to say good-bye: I learned the news when she didn't show one afternoon and I called her grandmother's house. The grandmother told me that she didn't have an address for her. I didn't believe her and so I argued with her, and she finally told me that Sally's mother had told her not to give it to me. "She wants you to know that she's Sally's real mother," the grandmother said. "Not you."

"I know that. You don't have to remind me of that," I said, and broke into tears.

After that, I kept going to the Garage, but I thought it important that I meet men and get on with my dream of having a family. I signed up for bird walks in Central Park, a tai chi class on Broadway, and then in July I was on my way to the island of Crete for the beginning of my bike trip.

I found it a great relief to get out of the city and to a place that I had never been with Jack. Though I wasn't really ready to meet a man, I talked to quite a few on the trip. It was nice to know that I was still attractive to some men—I seemed to have forgotten about that over the last year. Soon after returning from Turkey I took a rafting trip down the Snake River in Idaho, and when I returned I bought my old Volvo station wagon and began visiting friends outside of the city. I thought I was truly starting to become myself again.

Then one evening after returning to New York, I was on my way home from work when I spotted Jack in a crowd of pedestrians a block away on Sixth Avenue. Once again I felt that tectonic shift—not merely because I had finally seen him, but because I could immediately tell just by the way he was walking that something in his life was different. Sure enough, as other people moved out of my line of vision, I saw a woman by his side. She had blond hair; she seemed jovial and outgoing. Then I realized the woman was holding his hand. I was shattered; right away I had the feeling that she was the real reason we'd separated. I turned up Ninth Street, stepped down a flight of stairs for the PATH train in order to avoid him, and stood there on the landing in a trance.

When I came back up to street level, I felt as though the earth had shifted and the world was now an entirely different place. The whole city was even less my home than before. I walked to the subway at Seventh Avenue and boarded the IRT bound for the Upper West Side. At Forty-second Street I climbed the stairs and walked through Times Square. Although I always hated Times Square, I was suddenly comforted by its neon lights and commercial anonymity because Jack avoided this part of the city. As I approached my apartment, I became increasingly desperate. I thought my place would be a refuge, as apartments are in New York, but when I was finally inside, things took a turn for the worse. I started to make myself some tea, but couldn't wait for the water to boil and climbed straight into bed. I lay there curled up in a ball with a lump in my throat. I had always had this idea that I could pick up the phone and call Jack if things got really rough, and now that things had gotten rough, that was no longer an option.

After lying in bed for an hour or so, I got up and went out onto the street. I dialed Jack's number from a pay phone—I didn't dial from my apartment because I didn't want him to *69 me. He picked up after several rings.

"Hello?" he said in his naïvely friendly tone of voice.

I said nothing.

"Hello? Hello? Who is this?" He sounded confused. I remained quiet. He hung on to the line without speaking long enough for me to believe that he knew it was me. The moment he hung up, I thought of calling him back just to hear his voice again, but then he would know for sure it was me.

For months my thoughts revolved around both Jack and his girlfriend, whose name I learned was Simone Belvac. I was caught between two terrible alternatives—I felt that Jack left me either because he knew about my relationship to Peter or because he really wanted to be with Simone. I didn't know which was worse. A subtle pain poisoned my life. Seeing a friend, going to a movie, even attending a party seemed part of a larger scheme to hide from my feelings. I knew I was idealizing the past, looking more toward the beginning than the end, but I couldn't help it. I longed for simplicity. The only thing that gave meaning to my life in New York was my work at the Garage.

Finally, a few months later, I learned from a mutual friend that Jack and Simone had moved in together. I thought this fact—the fact that he was clearly moving on with his life—would force me to give up the past and get involved with somebody new. I began seeing Dr. Belheim again. I saw her for two sessions, but suddenly even she began reminding me of my life with Jack. That was when I decided to look for a whole new venue.

Once I'd signed Penny's lease in Atlanta and returned to New York, I put up flyers at the Pratt Institute in order to find a replacement for myself at the Puppet Garage. After interviewing half a dozen young artists, I chose two women that I liked—they seemed innocent and full of optimism, like I had been ten years back—and then prepaid the rent with what was left of the five thousand dollars. I had the addresses and phone numbers of some of the individual children. I promised them that I would be back to visit them.

"Can I get you something to drink, miss?" I was startled by the flight attendant. This one was younger than the other one; she had bright red hair and silver earrings. Her cart arrived parallel to my aisle.

"Ginger ale," I said.

She reached over the young girl who was still reading her magazine and set a cup of ice cubes and the can down on my tray. Then she moved on down the aisle. The captain's voice came on over the speakers. He told us we were just leaving the U.S. mainland and that we would arrive in San Juan in under an hour.

Chapter Twenty-one

At the airport in San Juan, I made the quick connection to a small, twin-propped airplane and was airborne again within half an hour. Then we were flying over an ocean that seemed to soften in color the farther south we went. Below us I could see cruise and cargo ships and the shadow of my plane as it passed over the long white wakes. The shadow passed over green and mountainous islands, some no bigger than a city block, others miles long. Another stretch of water went on for twenty-five minutes with fewer ships and no sign of land. Then we started to descend over an island with square, cultivated fields and a small industrial-like port to one side and a runway in the shape of a cross. The plane dipped and banked so sharply that I could see straight down into somebody's backyard: several ramshackle buildings, chickens and two shabby-looking donkeys tethered to a dilapidated pickup truck. The landing was rough, the wheels screamed as they touched down, and the glare from the runway shone brightly in my eyes. Then I stood up in the narrow plane with the handful of other passengers and waited to get off. I looked at my watch. Jack's direct flight was due to arrive in twenty minutes.

A haze of moist heat engulfed us the moment we descended the stairs onto the tarmac. My legs were slightly weak. I stopped to get my bearings while other passengers slipped around me. Palm trees bordered fields of pale green grass. It didn't strike me right away that I was in the tropics, but there was something different about the colors and the smell of the grasses and even the silence of the small airport. It seemed amazing that I'd spent so much of the flight in my head and in the past, and yet suddenly I was in a foreign country. It occurred to me that it was wise of Jack to choose someplace so different from what we knew.

The airport had but one large room, with tall empty desks to one side and a collection of clocks showing international times. I crossed the polished linoleum to a small café against the far wall with a zinc counter. Setting down my bags, I climbed onto a stool. A boy was wiping down the counter, whistling to himself. When he reached my section of the counter with the sponge, he looked up at me. I was surprised—he had dark eyebrows that reminded me of Andrew. Suddenly I began thinking of all that had transpired in the last twenty-four hours. I recalled our swim together in Andrew's pool, putting my arms around him in the water and kissing him and then walking through his house, trying to picture what I would do to his house to make it feel like it was partly mine. . . . If Andrew hadn't come to the airport, everything might have been different. I might have returned to Atlanta and married him.

I thought of how he'd called me a lapdog. *It's only a word, a name,* I thought. I began wondering if I could forgive him for that one word. Maybe I'd write him a letter and try to explain what had happened, tell him that I was very

lucky and unlucky at the same time to have married somebody like Jack. It was different from other loves. . . . I had
no idea how I would phrase it or even the purpose of such a
letter.

The boy asked me what I wanted, and I told him a decaf
espresso. After setting a spoon on a napkin, he pushed a
step stool under a large silver espresso maker, the kind you
rarely see in the States—another reminder of how far I had
come. Outside, I could hear the propellers of the airplane
pick up speed to take off again; then the plane was a distant
hum, and the airport was silent. Soon the other passengers,
having claimed their luggage, pushed through the glass
doors to meet friends and board taxis.

As I drank my espresso, I took the picture that Jack had
sent me out of my wallet and turned it over.

Dear Maddy,

*There's something I've been meaning to tell you
since our fateful spring, something that I wish I had
been more honest with you about . . .*

I had the feeling that the next few days would be pivotal
to my life. I crossed my legs in hopes of relaxing and tried to
imagine what Jack was doing on his plane at that moment.
I could not picture him anymore. I could not decide how tall
he was, or how wide. At best he was a blurry figure, like
Claude Rains in *The Invisible Man,* just an overcoat and
pants and footsteps in the snow.

Ten minutes later I heard another airplane buzzing the
airport, then caught a glimpse of its tail as it flashed by the
window. It was his flight, the one from New York. I paid for
my drink and dashed into the women's room. My hair was
pulled back into the same boring ponytail that I'd worn

around Jack for years. I brushed it out and then stepped into a stall and changed into a different blouse, one of the ones that I'd bought on the day Jack sent me the gouache. Standing back from the mirror, I decided that he'd know right away that I was trying to be sexy. I didn't need to impress Jack the way I did other men. I changed into another blouse, this one toned down. Meanwhile a woman in a black tank top barged through the bathroom door carrying her luggage. She was dressed like a New Yorker, one of those women who scare me, who aren't the least bit afraid of flaunting it, nipples and all. I stood statue-still at the sink, thinking how Jack was probably right outside looking for me.

"*Excuse* me," the woman said brusquely, and I moved aside. Taking a deep breath, I lifted my bags, and stepped out into the lobby. Sure enough, Jack was standing midfloor, facing the other way. He was wearing his familiar lumberjack boots, the kind more appropriate for the woods of the far North, and for a second I recognized how different he and Andrew were, how they truly were opposites. He seemed much smaller than I remembered him—a miniature Jack—as if he'd taken some *Alice in Wonderland* potion. I was relieved. I expected him to be looming over me like a shadow.

"Excuse me, Mr. Martin," I called.

He turned in my direction; he was wearing dark sunglasses. He rushed over to me and hugged me. I thought I could feel him crying. He held me tightly, almost smothering me, and he wouldn't let go for the longest time. Then he pushed back from me, dried his eyes on his sleeve, attempted a quick smile, and started walking for the open door.

"I've got to get my suitcases," he said.

"Suitcases?" I followed, falling behind quickly. "Suitcases?"

He looked around at me nervously, a little lost as to what I was saying. It was just like him to save the packing for the last minute and then throw half of what he owned into a couple of bags.

We stepped outside, and there on the tarmac was an orange baggage cart with two swollen blue suitcases, so heavy that they fell to the ground as soon as he pulled at the handles.

"What's in there, a body?"

"A body?" he said. "No." He was so nervous he didn't realize that I was making a joke—and I had thought I was the one who was supposed to be nervous. Dragging the bags behind him, he started looking for the exit on the taxi-stand side. "Jack, slow down, would you?"

"Ten minutes until the next ferry," he said, out of breath.

"There's got to be another one after that."

"Sure—but it's in an hour or something." I rushed along behind him, wondering if he had gotten off the plane thinking that once he was on the boat everything would be all right.

Jack raised his hand for a taxi parked just on the other side of the loading area. A short black man took a drag from his cigarette, stepped on it, and then took his time getting into the car. A cloud of blue exhaust coughed out of the back as he started it up. Jack began to pace.

"No emissions standards down here, I guess, huh?" he said.

"Jack, are you all right?"

"Yeah, fine," he said, but he wasn't very convincing. I could see crow's-feet at the corner of his eyes. I remembered faint creases there before, but not crow's-feet. The chest hair flowing from his Hawaiian shirt was certainly grayer than before and looked like it had been clipped a little. Despite these differences, I could already feel something deep inside my chest radiating a subtle message of relief. Here I was—at last.

"Beautiful," he said as soon as we were in the back of this rickety, musty old American car with the shift on the column. I wasn't sure what he was referring to.

The driver wore one of those hats that cabbies wear in movies from the thirties. He glanced in the rearview mirror at us. "Which ferry?" he asked.

Jack started rifling through his pants pockets, looking for the schedule as if the world were coming to an end. "Nobody said there's more than one."

The driver winked at me in the mirror and kept driving.

"Jack, I think he's kidding," I said. "Hey, *nice* shades."

He took them off and I smiled. "My flying goggles." His tone of voice became subtly more fragile. For years, flying was one area of his life that he couldn't so much as kid about. I always assumed that Jack's feet were so firmly planted on the ground that flying was against his nature in some intrinsic, subconscious way. "I reached new heights with these on—I think we were at like twenty-five thousand feet, something like that."

"You're the only one I've ever met who keeps track of those things."

"It makes a difference."

"Hey, I'm glad you made it."

It is hard to describe how I felt at that moment. I was in a land that was so different from what I was used to—sharp, spiky plants, faded, sun-beaten palm trees, and no doubt an alligator or two sunning itself on the banks of a swamp, and yet I was sitting next to the most familiar person in my life. Even his smell, which had clung to me since the moment he hugged me, was as old and familiar as a saddle.

We came down to the boat landing, where the ferry was churning water, preparing to depart from the dock. It was a smaller ferry than those for Martha's Vineyard. A crew member was just unhooking the rope. "How much do we owe you?" Jack yelled to the cabbie. After tossing the fare and a far too healthy tip onto the front seat, Jack paced back and forth near the trunk, waiting for his bags. He kept glancing toward the boat as if to keep it from motoring off.

"Where do we buy our tickets? Aren't there any signs around here?" he said as we made our way along the dock. Jack paid for our tickets on board from a big roll of cash. He was truly on edge.

Dropping our bags below, we climbed to the top deck and held the railing as the boat set out for the island of St. Marie. The sea was exactly that Caribbean blue-green that I had envisioned for years, almost too clean to be real, too perfect. Neither one of us really belonged here, not the two of us who had walked the grungy streets of the East Village to save the extra dollar or two for Odessa's pierogis. As I'd gotten into the habit of doing since deciding to leave New York, I went through the process of sizing up a place as if I might someday move there. I didn't care for the picture-postcard cleanliness of it, but I decided that for now it was a good thing—after the mess that I'd made of things in New York.

Jack was now standing next to me, tapping the rail. Our eyes met and he grinned nervously, almost sheepishly. Maybe Simone had given his ego a run for the money; he had that air of damaged goods about him. "How about a beer?" he said.

I shook my head.

"Are you sure?" he asked. "Might help you relax."

"For some reason, I am just that." I was almost telling the truth. "Besides, it's policy."

"Oh, nearly forgot about that." He turned and crossed the deck for the bar.

My policy about daytime drinking dated back to my college days, when I realized I wasn't going to make good on all the money my parents were dropping on my education. My name wasn't going to end with the letters MD or Esq. or MBA. To make up for it, I adopted a certain work ethic along with a strict policy of not drinking in the daytime. Sixteen years later I abided by it more out of habit than anything else.

"Jack," I called out. "Seabreeze."

He took off his glasses and came back to me. "Seabreeze? Are you talking about the drink?"

"Don't act so shocked."

"That sounds . . . that sounds"—he hesitated—"very, um, upper percentile. You aren't voting Republican now, are you?"

"Jack, go get your beer."

"Maybe I'll make that two seabreezes." He put the glasses back on and smiled. They looked ridiculous on him—they were far too glitzy. I didn't want to laugh at him—it seemed somehow too intimate—but I couldn't help but giggle as he walked away.

Holding the deck rail, I looked over at him slyly, my hair blowing across my eyes and mouth. He was standing in line for the drinks, talking to a woman ahead of him with reddish hair. She stood with a young girl to her side, probably her daughter. She was laughing at something he had said, and from here she looked beautiful. Something about her slender body had that *I-jog-on-the-beach-at-dawn* look. Jack took off his glasses and pointed with them back at me—I had obviously entered the conversation. I quickly turned toward the water.

When I looked back, he held the two drinks and he was talking to somebody else, a couple in bright green Windbreakers standing right behind the woman. Again the conversation was lively and Jack was doing the entertaining—I could see the two of them laughing. I thought how I had probably met more people any given month with Jack than in an entire year alone in Georgia. The couple became even more animated as he talked on and on, the ice in our drinks melting.

Then he came walking toward me. "Those two want to have us over to their *time-share*," he said. He and I used to laugh at the very concept of time-shares. It was reverse snobbism; we couldn't afford one ourselves.

"Who was the redhead?"

"Divorcée, used to come here with her husband. She said she's heard my name somewhere—she works in film."

"All that while waiting in line?" He had a way with people. I took a long sip—delicious, far better than a drink in the evening.

I insisted on getting the next round and crossed the deck to the bar under the blue-and-white-striped tent. I was feeling a touch giddy; I couldn't help but stare at the bartender's tanned biceps as I ordered two more seabreezes. The price was higher than I'd ever remembered paying for drinks outside of Manhattan. Everything, particularly the twenty-dollar bill I took from my back pocket, was starting to feel a little unreal. As I walked back over toward Jack, I began thinking how comfortable I felt around him already, despite my initial nervousness.

I stared out at the perfect blue of the sea, sailboats and yachts and the faint outline of a cargo ship on the horizon.

"Doubles," Jack said.

"*Doubles?*" I said. "Is that why these were so expensive?"

"Were they?"

"Two bucks back from a twenty," I said.

"You don't say."

"I do," I said. My eyes were watering a little and my words were starting to get sloppy.

"Wonder if there are sharks down there?" Jack said, leaning over the rail.

"Sharks? Who cares? Plenty of other things to worry about."

"Hey, you didn't hear about those preppy newlyweds on their honeymoon in Hawaii, did you? I read about it in the *Post* a few days ago. The newlyweds went to a big fancy preppy resort, had a great time doing their preppy thing, and then just before they were about to leave, they went swimming. Suddenly a great white came along, the real Jaws, and gobbled up the wife."

"That's awful."

"Here's the irony. You know how preppies always try to wear the happy face for every occasion? Well, the story said the guy just returned to work like a week later—I mean, sort of as if it never happened: the wedding, the wife, the whole thing. He just went right on with his life. Couldn't you see everyone slapping the guy on the back? 'Hey, how'd the honeymoon go, big guy?' 'Pretty good . . . Oh, yeah, except for one thing—a wife ate my shark.' "

I looked at him, trying to figure out what was wrong with that sentence. "You said 'a wife ate my shark.' "

We looked at each other for a long moment. Suddenly he started laughing, and then I did too, but not without a secret, underlying feeling of discomfort.

As we got close to the island, we could make out its shore of reddish cliffs and deep green vegetation leading up the slope of a mountain. Two villages of cottages with red roofs were nestled in the hills, joined by a fine line of white beach. Our ferry slowed as it entered the still waters of the port and then bumped the rubber tires on the landing dock. A small minivan sent by our lodge awaited our arrival, the driver leaning against the open door. The van took us up a steep cobblestone roadway, past the town of cottages and low white buildings, and then up an even steeper hill to the lodge office, a single-story building with smooth plaster walls overlooking the sea. We checked in and then went outside to find our cabins among the sandy trails. There were a dozen or so of these identical bungalows with red corrugated roofs on a hillside leading down to the sea cliff. Jack's was closest to the cliff, twenty or thirty yards below mine. I set my bag down inside my door and told him that I would meet him in just a bit. The windows were wide open and a breeze caught the curtains.

Lying down, I stared at the ceiling; I was dizzy and slightly nauseous from the drinks on the boat.

I thought how extraordinary it was that I was here, far from Atlanta, far from New York, far from Andrew. I thought about the ring he had given me—it seemed ages ago. Strangely enough, a part of me missed him—I hadn't considered what it would be like to be without him so suddenly.

After a while I decided that lying down was probably not the thing to do after having too much to drink. I downed a cup of water in the bathroom and then slipped into a bathing suit and followed the path to Jack's cabin. I knocked on his door and turned to wait for him to answer. I could hear him rustling around inside and I started to become anxious about seeing him again. Then he stepped from his door in a pair of flip-flops, holding a fully stuffed canvas carry bag. He wore a well-faded Hawaiian shirt that hung down over his bathing suit. He half smiled at me, his brow low. I couldn't tell what he was really feeling. Maybe he felt vulnerable, having poured his heart out in the letters to me. I followed him down the path to the steps above the beach.

Brightly colored umbrellas checkered the white sand. Kites rippled and soared, and shouting and screaming children dashed back and forth between sandcastles, their hairless chests puffing up and down. A black man was hawking beer and mangos. Jack set his bag down on the warm sand and unfolded an army blanket that must have taken up half of one of his suitcases. Who else would bring a woolen army blanket to the tropics? He spread it out, took out a book and canteen, and then collapsed onto his back.

I spread my small towel next to his and then looked down at him as he lay with his arm over his eyes. The haze from the alcohol was wearing off, rolling out to sea. I felt disoriented again, and naked. There was really nowhere to run if things didn't work out. It was just the two of us and our history—all the wonderful times and all the terrible ones that we'd been through. I was about to tell him to put sunblock on—he would soon be bright red, and I knew I was the only one who paid attention to such details. Instead I dashed across the sand and into the waves.

Diving deep, I swam along the sandy bottom before rising to the surface and turning toward shore. Jack was standing up now, shading his eyes with one hand. He seemed to tower over the beach. Yes, he still had quite a presence, an aura about him, a magnetism that people noticed everywhere he went. He was striking-looking; he had high cheekbones and a naturally open smile. There was so much color to his face whenever he was turning on his charm. It made him seem even more animated than he was. He raced down to the water, gaining momentum, landed with a great big splash, and disappeared beneath the surface.

He came up just in front of me, his thinning hair streaked over his face. His eyes opened wide and locked on mine, and for a long moment—not unlike that first night in college—I couldn't turn away.

Then he burst out laughing. I thought for an instant he was laughing at me. Then I realized he was happy and so was I. We began to swim far out into the ocean.

Chapter Twenty-two

We kept busy after our swim, playing Frisbee, building castles, and burying ourselves in the sand. We attempted the *New York Times* crossword puzzle together and we were still able to get only a few words. Late in the afternoon we packed up and climbed the stairway for our cabins. At the top of the steps above the beach, I hesitated, unsure of how to leave things for the evening, since we hadn't talked about dinner.

"See you later," I said, not knowing what that meant.

"All right, see you," he said, and then went on.

The deep sand along the path to my cabin must have been baking in the sun all afternoon; it was hot against my feet. Once inside my room, the door closed, I put my nose to the fresh flowers on the dresser. I was saturated with sun and salt water. I got in the shower to wash the salt from my hair and stood under the spray soaping myself for a long time. After dressing I lay down on my bedspread to read my novel. I couldn't concentrate. I rolled onto my side and closed my eyes. The cabin was just close enough to the water for me to hear the faint sound of waves sliding back and forth against the sand below the cliff.

Jack and I had driven up to Martha's Vineyard shortly after the end of our first school year together. Before then we'd taken a brief hiatus, each of us visiting our parents for a week. I'd lied to my parents about what I was doing for the summer, told them I was sharing a room with a girlfriend on the Vineyard. As my father put me on a Trailways bus bound for the Cape, he suddenly became sentimental, giving me a big hug and kiss, as if I were going off to a foreign land. He must have sensed that I'd finally fallen in love. Only one stop later in Hartford, I got off to wait for Jack, who would be driving his father's car. I remember all the anticipation of seeing him again after being apart for only a week. Then suddenly I saw this big blue car pull up into a slot reserved for buses, and Jack got out and looked at me across the roof while a bus driver shouted at him to move. His hair was a mess, his face red. He was blushing and so was I. I hopped in his car while the driver continued his tirade. We were laughing and Jack gave him the peace sign through the window as he backed out. Jack wasn't very good at maneuvering his dad's great big car—he called it the Hog. Jack had reserved a site at a Vineyard campground with the idea that we'd live out of his car until we found a permanent place. Right away we felt like grown-ups, driving down the highway, stopping wherever we pleased. Jack pulled a pack of cigarettes out of his pocket, pushed in the lighter, and lit one. "What the heck are you doing?" I said. He never smoked.

"I don't know, just bought these. How about a drag?"

"God, no," I'd said. But not far down the highway I took it from him and inhaled, coughing my lungs out for a full five minutes. "Disgusting," I said.

"Aren't they?"

I laughed. It made me dizzy and giddy and Jack kept fanning the smoke away from his face.

"You're nuts," I said.

"And so are you."

I recalled our confusion once we were in the ferry parking lot in Woods Hole about how to get the Hog on the boat—mishearing the directions from the attendant about where the standby line started and getting into the wrong line and then into the right one and then Jack leaning against the horn without meaning to. We dashed into the terminal to buy our tickets but stopped to get ice cream before returning, only to find all the cars behind us had moved ahead and our car was parked all by itself in the middle of the lot. A woman was standing outside her car shaking her head. I can still remember her scowling face. At last we drove onto the ferry, curious as to how we'd ever back the car out, since Jack was not a good driver. Then we climbed onto the deck and stood against the rail. I could feel Jack's fingers around my side. He held me like that all the time back then, wouldn't let me stand two feet from him. That night at our campsite we ended up sleeping in the backseat of the car, making love with my back pressed against a cold seat belt buckle. I knew even then that I'd never be able to separate the ocean, no matter where I was, from what I felt with him that summer.

I opened my eyes—I must have dozed off. On the wall next to the window I noticed a plaque shaped like a heart. At the center of the red heart was an eye painted so realistically that it seemed to be staring directly at me.

I sat up quickly, amazed. The design was exactly like the one I'd seen in Maggie's diary, her so-called vision during her third suicide attempt. I took it off the wall and examined it. There was no signature or sign of who had made it. The piece itself was ceramic. I was surprised I hadn't seen it before. As I was looking at it, I heard footsteps come up to the door, a hesitation, then a light knock. I opened a small dresser drawer and placed the plaque inside, facedown.

"Who is it?" I said.

"Me." The door swung open and Jack stood in the doorframe, his arms to his sides. He looked taller, thinner, and handsomer than I remembered him. I realized that this man I'd married was somebody who would have caught my eye on the street had I not known him. I was about to tell him how terrific he looked when I realized that somebody must have chosen his outfit for him. His shirt with the two vertical stripes over the pockets had a slightly French look.

"What's this?" he said, picking up my novel and flipping through it casually. Dropping it on the bed, he stuck his hands into his pockets; he'd lost his confidence again. "Got a cab waiting in town." He kept looking away. "Aren't you starving?"

"I wasn't thinking of food—but yeah, now that you mention it," I said. It felt claustrophobic standing in such close quarters with him. Strangely enough, I was afraid of touching him; even accidentally bumping into him would be overwhelming.

He stepped out the door, motioned for me to follow him, and then began walking away. The sun was behind him. Standing my ground, I crossed my arms. "Jack, what is this? What are you, the pied piper?"

"I've made reservations at a place across the island," he said, turning to face me. "I'm abducting you."

"Oh, really?" I said, arms still crossed.

"Come on now. Come peacefully. I'm armed and dangerous," he said and smiled. We stared at each other for a long moment, and I thought I really should stand my ground and tell him that I did not intend to follow him around the entire time we were here. But then Jack continued to stare at me in that overly serious way that used to make me laugh.

"Stay where you are," I said. "Don't move."

Stepping back inside my cabin, I slipped on a light cotton skirt from my closet. An innocent, childlike pattern of fish and insects disguised the fact that the fabric was practically see-through. I'd bought it in Greece on my bike trip; it was the raciest thing I owned. I then pulled a cotton tank top over my head and tied a matching cardigan around my shoulders. The delicate silver necklace that I slipped on showed off my long neck, which I knew Jack was partial to. After brushing my hair, I touched my lips with just a trace of lipstick.

Slipping outside, I closed the door and leaned against it. I wanted him to notice me. I stared at him with one hand resting near my hip, sort of like a gunfighter in a bad Western; and then I strode boldly past him through the sand.

"By the way," he said as he caught up, "you're still stunning." We walked alongside each other without saying a word.

We came into town by way of a flight of worn stone steps that ran along the clapboard side of an alabaster church with a square steeple. The streets were covered with sand and crushed seashells. A skinny hound with a reddish coat sat on its haunches by the fountain in the town square. At the taxi stand a big green Oldsmobile was waiting, something rescued from an American junkyard thirty years ago. The driver was craning his head around impatiently. Jack had always been late for everything when we were together; that part of him hadn't changed.

Chapter Twenty-three

We stepped out of the taxi in a neighboring fishing village and crossed the street to the entrance of an upscale French restaurant on the harbor. Jack raised his fingers to the maître d'. "I just made reservations—"

"Are you the Martins?"

Jack nodded and then put his hands in his pockets and casually looked at me to check my reaction to hearing his name refer to both of us. It was a small, slightly unsettling detail, but I liked it and smiled.

We followed the host over to our table near a screened-in porch and canopy facing the harbor of moored yachts and sailboats. A waiter pulled my chair out for me and I sat down, and then he bowed his round head. "Good evening, my friends," he said graciously. He recited the specials with their elaborate seasonings and sauces, smiled, and then left us alone. After mulling over the wine list for a while, Jack called the waiter back over and ordered one of the more expensive Bordeaux on the list.

We both looked over menus for a long time, choosing

our entrées and appetizers—we decided to share everything, just as we had always done in the past. Closing my
menu, I looked around the restaurant. It was a beautiful
place that was almost perfectly quiet except for the sound of
faint piano music. I glanced at Jack and then away. This was
far more intimate than the beach; I didn't know what to say.
I had the feeling that he didn't either.

"One thing I kind of like about being in a foreign country," he said finally, "everybody calls you 'my friend.' "

"Really?" I said. "I thought you were always everybody's
friend anyway." I tried to laugh but suddenly realized the
subtext of my words. During our last summer together I had
yelled at him for being everybody's friend but mine.

He didn't seem to notice. He continued looking from
table to table, and then he caught my eye in the candlelight.
"Don't you get the feeling people think we're honeymooners?" he said.

"Not really."

"Let's go along with them, play it up—make up a grand
old story about our wedding or something."

"Jack—no. I'm not here to meet other people," I said, irritated. He sank deep in his seat and stared at me, as if he
realized the boundary he'd crossed. I was surprised at how
close to the surface my anger had become—I'd almost told
him to shut up. "I don't want to make a show of this."

"I'll tell people the truth, Maddy. I'll tell them that we're
exes."

"How about keeping our business to ourselves, Jack?" I
snapped. I felt invaded. I turned my eyes away and took a
deep breath.

The waiter brought our bottle of wine over and held it
up to Jack, who pointed at my glass. I tasted the wine and
nodded for the waiter to fill our glasses. We ordered our appetizers and entrées.

"Sorry," I said, after a few sips.

He smiled and then broke off a crust of bread and dipped it into a saucer of olive oil. I tried to think of something to say, but it kept crossing my mind that this trip was his and not mine. I knew that if I were to have a good time I should drop that notion quickly. There was a long, awkward silence between us. I began to notice voices from the other tables and the sound of silverware and dinner plates. Everyone under the canopy appeared to be having a delightful time—everyone except us.

"Well?" Jack said, breaking the silence and lifting his glass. "Here's to"—it seemed like he was trying to choose his words carefully—"to both of us." Instead of lifting my glass to his, I turned my head and looked the other way. "To both of us, as separate, independent human beings," he added. I raised my glass, relieved to know that he knew how I felt.

Another awkward silence as we glanced around the restaurant. A dish of steaming mussels passed by our table, trailing a rich aroma of leeks and garlic.

"So tell me, Maddy, what have you been doing with your life these last three years?"

As I searched for an answer I thought how ironic it was that such a simple question could be so difficult to respond to. I was not about to tell him what had transpired in the airport. "A lot of things—and nothing, at the same time."

"How so?"

"I don't know. I don't mean to be catty, but it is a big question you're asking."

"You went to Greece? I heard about some bike trip or something."

"Who told you that?" I still felt touchy—and raw. I was sitting across from the man who had been the center of my life for so long.

"It's pretty hard not to hear things—I mean, we still

have quite a few friends in common. How's Atlanta? Do you like it there?"

"Love it," I said.

"It makes a difference living where you want to."

"How's New York?"

"I could take it or leave it at times. I never pictured you in the South. You used to call yourself a Vermont girl. Don't you remember?"

"I appreciate Georgia. It's kind of great having a climate that doesn't punish you six months of the year."

He laughed. "All right, maybe I can see you in the South. I just can't picture you with a Southern drawl."

"You've been seeing too many movies. The South is not all Southern drawls."

"Have you got a nice place?"

"I've got two dogs and a parrot. Bella's doing great. We're in a run-down building with tons of style. I live right next to an elementary school. Kids start lining up at seven in the morning. What a racket they make. I've started to figure out who's who just by the names of kids who are out of line. I love being woken up to that sound."

"You would," he said, and then he was suddenly silent, fidgeting with his silverware. I had the feeling he too was realizing the potential traps that lay in the most casual conversation. I sipped the Bordeaux and then pushed back in my chair to cross my legs. The warm breeze felt soothing.

"What's going on with you?" I said.

"Well, let's see," he said. "I'm a lot more careful with money now than I used to be." He paused, and continued staring right at me.

"And?"

"I made a deposit into my IRA this year instead of getting nailed for an early withdrawal—how's that sound?"

"Doesn't sound like you."

"Oh?"

"Have you been shopping for a cane?"

He reached across the table to touch my hair. "Speaking of canes . . ." he said.

I looked down and saw a single kinky gray hair. "That's your fault," I said, rolling my eyes.

"Here's to insomnia." He raised his glass and touched mine before I had a chance to move it away.

"You've caught the bug, too, huh?"

"Every couple of nights; flocks of dark thoughts keep me up—like in Hitchcock's *The Birds*."

"Thoughts about what?"

"I keep wondering what the hell I'm doing with my life." He laughed a little. "I guess we had"—he stuttered—"I had different expectations for where I'd be now."

"What kind of expectations?" I asked.

"To be honest, I thought . . . Oh, I don't know. I thought a lot of things."

"Like what?"

"I thought I'd be in a different place in life. It's nobody's fault but my own. Come on, Maddy, you know what I mean."

"I honestly don't."

"I thought I'd have a family by now."

He turned to ask a passing waiter for more water and then got up to go to the bathroom without allowing our eyes to meet. I couldn't quite believe he'd said that. I waited for his return.

Finally he came out of the bathroom with his napkin still in his hand and slipped through the busy tables. "Maddy, sorry about that," he said the moment he sat down. "I deserve every bit of your anger. I was a jerk and I've paid a price, and I know you have too. I'm sorry. I really am."

I turned away from him, my face flushed with anger; I could still picture the times I'd asked him about having children. I was out on a limb back then and he'd let me hang there, and all of this was back in a flash. All the romance of this dinner vanished; the nerve he had touched was still alive and raw.

The appetizers arrived but I didn't even acknowledge them. I didn't quite know what to do, except perhaps to leave.

"Look, Maddy, again, I'm so sorry. But will you hear me out? Please?"

I didn't look at him, just looked away with my arms crossed.

"About a week ago, Maddy, I showed up on your parents' doorstep."

"What?" I said, turning back to him. "You brought them into this?"

"Now wait a minute—"

"You wait a minute—you brought them into this? I don't talk about these things to them myself, Jack—and you brought them into it without telling me? What did you tell them?"

"Just a minute—let me explain."

I dropped my napkin next to my plate. I was getting ready to stand up and take a taxi back to my room.

"Maddy, please listen to me first—and don't be mad, especially at them. I begged them not to tell you. I was on my way back from Boston last week when I pulled off the highway and drove to your old neighborhood. They were on their way out to a diner, pretty surprised to see me, let me tell you, but they told me I could join them. The next thing I knew I was sitting in the Windmill Diner on Route 4, confessing to them that I was still in love with you, that I'd written you a letter and gotten a cool response."

I sat with my arms crossed, watching him.

"I asked them for advice—as their former son-in-law—told them that I was thinking of showing up where you worked and taking you to lunch. But your mother cautioned me about that. She didn't tell me outright, but she let me know in so many words that you might be seeing somebody—and she also let me know without saying it that she didn't have a good feeling about him. Then your dad chimed in and said that I needed to do something big—not just show up on your doorstep, not just send you letters, something to make you understand how serious I was, and he told me that I should do it soon, like right away. Your dad's cool. He knows you better than you think. They both wanted to see us together, but that's not why I'm telling you this."

I stared at him, waiting for him to continue.

"The reason I'm telling you this now is that before I left the diner, your mom took my arm and said, 'If you do see Maddy, tell her to remember what I said about forgiveness.' I wasn't quite sure what she meant."

I stared at him, knowing exactly what my mother had meant.

"I don't mean to be presumptuous, but I have a feeling I know what she was talking about. She's right. This is what this is all about, this thing between us. And I'm sorry. I know that wasn't cool seeing your parents like that, but I couldn't help myself. I missed them too."

I still wasn't sure what to think of all this. Now everything was mixed up in my mind, my parents, Jack—and Andrew. I had had the feeling they hadn't liked Andrew, and now it was confirmed. Maybe that was really why I had ended it with him at the airport; maybe that was why I was back here with Jack—because they loved him so much.

Our appetizers were getting cold sitting on the table between us.

"Are you okay?" Jack said. "It's a lot—I'm sorry. I've come at you with a ton of bricks."

I turned my eyes from him. "Whatever, Jack. You're who you are—I'm who I am." I took a deep breath.

He took my plate from me. "Some shrimp?" he asked.

I shook my head. He pointed at the plate of baby squid and I shook my head again. "You're not going to eat anything, are you? I didn't mean to ruin things like this."

He forked shrimp and squid onto his plate. He pressed on one of the squid and ink came out onto the plate. "What the hell? They left ink in this thing. What the hell? Should I call the waiter over?"

"Don't call him over."

"Well, what's going on with this ink thing?"

I tried to smile but I was in no mood for humor. "It says on the menu that it's cooked in its own ink." I repeated what the menu said in French.

"Oh," he said and began eating. "You know, your dad ordered liver and onions at the diner, and your mom—guess what she ordered?"

I stared at Jack as his mouth was becoming blue with squid's ink.

"Come on," he said. "We were eating in the Windmill Diner. What did she order?"

"Your mouth is turning blue, Jack."

"What did she order?"

"Jack, I don't know what she ordered."

"Chicken fingers. Has she ever ordered anything else? The waitress didn't ask them what they wanted. She only asked me."

"Jack, your lips are turning dark blue," I said. I had to laugh. Then I noticed somebody standing just far enough away from our table to catch our attention—the woman with the light red hair from the boat. She was one of those beautiful women whose delicate features make them look both feminine and physically strong. Her skin was lightly freckled and her lips were a light red, like clay.

"I figured out how I know your name," she said to Jack. "Hope I'm not intruding. . . ."

Jack self-consciously tried to wipe the dye from his lips, and then he looked at me to see if it was all right to talk. I nodded my head. I was glad somebody else had come along to take the pressure off the conversation.

"You're a writer—a screenwriter?"

Jack nodded.

"A client of Elaine Price?"

"Yes."

"Price pitched your script to me. You're almost finished with it, aren't you?" she said.

"Yes, but how do you know Price?"

"I'm Julie Berman."

Jack turned and looked at me, amazed. I knew who she was as well as he did—a very successful Hollywood director whose movies we both loved. She smiled in a way that made her seem humble, even genuinely shy. There was something almost bigger than life about her, the way one pictures famous actors and actresses. Jack praised a few of her films and I knew that he meant it; he simply didn't have the ability to lie about things like this.

Berman and Jack talked a bit about the script and then she turned to me. "Isn't this funny? I was thinking about his script on the plane down here."

"Do you want to see it? It's just about done," Jack said.

"That would be wonderful," she said.

Jack told her he would have somebody overnight it from Brooklyn. She thanked him and then gave him the address where she was staying. After excusing herself, she crossed the room to her table.

I was still trying to take this all in. I wasn't used to actually seeing somebody—anybody—ask him for his work, let alone someone renowned. Berman was one of the few women directors of both small artsy flicks and big-budget commercial pictures. She'd also directed a Broadway play. I was happy for him—despite everything.

"Jack, your lips are still blue, but congratulations," I said.

Our entrées arrived at that moment. I was suddenly hungry again. Jack refilled my wineglass and I began to eat.

"Now tell me what's going on with this agent," I said.

He pushed back in his seat and looked down for a moment pensively, as if trying to think of a way to start his story.

"Well," he said. "It's Peter's doing—sort of." He looked up at me and I averted my eyes. Peter was the last person in the world I wanted to hear about at this moment. "Put it this way," he said. "The more I used to read about him, the more I began comparing my whole life to his. You know what I used to say—writing's a private thing, not a game. Every writer is his own private world, and there's no sense comparing yourself to another writer. But I couldn't seem to help it with Peter. Have you heard the latest about him?"

"No." Nobody had told me, and I had never asked after that day in the airport.

"You didn't happen to see that last piece of shit with De Niro in it, did you?"

"That comedy?"

"Yes, just that, but it wasn't meant to be funny. Peter directed it—what a waste of De Niro's talent." He stared at me a moment, as if to emphasize his point; then he went on. "Anyway, it made money at the box office, a ton of money, and so he's big-time. Real big-time . . . It's not good to compare yourself to somebody like that, not good at all."

I nodded my head.

"A couple of years back, I reached a kind of boiling point. I guess this is a kind of confession—to you," he said. "You see, what happened to me in New York was what happens to so many people there. I lost sight of my original vision. I began putting my success above human relationships, the people I cared about most, the things in life that are truly meaningful. I was thinking about my success and the success of others. I was jealous of certain people. I didn't admit it—oh, no, not me. I acted cool as a cucumber, but inside I was tormented by the fact that all these others were getting attention and I wasn't.

"Anyway, Maddy, in a brave moment, I blew off the whole competition thing, decided if I was going to do anything, I'd do it for myself from that point on, so I announced to everybody that I was quitting writing for good. Actually, I was thinking of doing something important. I kept thinking about the Puppet Garage, something meaningful like that." He refilled my wineglass and then his own. "Then something happened a few months later, something downright strange. I was kind of messing around on my computer, writing a letter to a friend, when the next thing I knew I was telling a story. I finished it in a day, read it over—it was really fresh, so I wrote it out in script format. The night I typed the last line—it was a Sunday night—I met this young woman at a party, an undergraduate who was interning for some agent—I didn't know who. I told her a bit about the story and she told me she was heading to Hollywood and would read it on the plane if I got it to her in the morning. Well, she did read it, and then a day later Elaine Price called me from her home in Beverly Hills. She's nuts about it."

He used to talk about her and so I was truly amazed.

"I have to confess, you taught me a lesson in New York

the way you quit the pretentious art scene and started doing something you loved so dearly. You were my inspiration. Deep down in my heart I really had to stop caring about what other people thought of me. I had to do it for myself, and yet it also had to be a generous act. I knew that when I started out writing, but I had to relearn it on a whole new level. It was then that I became a writer." Jack was staring into my eyes. I was afraid that I was blushing.

Jack lifted the tablecloth and began looking underneath. "What kind of shoes do you have on?" he asked.

"Shoes?" I said. I suddenly noticed that our bill had come and Jack had laid cash on the tray.

"Come on, up for dancing?" he said as he got out of his chair. We stepped outside and into a taxi and headed across the island to a nightclub. I was still thinking about Jack's sudden success and his telling me that I was his inspiration. Soon the driver was acting as a tour guide, pointing out famous beaches and landmarks, and telling stories about hurricanes and celebrities.

The island's capital was much larger than the other two villages, with two high-rise hotels lit up with neon. From the cab we crossed a footbridge to a nightclub, a single-story, windowless building with palm trees and alligators painted along the sides, and we were swallowed by deafeningly loud music. Jack and I sat down at the bar and ordered frozen piña coladas. As I sipped from my drink, I noticed that the place was filled with teenagers no older than we were when we first met.

"You know, I didn't mention it, but when you were talking to that director, you looked absolutely crazy—your lips were bright blue," I said.

Jack laughed and then grabbed my wrist and we headed out to the dance floor.

*   *   *

It was three in the morning when we climbed out of a taxi and hiked the sandy trail to our cabins. The sand was so fine and soft that we felt like we were walking in place. I could taste nicotine on my tongue. All the young people in the bar had been smoking and Jack had bummed a cigarette from one and persuaded me to take a drag. As we reached the fork in the trail, Jack suggested we meet near the kiosk the next day in the afternoon, and then, after a quick kiss on the cheek, he turned and walked away.

"Hey, thanks for the evening," I called. He turned and waved at me and then went on. I climbed the trail to my cabin and got into bed. At that late hour I expected to pass out right away, but I was beyond sleep, and so I lay there thinking. I'd been feeling so many different things with Jack all day that it was a relief to be alone. Then the memory of Peter started haunting me again.

An hour later I noticed the curtains were lighter: dawn. Then something on the wall caught my eye—the plaque that I had placed in the dresser was hanging up again. I got out of bed and studied it. I opened the drawer in which I had put it—it was empty—and began looking around the room to see if anything else was disturbed, but nothing else as far as I could tell had been touched.

Chapter Twenty-four

I got up close to noon after having fallen into a deep sleep and went to the plaque again. I was a bit surprised to see it was still hanging there. I hid it in the drawer again and then walked to the center of the village to get a bite to eat. I was anxious about seeing Jack. The village was abuzz with islanders from the surrounding hills, hawking fruits and homemade wares at an open-air market. I passed through a long green tent amidst the din of chicken squawks and pig squeals and the nervous purr of pigeons. Bins were overflowing with ripe papaya, mangoes, and pale yellow berries that I had never seen before. I stopped and asked a man if he could suggest a place for breakfast and he gave me directions to a well-known café that served Creole food. It was called Madame Serle's. "Everyone's there," he said, and smiled.

I managed to find an empty table on the dusty terrace of the packed café with a view of the town square. Madame Serle, a matronly woman in a big blue apron, shuffled over to my table and took my order. A toothpick was stuck in the side of her mouth that she sucked on like a little cigar.

I was just finishing breakfast when I noticed Jack in the crowd across the square. He was with Julie and her young daughter. I could tell by the way she and her daughter were smiling and laughing that he had already charmed them. Jack noticed me, came over, and introduced the daughter. Her name was Lizzy and she had wild, curly hair and intelligent blue eyes. I chatted with her for a bit. She carried a stack of Tintin comics under her arm. She was a big fan of Hergé, she said. I too had read him as a child and so I thumbed through one of her books, remembering the beauty of the drawings. It was the sort of art I liked—beautiful but serving a purpose other than to be sold in a gallery. Then I turned to Julie. She said that she was anxiously awaiting the arrival of Jack's script.

"You won't be disappointed by it," I said, surprising myself. "It's a fabulous story."

"Well, please get it to me soon," she said to Jack. Then she and Lizzy excused themselves. At times in the past I had felt hurt by his gregarious nature, but I was seeing it in a different light now.

"Hey, do you want to be my agent? Two is better than one," Jack said.

"Sure, I'll be your agent," I said.

"How did you sleep?"

"I feel great."

"Isn't this a fabulous town?" He looked around. "Whoever thought this could have happened—the two of us meeting up here like this?" He continued looking around. "There were times in New York when I wondered if we'd see each other again." He took a deep breath and looked me up and down. His nervous edge was back. For some reason I expected him to say something about us, about our breakup. "By the way, did you read that thing on your door, you know, the legal notice in fine print?"

"What thing?"

"You know, about that strange law they have down here?"

"In fine print? What law?"

"That if you don't go snorkeling at least once while you're here, they'll—"

"Oh, sure, Jack, they'll what? Incarcerate us?"

"No, just confiscate everything we own."

"Well, sounds like we'd better get on the stick," I said.

We returned to our cabins to grab towels and bathing suits and then strolled through the streets looking for a place to rent snorkeling equipment. It reminded me of the French Quarter in New Orleans, with gingerbread-style wooden porches and balconies on almost every building. Music blared out of apartments and children played ball in the narrow streets. A woman was beating sand from a small rug, leaning so far over a railing that I was afraid she might fall. We stopped and flipped through a pile of tie-dyed T-shirts; a young man was selling them from the hood of a rusted VW Beetle. I picked one out that said ST. MARIE over a palm tree, and Jack paid for it. I could tell he really wanted to buy me something.

At the far end of town we discovered a bike shop that also rented snorkeling equipment. I stepped up to the counter and told the thin, dark-skinned man what I wanted.

"I'll need a credit card," he said. I took out my card and he copied down the number with meticulous care and then ran it through the machine by hand; he was certainly in no rush. Jack raised his eyebrows slightly and whispered that we were lucky to be the only ones in line.

After fitting me with mask and fins, the man asked Jack for a credit card too.

"I carry only cash." It was part of Jack's philosophy about money to use cash instead of plastic. He liked to have a lot of it on hand so that he might give it away at a moment's notice.

"Can't do it then," the man said.

"I'll leave you enough to buy the equipment twice over if need be," Jack said.

"It's our policy."

"Now wait a minute," Jack said firmly. "I happen to have enough cash on me to cover anything."

"It's the policy," the man said, shaking his head.

"That's absurd."

"Put it on my card," I said, stepping forward. "My husband is just a bit of a nut. He's strictly a cash man."

"Your husband? You should have said something," the man said. He was a peculiar little fellow; he would not look at Jack as he fitted him with the equipment. Soon we were walking down the road, mask and fins dangling from our fingers. Jack touched my back and thanked me.

On the beach we put on our bathing suits and then sat down in the shallow water to slip on the fins and masks. We peered at each other through our lenses. It was a ridiculous moment, as if fate had forced us to wear silly masks for being such dunces about our lives. Then we were gliding over the beautiful coral. We swam for a long time, pointing out schools of fish and sea creatures and interesting formations of coral and sand. I became even more comfortable next to him than I had been on land. I swam alongside him; sometimes our hands touched.

Then the vibrant colors triggered a memory of the Puppet Garage in Brooklyn. One afternoon I stood in the middle of the floor alone before the children had started to trickle in and simply stared at the pictures that the many young artists had done. I'd hung them everywhere in the room. Suddenly they seemed to float before me and speak to me in some secret language. *So this is what art's really about,*

I thought at the time. Now the reef brought that wonder back to me.

We spent the rest of the day on the beach and then later went out to dinner at a less expensive restaurant, more our style, more like the kind of place we might have found in the past. We were pleasantly tired from sun and water. Our chairs were facing the square and fountain and there was plenty to look at. We played a game of guessing the nationalities of people in the passing crowd and then trying to overhear them speak so as to know if we were right.

"A German."

"A Russian."

"You're nuts."

"A thousand bucks says he's a Russian."

Later in the evening, a fire-eater fell to his knees and blew a yellow-and-blue flame high above the fountain—a kind of hush, then a puff, and black smoke drifted toward the sky.

We took a walk, kicking off our shoes and stepping into the waves in the starlight; the foam tickled our shins.

Then something happened that I still cannot explain—I realized we were holding hands and yet I had no memory of when this started. Jack kept walking along the edge of the waves with me as if he hadn't noticed anything either, as if we had just stepped back in time a dozen years. It was not until we arrived back at our cabins that I became unsure of how far to take this. I loved the feel of his hand in mine, but I knew it was getting late. At my door I turned and let go. I saw that he was standing still, the light from a nearby cabin shining faintly on his face.

"Care to sit outside here, have some tea or something?" I said when we reached my cabin.

"Love to," Jack said.

I made tea and then sat down next to him. We could hear the ocean far below the cliff.

"Hey," Jack said, looking at the sky. "Two moons."

"Do you think he's still alive?" I asked, recalling the crazy farmer that we'd lived behind on Martha's Vineyard.

" 'The litmus test for marriage is a driving lesson by a spouse,' " Jack quoted the old man. " 'Marriages that pass that will last forever.' " The old man had been watching Jack teach me how to drive his father's car—me starting and stopping. I'd nearly given both of us a heart attack back then.

As I sat outside with Jack, the smell of the ocean brought back those days. We chatted for a while, and then we were quiet again, as if we'd run out of things to say.

"Pretty strange, isn't it?" Jack said suddenly. I waited for him to elaborate. "I mean, after all those years of it just being the two of us?"

"Of course," I said. I was suddenly uneasy.

"So you really are seeing somebody?" he asked cautiously.

"I was," I said.

"I guess I knew by the way your parents acted," he said. He sounded disappointed. "Was it serious?"

I took his hand to comfort him and squeezed. "Well, yes. I nearly married him."

"You're kidding."

I squeezed his hand harder. "It's totally over—I doubt I'll even see him again." I believed I was telling the truth.

"In Atlanta?"

"Yes."

I could feel him tense up at hearing this; then he seemed to calm down and again there was silence. I leaned back and stared at the stars.

"Jack," I said quietly, "I saw you on the street holding hands with somebody in the Village." It had never crossed my mind that I would get up the nerve to tell him this, but now I felt as if a weight were off my shoulders. I told him how I had ducked into the PATH station entrance to avoid him.

He apologized, and then he seemed at a loss for words. "That must have been Simone," he mumbled. "I learned a lot from her. She was so different from you."

I could feel the intensity of my jealousy of her. As irrational as it was, I hated her, hated her for the mere fact that he had liked her.

"You guys—what happened?" I asked.

"Talk about over," Jack said. Then he turned to me. "You're a lot stronger than she ever will be. She's the sort of person who believes that everything works by magic, that love is just this thing that happens to you, like taking a drug." He laughed a little. "She's young too, twenty-six."

I was thinking about what he said. "You must have hurt her," I said.

Jack was quiet. "Some things are hard to avoid."

We sat there not speaking. I felt jealous still and wondered if he felt the same way. I knew that I would always miss that innocent closeness that we had felt for so many years.

"Sometimes life is just so out of your control," he said. "You think you know and then you don't. Last year a friend told me that she felt like she simply could not survive without her husband, that she would rather die than lose him. Then just a few weeks ago I heard that she asked him for a divorce. I also heard that she'd fallen in love with somebody else. I was amazed. The strange thing about love is that I feel like I know less about it than I did ten years ago." His arms were crossed over his stomach and I could see his eyes searching as if he were thinking. "I know that it's kind of heavy—I was going to try to avoid the heavy stuff, but I have to tell you that I've looked in the mirror these last few years. I play the part, you know. I'm at ease with people, but really I've always been scared shitless of everything, my intellectual abilities, my skills as a writer. Maddy, I think all that fear kind of put my head in the clouds. What I'm trying to say is that I wasn't there for you so much of the time and I never explained it, never admitted that it was all about being afraid. I'm a good actor, that's all—and so, in a way, I was lying to you about myself."

"Jack, those aren't real lies."

"They are." He stared at me. "I don't know how you stood it. It was so damn self-centered of me to make you put off having a family."

It was good to hear him admit this again. "I was in love with you. Everybody has—"

"I was a jerk—I have no excuses." He was silent. "A few months ago I did something really stupid. I took a trip upstate, having fooled myself into thinking that I was going hiking. But really it was to check out the rabbit house, to see who had bought it and what they had done with it. Maybe I wanted to punish myself, or maybe I've never been able to simply let it go, the thought of our living together there and the life we almost had together." He stopped and looked at me. "Anyway, when I got there I saw a for-sale sign up. The place was exactly the same, untouched. And so there it still stood up on that hill, the spirit of our marriage, of our love for each other despite all its imperfections. The place smelled, of course, but I didn't mind the smell now at all. The door was unlocked, so I walked through the rooms upstairs, the grand bedroom with the splendid view. I could not believe the dreams I'd had in that room with you, if only for a weekend. I saw the small bedrooms, imagined the guests we might have had, and the children. I could practically hear those tiny feet running up and down the stairs. For a good hour and a half I paced up and down the empty rooms feeling like a failure on the most profound level. How had I done what I had done to you; how could I have been that self-centered to have kept you from fulfilling your dream that was really my dream too? How had I lost touch with something so important? Then suddenly I had an idea—whoever had bought the house couldn't really want it, even if it was that inspector who got it. What if I managed to buy it back and then get in touch with you? I wanted to come at you that way, knock you off your feet. I had this realization that the past was not lost, it's never lost.

"I got all excited, beside myself with hope. I drove out of there to pay the Realtor a visit. But the moment I entered his office, he knew what I wanted. He told me the asking price was outrageous, triple what it had been before. He told me the owner was cavalier about selling it and scoffed at lower offers. I drove back to the city alone and then I sort of lost it. I pulled over on the side of the highway and started crying uncontrollably." He stopped talking; his face was dark as he stared at me. "I still love you, Maddy. I still believe in what we had."

He covered his eyes with his hands. I put my arms around him and held him. Then he broke away and looked into my eyes. I'm not sure who kissed who first. I only knew that I was so happy to be in his arms again. We held each other for the longest time and then moved into my cabin and onto the bed. We made love all night and into the morning.

We stayed under my sheets all day. There was a certain distance between us; we were strangers in a way, and yet in another way we were closer than ever before. The jealousy that we'd felt the night before was still there at times, but as long as we were in bed together, we'd make love and then feel closer and begin talking again.

That afternoon I took the photograph out of my bag, the one with his writing on the back.

"You know, I have a confession to make," I said. "I came all the way down here, not to see you, but to ask you what the heck you were planning on saying on the back of this photo."

He looked at the photograph, and then he got out of bed and sat at the table writing something on it. After getting dressed to go outside, he dropped the photo on the end of the bed and then stepped out the door. The moment he was gone, I felt the vacuum from his absence, as if a part of me had just left the room.

I leaned over and picked up the photograph.

Dear Cricket,

> *It took me three years to realize this. The real reason I hesitated about having children with you is because I felt so much the first time that we tried that I was afraid of trying again. That's the one thing I left out last night when I told you how scared I was. Now that I understand that, I'm no longer so afraid.*

> *Your Loving Ex,*
> *Jack.*

Half an hour later, he burst through the door with grocery bags in his arms, a smile on his face, his cheeks bright red. He laid out a banquet fit for a king—baguettes, wedges of cheese, bottles of red wine, and a bouquet of flowers. That night I fell asleep in his arms. When I woke, we were holding each other so tightly that I could hardly breathe.

Chapter Twenty-five

The next morning we finally staggered out the door like two bears from a winter cave. It had been a day and a half since I'd seen the sky. After a short swim, Jack suggested we split up for a few hours. His script was supposed to have arrived the day before and he wanted to make a call. We kissed and I went up the trail to my cabin.

I decided it was time to make some telephone calls to tell people that the wedding was off. I'd call my parents first, and then Jennifer and ask her to make the rest of the phone calls. I thought about what I would tell them. I decided to put off the calls for another day or so. Instead I began to browse through a guidebook in my room. The island's history was more diverse than I knew. I read about the waves of settlers to the island from different countries over the years. At one time there were wild panthers in the jungle, imported from India. I read about hiking trails, wild monkeys, and wild boars. A poisonous snake, some relative of the coral snake, inhabited the eastern end of the island.

Then, as I looked down a list of museums, my eye rested on *The Estate of Maggie Comane.* There was no information about the museum other than the hours and its location just outside of town. I was too curious to let this go. I glanced at my watch and saw that I had time for a short visit, and so I borrowed a bicycle from the proprietor and rode out of town. There was little traffic on this wide dirt road without houses. Only a rickety truck carrying a load of grapes and trailing a noxious plume of diesel exhaust passed me. Turning off, I glided through an open gate and found myself on the grounds of the estate. At first I did not realize what I was looking at—the house was located at the top of a hill with trees on either side. Then I was astonished. It was *the house,* the exact one that Jack and I nearly bought, only it was perfectly kept, the shingled siding painted blue, the porch banisters a fresh, glossy white. The house looked huge, even monumental. Low hedges and small gnarled fruit trees bordered it. I turned around. Instead of looking out over a valley with farms, the view was even more dramatic— a carpet of tall, dark green forest leading down to the sea.

After parking my bicycle in the gravel lot near the front door, I stepped into the shade of the porch. Just inside the door an older woman sat next to a cash box at a desk. Behind her, I could see Maggie's name engraved in brass and the dates 1914–1987. I paid my five dollars, picked up a brochure and floor plan, and followed a strip of rug into the kitchen. Hanging in almost every room was a ceramic heart with an eye painted at the center. There were also sculptures of rabbits on shelves and tables—white rabbits with pink eyes and waistcoats. I wondered what on earth had happened to Maggie that she was able to put her life into such order—or maybe it had been put in order after her death. I stopped and studied the floor plan. Just as with the rabbit house, above the rooms were names like the Burrow

and the Hole. I wandered from room to room. Framed on
the wall in the small room between the dining room and sitting room were pages of handwritten text that looked like
original manuscript pages to some version of *Alice in Wonderland*. I climbed the stairs and peered into small bedrooms, a sitting room and an office with a writing desk and
quills. Finally I came to a large bedroom with the magnificent view of the sea across the jungle valley. There was a
large dresser with a tall mirror and on its surface a hand
mirror, a hairbrush, and a silver comb. Although there were
signs on various tables that read DON'T TOUCH, there was no
such warning on the bed, a canopy bed with a very plush
pink cover and thick, fluffy pillows. I sat down on the bed
and opened the brochure.

The Strange Death of Maggie Comane of St. Marie.

In 1980, Maggie Comane, a wealthy and eccentric
woman in her late sixties, moved to St. Marie from
America. She fell in love with the island and eventually built a mansion three miles into the jungle. The
house, which is now preserved as a museum, is like
nothing anyone on the island has ever seen before—
something more akin to Victorian England. Much of
the oak and maple needed to build it had to be shipped
in from North America. . . . The museum is preserved
by money left in a trust by Ms. Comane.

I skipped a page.

Maggie Comane, it is said, began making her mark on
St. Marie even before setting foot on the island itself in
1980. While on the ferry ride here, Maggie got into a
discussion about money with a young French painter

who made his home on St. Marie. Maggie told the painter that money should not concern people, that it is ultimately meaningless and that it kills the dreams and aspirations of the average citizen. Money, she said, is a boundary, a way of separating oneself from the world that must be defied and ignored at any cost. The young painter took offense, citing the many poor people in the Caribbean and elsewhere. Depending on who you were, money could be very important, he said. The discussion became increasingly heated, the painter calling Maggie delusional. Maggie did not seem to take offense at any of the man's name-calling, and instead handed him a check made out to cash for five thousand dollars. Certain that the check was a farce, the man tore it up in front of her. Ms. Comane then proceeded to write him another one, this time for ten thousand dollars, which the man discarded in a receptacle. Meanwhile, a young boy working on the boat fished the check out of the garbage and cashed it that afternoon on the island. A week later, to everyone's surprise, the check cleared. When the man learned about this, he demanded that the boy give him the money from the check. A rather lengthy and ultimately bitter dispute between the boy's family and the man was not resolved for several years until the man moved away from the island.

I turned the page.

Maggie claimed that she had spent her life as a shy person overshadowed by an extraordinary love affair that ended in tragedy when her lover died of a heart attack. Soon after the death, she descended into madness, which brought her close to death numerous times. She finally began to rehabilitate herself when she set off on a journey to find something that she described as love. It was when she stepped foot on this island that the metamorphosis of self that she had been looking for finally began. She shed her old ideas of love. "I did not merely adopt new ideas of love; I became them," she said. "My old idea of love, the love that I felt for Gwen, was not true love but only a beginning. True love has nothing to do with the image of oneself or even the image of another; it has nothing to do with possession, nor dependency. Instead, it has everything to do with tearing down the boundaries between your heart and the rest of the world. I started with this island, this island became my self, and then eventually I expanded my boundaries to the rest of the world. It was on this island that I finally discovered my dream and on this island that I've finally mustered the courage to step into it. Therefore, I've completed what I only started with Gwen. I've stepped into the world."

I skipped a few more pages and came across a black-and-white photograph of a lookout point on a bluff with steps leading up to it from a rocky beach. There was police tape at the top of the bluff as well as on the rocky beach below.

Ms. Comane's death was immediately labeled suspicious because of her controversial nature. Though most of the inhabitants of the island believed her harmless, some considered her psychotic and dangerous, especially to youth, and so to the police it seemed a more likely scenario that she was pushed off the bluff rather than that she jumped. However, a thorough investigation did not turn up a single lead and eventually the case was closed.

There was a kind of postscript at the end that read:

Soon after her death, rumors began to circulate that the ghost of Maggie Comane haunted the island, and even today daily mishaps and travails are attributed to her so-called presence. It's also believed that the island has an unusual number of broken hearts among lovers. As a means of appeasing the so-called ghost, some islanders hang on the walls of many houses a small ceramic heart with an eye painted on it that's a replica of the pendant that Maggie was wearing when she fell to her death. To this day, the tradition continues among islanders.

A feeling of sadness swept through me. I thought of what Maggie had written in her diary about stepping into your dream and living it and I thought of her sad end. Then I heard footsteps and looked up into the face of the woman from the front desk. She wore a gray dress, and she was standing just back from the edge of the bed, smiling, though it was difficult to tell whether she wore a friendly or a hostile smile. She shook her head ever so slightly. "Didn't you read the signs?" she said sternly.

I apologized and got up and moved toward the door.

Outside I turned and looked at the house. I wanted to get back to Jack to tell him about it. I folded the brochure, put it in my pocket, and then rode down the gravel road between the hedges and through the gates. Twice I got off the bicycle to push it, then coasted down the other side, and finally glided into the village.

Chapter Twenty-six

At our lodge I returned the bicycle and then ran down the hill to the cabins to look for Jack—I was so excited to see him.

"Jack," I yelled near his cabin. "You won't believe what I saw. You just won't believe it."

Then I stopped a few feet away from the door, surprised by what I saw sitting next to it—a FedEx package similar to the ones he had sent me. Assuming this was the script, I picked it up and knocked on his door, but there was no answer. I climbed the hill toward my room with the package under my arms. The return street address was Jack's in Brooklyn, but the name on it was Simone Belvac. I was confused; he had told me that she was living in Manhattan and that they were out of touch. I stopped outside my door and carefully tore it open.

I looked at the title of the script—*Kissing Your Ex*. It was the title that Peter had given him. I opened it up and began reading. The story started in a supermarket on the Upper West Side, a man and woman bumping into each other, fumbling with groceries as they spoke to each other. In the margins were somebody's notes, questions, underlined words, and deletions. I suppose that was what inspired me to reach back in the envelope. There was a note inside.

> *Dear Jack,*
>
> *Sorry if I'm a bit late getting this off to you. That's great that you met Julie Berman; in fact, it's incredible, and just like you to have that kind of luck. I know good things are coming your way. By the way, our apartment feels so damn empty without you. I know what I said before, but I now believe that this trip of yours is a good idea. You need to focus on your writing now that you're on a roll. Our friends have been wondering what's become of us. I told them the whole truth and nothing but the truth. As you said last night, love is never simple.*
>
> *I'll see you at the airport at nine tomorrow night. I miss you. By the way, this is the only copy I could find.*
>
> *Love,*
> *Simone*

I stood there in the hot sand of the trail just below my cabin unable to move. It seemed like some sort of cruel joke that he was playing on me, and yet I couldn't reconcile my image of him with this. Clutching the letter, I walked into my cabin, closed the door, and sat on my bed to read it over again. My eye fell to the line, *I miss you.* I began going over the time Jack and I spent together on this island, examining his behavior, from his nervousness in the airport to his reserve when it came to talking about our lives when we were apart—and I'd thought he was merely being polite.

Then I had a sudden sense that all of this had happened

before, a powerful déjà vu. I felt like I had always been more vulnerable than he was. He always seemed to have one foot out of the relationship; that was the real reason he didn't want to have children with me back then, not what he'd just written on the back of the photo.

When I looked up from the letter, I noticed a note on my dresser and picked it up. It was handwritten. *M—At the Madame's, Love URX . . .* I sat there for a moment trying to decipher the meaning of it—it had a kind of hazy familiarity. Then I realized it was shorthand for "your ex" and that it was written in Jack's handwriting. I did not know why it had been left there rather than on my door.

The anger that I'd felt toward him was back. I was tempted to return the package to his door and leave the island, let him figure out what happened. There was nothing he could say to hide the fact that he was living with another woman.

I saw shadows of somebody's feet at my door. Thinking it was Jack, I quickly put the script and note back in the package. I heard a loud knock.

"Who is it?" I said, startled by the sound.

"Cleaning service," a woman with an accent answered.

"I'm busy," I said. I opened the door and saw a woman making her way down the hill with a vacuum cleaner in hand.

"You can come in," I called. She turned around and began coming back up the hill. For a second I thought it was the woman in the museum—they looked almost exactly alike. She slipped by me at the door and put her vacuum cleaner down.

I picked up Jack's package and walked toward the village to find him. I did not know what I would say to him. I guess I just wanted to see his face when I confronted him, to experience his lying directly to me, to see if such a thing were really possible. I felt like I had nothing to lose now, nothing at all. I walked along the trail and then down the steps past the church. Crossing the square, I spotted Jack sitting on the far side of the crowded terrace talking excitedly with Julie.

Jack rose to his feet and kissed me. "Hey, what's that?" He pointed to the package in my hand. "Did that just come?"

I nodded.

"Now that's luck," he said. "Julie and I were just trying to figure out what to do about getting her a copy." I smiled at Julie. "The place across the street does photocopies. I'll be right back—you two don't mind, do you?" Then he was gone. I had the note in my pocket. I looked over at Julie.

"Jack was telling me about you two—an incredible story," Julie said.

I nodded. I was still thinking about what I would say to him when he got back.

"Jack told me you're an artist," she said. "An incredible artist."

"I quit," I said. "He's always telling people that, but that part of my life is over—at least in the way most people think of it."

Suddenly Jack reappeared and gave us both copies of the script. Then Julie stood up, thanked him, and told him that she was leaving early in the morning but that she would be in touch through his agent. She shook our hands and departed.

"So where've you been, darling?" Jack asked.

"I was looking for you. Where were you earlier?"

"I bumped into Julie. We took a little tour of the town— it's just so beautiful around here."

I took the brochure from the museum out of my pocket and put it on the table. Jack picked it up and started reading it. "Wait a minute, is this—"

"The woman—from the house upstate."

"This is her?" he said, reading. I watched his eyes moving back and forth across the page. "She rebuilt the rabbit house? This is wild," he said, and then skipped to the part about Maggie falling from the bluff. "This is a terrible—what a sad ending," he said.

He looked up at me. I could feel blood in my face from the anger.

"Hey, you look upset."

I looked across the square to the fountain. I had no idea how to begin. "Jack, we talked about a lot of things these past few days, but one thing we never touched on was why we really split up. I don't think we ever really got to the truth. I mean what happened, what really happened—I think it's time you were honest with me."

He stared at me a moment before answering. "I never stopped loving you, Maddy, not for one minute."

"You ended up with somebody else pretty quickly, didn't you?"

"That just happened. It was lucky. I met somebody I liked and she liked me."

"She was somebody you knew before you moved out, Jack."

"Are you implying—"

"What's this?" I pointed to the return address on the package.

He laughed a little. "Oh, that. She's just watering my plants. I couldn't think of who else to ask to send the script."

"She's coming all the way over from Manhattan for that?" I asked. I knew that what I was doing was destructive, but I pressed on.

"We're still friends."

"Jack, do you remember that night we camped out at the

rabbit house? Do you remember what you said? You said it would be horrible to lie to somebody you loved. Do you still feel that way?"

"Maddy, what's gotten into you?"

"I'm just curious—you told me you still love me."

"I do."

"Then why are you lying about Simone?" I took the note from my pocket and put it on the table. It didn't take him long to read it; then he crumpled it up and put it in his pocket. He glanced at me quickly, then away. "I can explain. She's a bit of a nut."

"Are you two still living together in your apartment in Brooklyn?" I said.

Jack started to shake his head, and then he stopped and looked at me. "It's not what it might seem like—"

"So you *are* living with her?"

"Maddy, it's a New York thing—she hasn't been able to find a new apartment—"

"You lied to me, Jack. You told me she lived in Manhattan."

"I didn't want to hurt you. I'm sorry."

"You didn't want to hurt me? You invite me down here while you're still living with this woman you've been with for all this time and you don't want to hurt me?"

"Maddy, it's not like that. Our relationship has been over for a long time. It's complicated as hell."

"What the fuck could be complicated? You're going back to live in your apartment with your girlfriend after seducing me down here. You know, I was engaged when I came down here. Do you hear me? I was engaged to some guy. And I broke it off to come down here to see you. You asshole, you ruined everything. You fucking ruined everything!"

I jolted the table and a glass fell over. Then I ran through the streets to my cabin.

Chapter Twenty-seven

I drew my curtains and threw myself down on the bed. I wanted to cry but I couldn't. I was alone again, so alone and so bitter that I couldn't even cry about it. Then it occurred to me that Jack would soon come knocking. The last thing I wanted was to listen to his stupid excuses through the closed door, so I grabbed a towel and my book and dashed down the trail to the beach. I walked to a remote spot, left my belongings in the sand, and walked on. I needed to get far away. I was disgusted. He wasn't just in a relationship with her; he was living with her, and that meant he was sleeping with her. I could tell by the very tone of the letter that it was still very much alive—*love is never simple*. There was nothing to do now but locate a pay phone and find out when the first flight out of here would be.

I walked briskly down the beach, my eyes on the sand before me. I could not believe that an hour ago I'd been imagining spending the rest of my life with him. Now I never wanted to see him again. To make matters worse, Simone knew nothing about where he was. Once I was out of the picture, as I would be shortly, he could return to New York as if he'd been working away on his script and get back on track with her. She was so much younger than I. She and Jack had plenty of time to iron things out, and then she could bear him as many children as he wanted. And where was I? Thirty-seven years old. I'd done everything in my power to start a new life for myself. But in my heart of hearts, I had been waiting for Jack to contact me, and then he had sent me those letters. . . .

He calls and you come, Andrew had said. He was right after all: I was Jack's fucking lapdog and I had ruined my life for him.

Far out on the point, I could make out a strip of breakers. I asked a teenage girl where I might find a telephone, and she pointed to some wooden steps leading over the dunes. On the other side was a short boardwalk with storefronts— a bar, two surfboard-rental shops, and a concession stand where a skinny girl in a bikini was paying for a hot dog. I went into the back of the bar to the pay phone and dialed the number to my airline. I'd take the earliest flight off St. Ann in the morning.

A recording came on that said the circuits were busy. I tried again and got the same message. I slammed down the telephone.

"Hey," the bartender called as I was leaving. "Some of us like to use that thing."

I did not look at him as I passed outside. The girl with the hot dog was walking away. I purchased an iced tea from the concession stand and sat down near the entrance to the bar before trying the number again.

A few surfers came over the dunes with their boards, set them down, and went inside the bar. Minutes later they came out and headed back toward the beach. A blond-haired boy wearing a headband stopped before crossing the dune, came back, and leaned his board against a post. He lingered near the post. I turned and saw that he had taken off his headband and wound it around his wrist. He was looking at me, pulling the wrapper off a chewy energy bar with his teeth. His wet hair was sticking up straight in places. His skin was tanned.

I could feel him still looking at me as he came over and sat down on the boardwalk near me.

"Hey," he said. "Nice day, huh?"

I pretended that I didn't know he was talking to me.

"Can I get you something to drink?"

He moved closer to my peripheral vision. I held up my iced tea and shook my head without making eye contact.

"From the States?" he said.

I thought I might not answer him. "Ohio," I said.

"Ohio's cool. What brings you down here?"

"Whoever said Ohio's cool?"

"Nobody—I did—what brings you down here?"

"Actually, it's personal." I turned my face away from him.

"Sounds like you're having fun. What did you do, come down here with that screwy guy?"

"Who are you talking about?"

"I saw you with some guy." He tore at the energy bar with his straight white teeth. He hardly looked at me, just expected me to answer him.

"How old are you?" I asked, looking him up and down.

"How old are you?"

"Twice your age, at least, but I asked you first." I guessed he was no more than twenty-five.

"You're a funny girl—"

"Thanks, but I'm not a girl—I'm a . . ." I didn't want to bother finishing the sentence; it seemed like a waste of time.

"So what happened?"

258 Brooke Stevens

"Aren't you afraid of missing that big wave of the season out there? I think I see some swells on the horizon." I sipped from my straw and looked away.

He laughed a little and then moved closer to me. "You're interesting," he said.

"What is this, spring break?"

"Hell, no. I work for a living."

"You work for a living? What, trying out different suntan lotions?"

He laughed a little. "You are funny. I'm a writer, *an intellectual,* a member of the *intelligentsia.* But I also happen to like to surf. It's my passion, or one of them." He pointed behind him. "He says you're bumming."

"Who?"

"The bartender."

"How would he know?"

"Watch my board?"

"I'm not watching your board." He disappeared into the bar. *Get up and move along,* I thought, but the weight of what had happened to me with Jack seemed to anchor me in place. I still could not quite believe I had gotten myself into this situation—a situation that I had feared for so long. A few moments later he came out carrying two frozen drinks with straws and set one down next to me. "Here, New Orleans Hurricanes. My bud used to work on Bourbon Street." He gestured toward the bartender. "He says you broke the phone."

"Really—what am I waiting around here for then? I'd better find another one."

"If I know Angel, there's some rum in there," the boy said, pointing to the drink.

"Are you trying to pick me up or something? Because if you are, it's a big waste of time."

"Why did you slam down the phone?"

"Anybody ever tell you that you're nosy?" I said.

He patted his nose. "Down, boy, down."

"First prize for persistence." I got up, leaving the drink on the wooden walkway. "But I've got to find another phone."

I walked along the boardwalk and then turned toward the small town. The moment I was alone, I had the sudden desire to brag to Jack about the fact that a boy a dozen years younger than I had tried to pick me up. Then I recalled Simone again—she was probably the same age as the surfer. I found a telephone in the back of a café, got through to my airline, and changed my flight for the earliest one the next morning. As I was walking away, I heard a loud wave break on the beach—much louder than all the other ones. I thought how a wave that big had broken inside me just now. It occurred to me that I should call up Andrew. I didn't know what I would say to him, and I certainly didn't believe that he would forgive me. I found another pay phone and began to dial his home and then I hung up.

Chapter Twenty-eight

Instead of taking a cab back to my cabin, where Jack could easily find me, I decided to stay in town and eat dinner. I found a new American restaurant, a place that neither Jack nor I would ever have been caught dead in when we were together. There were large trees around the patio, and I could hear insects in the branches as the light in the sky was starting to fade.

"Can I join you?" I heard. I looked up from my dessert to see the surfer. He was dressed casually, his linen shirt unbuttoned low and Birkenstocks on his feet. I could not help but notice the sun-bleached hair on his muscular legs. He pulled a chair out, turned around to a passing waiter, and asked for a glass of beer. "And another glass of wine for the girl," he added. Then he looked at me and winked. "I mean woman. Sorry." He smiled.

"You didn't ask me if you could sit there. And don't wink like that. It's tacky."

"You do want another glass of wine, don't you?"

I considered telling him to go away, but the proper moment came and went. My discovery about Jack was sinking in more with every passing minute. I went over all the tender things he'd said to me the last two days, despite knowing he was going home to somebody else. I tried to imagine how he could possibly make it up to me—by telling me he'd never see her again? Nothing could undo the telephone call he had made a day ago to her—nor the lies that he'd told me.

The streets were coming alive, a carnival atmosphere—young people, some with linked arms.

"I'm not trying to pick you up, as you suggested earlier. If I were, you'd know it."

"Oh, you're just ruffling my feathers—is that what it is?"

"You sound like you're from New York, not Ohio."

"Never heard of the place."

"You've lived there, haven't you?"

"I'm very busy right now," I said, and realized how silly the remark was, since I'd just been staring off into space when he'd come up.

He laughed.

"I've seen you before," he said. "You've got to be from New York. The West Coast wouldn't stand for all the angst."

I glanced at him and realized that I too felt like I had seen him before.

"You've been dumped, right?" the surfer said. This remark came so much out of the blue that I stopped swallowing my wine for a moment. I turned to tell him to leave, but as I looked at his smile, I realized there was something harmless about him, innocent, the way Jack had been for me once. I felt sympathy for him. It was as if he were asking this because he was afraid that something similar was going to happen to him, too. I continued to watch the passersby.

"First time?" he asked.

I looked at him to see what he meant.

"First time some jerk's gone and broken your heart?"

"How did you ever get to be so cocky?" I said. A gentle breeze wiggled the sleeve of his linen shirt.

"I told you I'm a writer, didn't I? An intellectual," he said and winked.

"Intellectual?" I laughed. "I didn't think there were any down here—about as common as icebergs." He looked at me, a bit confused. "You look like you've had a few too many rays on your head—I'm just being candid with you— a little advice from an old lady."

"I happen to be writing a book on the subject of heart-break."

The way the boy stared at me made me nervous; I wasn't sure why. "Sounds *just* fascinating," I said sardonically. "Tell me when it will be out and I'll be sure to buy a dozen copies and give them to my friends."

"You don't believe me, do you?"

"It really hasn't yet occurred to me to believe or disbelieve."

"I thought you'd be a lot nicer than you are."

"Look, you're right about one thing. I was having a bad day—and now I'm having an even worse night—so I apologize for that, okay? But honestly, you're not making it any better."

"All right, I'm sorry. I'm just giving you a little advice."

I looked away. An awkward silence ensued.

"Just what the doctor ordered—free advice from yet another man," I said without thinking.

"It's in our genes."

"Well, why don't you just . . . keep it in your jeans then."

The boy laughed. It took me a moment to realize the double entendre. I knew it had broken the ice with him, whether I wanted it to or not.

"Aren't you interested in the premise of my new book? I believe that having your heart broken is a rite of passage that everyone goes through in America, but nobody seems to know that it is, in fact, a rite of passage. They do not realize how dangerous it is to have your heart broken, nor its value. It's called *First Loves and Other Disasters*."

I tried to laugh. "It'll be shelved under humor with a title like that."

"This island happens to be a perfect place to collect case studies." The boy paused and stared at me.

"Why?" I said.

"Any chance you could talk to me about being dumped? I won't publish your name—*Maddy Green*." Now I was doubly baffled. He watched me, smiling, aware that he'd captured my attention. Then he slid a card across the table—my long-distance calling card with my name on it. "By the pay phone down the street. I saw you leave it there."

"Thanks," I said quietly, putting it into my pocket. I hadn't noticed it missing until now. "It's not worth interviewing me. I've never been dumped. And I'm making it my mission, right now, right here and now"—I lifted my wineglass—"to never, ever be dumped."

"And you've got a hell of a sense of humor," the boy said. "I'd really, really like to interview you before—"

"Before what?" I said.

"You've never been in love with somebody who's been interested in somebody else?" the boy asked.

"All right, here's a tidbit for you. I met my husband when I was eighteen. I'd never had a boyfriend before that, never even developed a healthy crush on somebody. I was too busy before that."

"Ah, one of those."

"What do you mean, 'one of those'?"

"Those are the worst kind."

"Well, surprise, we're divorced, and there were no big heartbreaks."

"And you're here with him on an island that's advertised as the ideal place for honeymooners?"

"No ads like that."

"They're all over." The boy pointed to a billboard on the building across the street: WHERE COUPLES HONEYMOON THEIR HEARTS OUT. Then to an item on the menu itself: *The Perfect Anniversary Dinner*. I smiled a little. How had I missed this?

"We're friends. That's the sort of relationship we have. All couples don't scream and pull hair, you know."

"Don't friends usually have dinner together when they're vacationing?"

"He's got a girlfriend," I said as if it didn't matter to me.

"I know. I saw him chatting her and her daughter up earlier. She's one of the more attractive women on the island, and your husband was sort of pulling his ear when he was talking to her—that's body language for 'I want to do it with you.' I know that sounds a bit crass, but it's true."

I was shaken. He must have been flirting with Julie even after all that had happened between us. That was the problem with him—even now he didn't really understand what he had done.

"We're friends, close friends," I said. "Close friends can withstand a lot. We never went through the shit that most do. Just decided to go our separate ways."

The boy scratched his chin, looking away and then back to me. "Sounds like you're holding something back."

"From who? You? Why would I do that? I don't really care what you think; if somebody had broken my heart once I would not deny it. This is ridiculous." I went inside the restaurant and reached for my credit card, but realized I'd left it on the table. When I came out, the boy was tapping it against his chin, smiling. I snapped it away from him and paid my bill.

The boy was still sitting there as I passed by him, his legs crossed at the ankles. "I hope I didn't upset you," he said. "If you'd stick around, I could tell you a bit more about my ideas."

"Not interested," I said. "Maybe you should buy yourself a hat—it will help you think better."

I took a cab back to my cabin, locked my door, and settled into bed. Again I had that feeling of wanting to cry but not being able to; I could not help but think how screwed up my life had become.

I heard a knock on the door. I didn't speak or move.

"Maddy?" It was Jack.

I continued to lie there quietly.

"Can we talk about this, please?"

I held the sheets up to my chin. He waited outside my door for a moment longer. "I'm sorry about what happened. I'm so sorry." I kept silent and still. Finally he tried my doorknob but found it locked. "Please don't leave the island." There was a short pause. "I mean it."

He waited for me to speak. I could feel the pain I was inflicting on him by not responding. It was not enough, of course, not nearly enough.

Chapter Twenty-nine

I woke at dawn with an even clearer under-standing of what happened the day before. I kept picturing their clothes mixed up in the same drawers. They were probably even sharing the same toothbrush. Maybe she was in his bed at that moment in one of his undershirts. If Jack really had wanted to make things happen with me, he would never have risked having her send his script here. The more I thought about it, the more self-centered it seemed. I had seen this side of him before, but I had never taken action about it. I thought of all the years I'd put up with this very hurtful side of him. I decided to take the first ferry in the morning so as not to have to deal with him. Packing my bags, I cleaned up my room and then suddenly remembered the towel and book that I'd left on the beach.

Dawn was just breaking as I stepped out of my cabin. There was a white coating of dew on all the leaves of the plants along the path. I slipped past Jack's cabin and down the steps onto the sand. I had to walk a considerable distance before I found everything at the foot of the cliff where I had left it. A note was resting on my towel.

Maddy,

Please don't leave the island. We need to talk. I feel sick about what's happened.

Jack

At first this seemed genuine. Then I crumpled it up. *No, Jack, you'll never, ever trick me again.* I walked back toward the steps. The beach ahead of me was deserted, the cabanas closed, and the chairs near the boardwalk chained together. The horizon was just starting to soften with the coming sun. Before reaching the steps to the cabins, I checked my watch. I had an hour before the first ferry. I turned and walked to the edge of the water, glanced around me to make sure I was alone, and then stripped off my clothes and dove in. Hoping that the water would soothe some of my bitterness, I swam far from shore and then stopped and turned onto my back. I stared up at the heavens. I could see the faint outline of the moon in the lightening sky.

Suddenly I felt as if the water were moving around me. It was the sensation of the whole ocean circling me gently. I knew it wasn't real and yet I couldn't seem to break myself of its spell. It felt as if I were in a whirlpool. I began to tread water and look toward shore for some sort of reference point, but even the island itself seemed to be spinning around me. I was starting to become dizzy, and it occurred to me that this was dangerous; I might faint. I noticed a strange feeling in my stomach, a mild tingling almost indistinguishable from the warm water itself. Suddenly I heard a voice: *A wife ate my shark*—the innocent mistake that Jack had made on the boat. I began to kick toward the beach but as I did, I felt like I was moving farther away from the island, not closer. *A wife ate my shark,* I heard again. I put more effort into my stroke, wondering if I wasn't caught in a rip current. I took stroke after stroke until I was lifting my arms heavily and letting them fall back into the water with a splash. I became exhausted quickly. Finally I could see I was making progress, and then at last my feet touched bottom and I began to walk out of the water. It was as if I had weights on my limbs. I wrapped myself in my towel and collapsed facedown.

As I recovered, still lying facedown, I thought of what had just happened, the whirlpool. It was the feeling of falling down a tunnel, and then I suddenly thought of rabbits. *Rabbits rule!* Then I noticed the tingling in my stomach again. I put my hand against my belly and closed my eyes. I wondered if I had been careful enough when Jack and I were making love. Then, all at once, I recalled that feeling in my stomach when I'd been pregnant the first time. I was sure it was the same feeling.

I sat up on the beach to put on my clothes and then looked back out at the sea. The sun was just starting to strike the water near the horizon. I was relieved, sure that I had narrowly escaped drowning, but I was sad. I could not believe that I was going back to all that emptiness of my life in Georgia. Andrew was no substitute for Jack, nobody was, that was the problem. You only get one chance at first love and nothing will ever compare to it, and yet mine was finally over. I couldn't live with him again. He hadn't changed. Maybe I hadn't either. As I climbed the steps to the trail, I began thinking maybe nobody really changes, maybe life is far more out of our control than we allow ourselves to believe. At the top of the trail, I noticed that Jack's light was on behind his closed curtains. I slipped by quietly. At my cabin I opened the door and flipped on my light. My two carry bags that I had placed neatly on my bed were gone.

I was astonished. I stood perfectly still in the doorway. Everything in the room seemed somehow faraway and foreign. I looked around the room slowly, no bags in sight. My breathing was shallow and fast. Then something dawned on me. Maybe I only *thought* I left the bags on my bed; maybe I had placed them *behind* it. I moved forward one step at a time, my hands trembling. I peered over the edge of the bed only to see that the floor was bare on the other side. I looked to the propped-open bathroom door. Again, my breath came up short. The bathroom was empty except for a wet towel pushed against the base of the shower. The bags were gone. I had been ripped off.

I tried to remember exactly what was in the bags. Mostly clothing, a few books—my diary; the thought of losing that was terrible.

And then I remembered the silly joke Jack had made about the islanders confiscating your bags if you didn't go snorkeling. All at once, I realized the obvious. He had hidden them to keep me from leaving. I sat down to collect myself. Not only had he persuaded me to come down here by lying to me, but now he was keeping me here by making me think somebody had stolen my bags. Rising to my feet, I headed swiftly down the hill toward his cabin. Blood rose to my face—a dam inside me broke. I came up on his door, raised my fist, and knocked rapidly and loudly. I had this feeling that he was waiting for me to come to him for help. Just as Andrew had said—*he calls and you come*. I was livid.

The door opened and Jack stood in his shorts and undershirt.

"You were in my cabin just now, weren't you?" I said loudly.

He stared at me, amazed. "Yes, I was."

"Do you really think you can get away with this bullshit?"

I pushed past him and began to search his messy room. I opened his closet to a pile of dirty clothes and then got on all fours and pushed aside his bedspread. Turning on his bathroom light, I saw a wet towel on the floor and a curled length of dental floss.

"What the hell are you doing?" Jack said.

"What the hell am I doing? What the hell are you doing? Where are they?" I shouted.

"What? Hey, come on, keep your voice down."

"The boat is leaving in half an hour!" He did not seem to care that I was leaving, or maybe it was part of his act. "Half an hour, did you hear me?" I stepped out his door and slammed it behind me.

"What the hell are you talking about, Maddy?" he called, opening his door.

"You may have gotten me down here, but you're sure as hell not going to keep me here. Where are my fucking bags?"

"Bags? I don't have your bags."

"You're not keeping me on this island. I don't know who you think you are, but we're finished! It's over between us, it's so fucking over, you have no idea how over it is. You think I'm your lapdog, is that what it is? Is that what you're doing to me?"

"I've always respected you. You know that. We had a pretty amazing marriage, and you know that too."

"Do you have any idea what it was like going out with somebody like you—self-centered, dirty liar."

"Liar?"

"You fucking promised me the moon. But you lied—you're a liar. You left me just when I needed you the most. You left me high and dry. You're a sadist too."

"What are you saying, Maddy?"

"Are you that thick? Do you realize how old I am? Do

you realize the situation you put me in? What about our life together, what about all your promises? What about the house apes, how about that? All your little jokes about them—running up and down the halls, you and me taking care of them, taking them to day care and to elementary school and to piano lessons and to Little League or whatever you wanted to do with them. You told me to follow my dreams and you knew what my dream was; you knew I wanted to have a family, and you held it out in front of me like a carrot. I went along believing you. Believing *in* you! And then you went and ended it with me. Sadist!" I was yelling. "Did you have some fun this weekend? You wanted to see if I still liked you. Have a big weekend with the ex. It must have been satisfying—huh—to see somebody throw their life away for you. That's right, I had a life before you called me, and you ruined it. It wasn't with you, but it was something, it was fucking something. What an idiot I was. What an idiot I was to come here, to see you again. What an idiot I was to ever marry you, to ever believe you and all the shit you told me over the years, and all the things we did to-gether." I began crying and Jack tried to reach out to touch me. I pushed his hand away. "You broke my heart once, Jack, but you're never going to do that again, never." I started walking away. "And just so you know, I never broke yours. I kept from breaking yours—" I said, turning back to him. I was crying so hard that I could hardly speak.

"How?" Jack said.

I was walking away, crying uncontrollably.

"How did you keep from breaking my heart?" he asked again.

I turned back to him again. "Look what you've done to my life, you bastard."

"I'm asking you a question, Maddy. You kept from breaking my heart how?"

My face was all wet and I was staring at him.

"Talk about lying," he said. "And *you* call *me* a liar."

Through my tears I could see him nodding his head, as if he were confirming something in his mind. I tried to turn away from him, but I couldn't.

"How do you think it feels to have the person you love do what you did behind my back, huh?"

"What?" I said.

"You know what I'm talking about. You're not going to stand there and deny it, are you?"

I started to shake my head but I stopped.

"Who was it with, Maddy? Who were you fucking behind my back?"

I was speechless. I wanted to say something but I couldn't. "Nobody," I said at last.

"Nobody?" he said, smiling. "Don't stand there like that. It's not going to do you any good to deny it."

"I never slept with anybody."

"Do you think I'm that stupid, huh?" He came at me, eyeing me as if trying to figure something out. "It wasn't Peter, was it?"

"No," I said, and I knew right away I hadn't denied it vehemently enough.

"You fucking asshole."

"I never slept with him, Jack."

"Get out of here." He came at me, shouting. He shoved me a little.

"Do you want to hear what happened?"

"I don't give a shit what happened!" Jack screamed.

"I broke his heart—not yours!"

"Just get the fuck out of here before I do something crazy—and I mean crazy!" Then he ran back to his cabin and slammed the door. I ran up to it—he had locked it. I banged on it.

"Did you hear me? You're the asshole. Nothing happened! Nothing!" I shouted.

I kept banging on his door until my hands were sore; then I turned and started up the hill, unsure of what to do. I could hear his words ricocheting around in my head like a stray bullet. Just before getting to my cabin, I saw something that struck me as odd. The door was shut tight and I was sure I had just left it open. Why would somebody come back to close the door?

I was suddenly sure that somebody was in my cabin. I climbed the porch stairs quietly, stood still just outside of it, and caught my breath to listen. Then I took hold of the knob and pushed the door open with my foot.

The room was dark from the drawn curtains. From the light of the door I could clearly see that my bags had been returned to the exact same position I'd left them on the bed earlier. They were resting at the exact same angle—the only difference was the zipper of one had been opened. Slowly I turned my head. I noticed a wineglass from two nights earlier, a dirty napkin on top of the dresser.

So many things flashed through my head in that moment. How could someone have done this? Then suddenly a realization exploded in my mind and I rapidly began adjusting my sense of reality. There was more to this world than met the eye.

Then something caught my eye through the window—the door to the cabin next to mine was wide open. I went down my porch steps, walked over to that cabin, and climbed its steps. I looked inside. It was empty—the room was clean and the bed was made.

Slowly, an understanding of exactly what had just happened came to me: When I returned from the beach, I had gone into the wrong cabin, an empty one similar to mine.

I stood apart from myself, feeling the momentum of my rage against Jack and yet my stupidity. I wanted to flee.

I gathered up the book and towel and then returned to my cabin. I picked up my two bags and walked as quickly as I could down the hill and through the village, where I could see the ferry idling at the pier. I stepped down onto the boat. Moments later I felt the deck moving; we had departed. I placed my bags down below, paid for my ticket, and then climbed to the upper deck and stared over the railing at the white foam of the ferry's wake.

I looked up at the cliffs and saw him standing at his cabin door in his bathrobe. He was looking straight at me, his tiny figure becoming smaller as the boat motored away.

It was then that I understood what had really happened, how we had tainted that which had seemed so innocent, how the seemingly incorruptible had become corrupted. All those years of feeling like we could die for each other, all those words whispered to each other every night and morning, all those promises and proclamations and presents exchanged and friends and opinions shared, all those nights of making love, of waking up in the dark together and whispering, of pressing my ear against his chest, of slipping off his underwear and letting him slip off mine. Of crying in his arms after we made love. It was almost too much to bear.

Chapter Thirty

After checking in at the airport, I brought my bags over to the café near the gate. The same boy who had served me at the start of my trip smiled brightly as he took my order. I watched him set the cup under the espresso machine and flip the switch. The black coffee poured into the small cup. "Isn't the ocean wonderful?" he said, as he set the cup down before me. "People flock to it from all over the world."

Somebody tapped me on the shoulder and I turned around. It was Julie Berman. "Where's Jack?" she said.

I shrugged my shoulders. "We have different return flights—actually I think he's leaving in a couple of days."

"I wanted to talk to him about his script. I read it last night." She was quiet a moment, thinking of something to say. I said nothing, hoping the conversation would end there. "There's a whole lot of feeling in it. But the end still needs work. I don't know what it is. It needs something, though, and I'm not sure how to fix it," she said. I stared at her, knowing that Jack was going to be disappointed. "It's his characters—they're too nice to each other. They need to get into it with each other—you know, scream and yell, the gestalt thing."

She was quiet and I realized she was waiting for me to comment. "I thought it was fine," I said.

"Well, tell him I'll be in touch through his agent." She walked across the airport to Lizzy, who was seated against the far wall.

I sipped my coffee and watched the boy behind the counter; he was busy serving the many customers who had just arrived. Then suddenly the strange tingling sensation that I'd felt in my stomach returned. I put my hand there to settle it, but it didn't go away. Then I took my bag out from the over-head compartment and found my small pocket calendar. I counted back and, sure enough, the past few days were the right ones for me to have conceived. I did not know if it could really be true. But I began thinking it must be. The longer I sat there, the more sure I was. All those years, all those promises, and here it was at last after we'd finally broken up.

I was crying now, and I reached into my bag for a tissue to dry my eyes. There, on top of my clothes, was a letter-size envelope with my name on it.

Dear Maddy,

I'm writing this in my cabin right now knowing how mad you must be at me. I understand your anger, but I want you to know the real circumstance by which I came to see you. First, I ended things with Simone months ago. You know me, Maddy; I did not have the heart to ask her to leave right away, but nor could I find her another place to stay. It may be hard to be-lieve, but I wasn't merely keeping her in the wings. Things are over between us.

Maddy, I also wanted you to know about an incident that happened before I contacted you. About six months ago in the Village I bumped into that woman who was moving into our apartment when you and I were moving out. She said she had been looking for me for weeks because she'd come across something that she was pretty sure we'd left behind. She reached into her pocket and took out a ring, a beautiful old ring that she said she found under a floorboard. I told her that I didn't think it was ours but she told me to look inside. Sure enough, there was an inscription that read To My Love, M.G. I laughed and gave the ring back to her. I told her it was a mere coincidence, and then I said good-bye. It wasn't until later that I began putting things together. I never told you this, but at the end of our marriage, I'd had suspicions that you were doing something behind my back. I could never tell whether they were just in my head, but it was one of the reasons I asked for the separation. I was afraid to ask you because I was afraid it would end things between us forever. Then this ring confirmed what I had hoped wasn't true.

You can imagine how I felt—so hurt and then so sad. I spent several days in bed thinking about how you'd betrayed me. Then I became angry and far more bitter than I thought I could ever be. In my mind, I reduced our entire time together to one and only one thing—the fact that you had lied to me. Hating you seemed like the only way to move forward, but that didn't work. I ended up feeling like I was only hating myself. I began to search for answers as to how something like this could happen. It took many months to admit to myself that I was not totally innocent. Then, for reasons that I didn't understand, I began thinking a lot about Zuzu. I kept thinking how we had never talked about losing her. Only then did I realize the magnitude of what I was denying you by not having children. As I wrote to you on the back of the photo yesterday, I was terrified of the same thing happening again. I wish we hadn't kept so many secrets from each other. I wish we'd confronted each other—even argued with each other at times.

I'm sure you're wondering why I asked you here, given what I had learned. Maddy, it's important for you to know that I'm not accusing you of having had an affair. I still don't know for sure and I don't need to know. I don't ever need to know, because I've already forgiven you. I understand our love seemed so simple and innocent for so long, but all living things must change, and life is so complicated. Nobody in the world can possibly know how much I still love you.

Jack

Chapter Thirty-one

I caught a ferry back to St. Marie and then a taxi to the lodge. I was still checked in, so I dropped off my bags in my cabin and ran down the hill to Jack's. I did not know what I would do if he was already gone. I peeked through his windows and saw that his belongings were still scattered on the unmade bed and floor, but he was not there, so I went down to the beach and looked over the many bathers under their umbrellas. I spotted Jack's woolen army blanket spread out in the sand, and on it was his canteen and an open notebook. I sat down and waited for him, looking in both directions for any sign of him. I thought of the depth of my betrayal of him—at least in his mind. Then a terrifying thought came to me and I stared out at the water. Maybe he had done something crazy?

I walked quickly toward the point to look for him. It was a long walk, nearly a mile, and finally I came to where the shore was cobbled with colorful rocks. I kept my eyes down as I stepped from stone to stone, crossing small tidal pools filled with mussels and hermit crabs. I could smell the decay of seaweed and hear beach stones rolling in the back-wash of the waves. There were large, dark rocks out in the water, slipping in and out of the swells like the backs of small whales.

I came to the very end of the point—a sea cliff with water against it. There was no way to go farther. The light was changing and there were bluish clouds. There were no people down here, and the beach seemed eerie and lonely. Turning around, I noticed something—wooden steps leading up the side of a steep bluff. I recognized these steps from the police photo at the museum—they zigzagged up the bluff that Maggie had fallen from.

At the top I spotted a small figure sitting on a rock near the edge—Jack, looking proud, staring out at the ocean with his feet tucked up under him and his arms around his legs. He wore his sweatshirt with the hood up and his sunglasses—his flying goggles, as he called them.

I crossed to the base of the wooden steps and started to climb. They were rickety and I held on to both railings, crossing back and forth up the side of the cliff, the sound of the ocean becoming more distant. There was dirt and grass and a field of reddish boulders at the top. I could see Jack on the one closest to the edge.

I followed a path through the grass close to the cliff's edge. I stopped below Jack and looked up. He hadn't acknowledged me; he was looking at the ocean.

"Hey," I called. "Are you okay?" I could not tell what he was thinking with his glasses on. Waves were breaking against the stony shore below us, and a cawing tern flew overhead. He continued looking out at the view as if I weren't there. "I read your letter," I said. I waited for a moment before speaking, watching him. "Jack, I'm so sorry for everything that's happened."

He continued looking away.

"I don't know if it makes any difference, but I feel like we're on the other side of something—something terrible. We're in a different place now. But I still love you. I don't even know how to tell you how much I love you."

I could hear the water washing against the shore below. His silence continued and he was very still.

"Jack, would you say something?"

The wind was suddenly so loud that I wasn't sure if he had heard me.

"Please—" I said.

"I don't want to fight with you," he said finally. "It's too late now. It's not working, Maddy—and it never will. I just want you to leave."

He turned back to the view. I stood there a moment considering what to do. I wanted to argue with him, to tell him how wrong he was, to tell him that it would never be over, but I knew it wouldn't convince him.

Finally I turned away and walked along the path next to the bluff. Reaching the top of the steps, I looked back at him. He was still sitting on the boulder, looking the other way.

I walked back toward him on the path, cautiously. "All right," I said, standing just below him at the bluff's edge. "I'll go, I'll accept that, but only if you answer one question for me. I've been meaning to ask you it since I met you." He continued to sit there with his back to me. "Why did you fall in love with me to begin with?"

The hood of his sweatshirt was up and I could see only the side of his face.

"Tell me why you fell in love with me," I said. "And you'll never see me again. That I promise you."

The wind came up again and he continued to sit there.

"Well, I know why I fell in love with you," I said. "Remember telling me about following my deepest dreams?

Coming from you, I understood what that meant in a whole new way. You trusted the world because you loved it and you loved every bit of it, and that gave me courage to do what I wanted to do. I changed the course of my life and became a painter. But things didn't work out for me. I quit, as you know, because I wanted to have a family with you. That's why, when you turned away from me . . . it was crushing, like all the oxygen in the room had vanished. Yes, somebody else did come into my life, and yes, I did have a choice to leave you for him. Do you want to know why I chose not to? I realized that you, Jack, you had been my deepest dream all along."

Suddenly he slipped down off the rock and came toward me along the edge of the bluff. He came right at me, his hair a mess, his eyes red from crying, and a crazy look on his face. I thought he was going to shove me, but instead he ran around me and along the path to the steps. Gripping the rails, he raced down the rickety steps to the beach. He went recklessly fast, zigzagging down, and when he reached the shore he ran across the stones, a small figure. He kept up this fast pace as he crossed to the beach of white sand and he became smaller and smaller until finally I could no longer see him at all.

And there I was, alone again, at the top of the bluffs overlooking the ocean. We had crossed a line and there was no going back. It was over—it was truly over at last, and I was exhausted. My legs felt weak. I walked recklessly close to the edge as I made my way to the steps, held both railings, and started to climb down. The ocean was beautiful, the water that soft early-afternoon blue.

At the bottom I started the long walk back to the cabins. A memory came to me of the first summer Jack and I lived together on the Vineyard—our last day on the island. It was late in the afternoon and we decided to ride our bikes to a private beach down a long dirt road. The beach was like our little secret when we first discovered it; few people, even if they knew about it, were up for the long trek in. The road ended near a saltwater pond with meadows of long sea grasses of different colors, mostly shades of green. A wooden bridge crossed a narrow saltwater stream where children went crabbing with white nets during the season. There were dunes dividing the stream from the sea so it was always quiet, and one could easily hear the gulls or even the wings of swans crossing from pond to pond. It was here that I learned how loud the wings of flying swans can be, which is testament to their strength. Saltwater ponds radiate a softer and somehow sweeter blue than freshwater ponds, and they are always touched by a certain melancholy because one senses the salt water yearning to return to the glorious ocean only yards away.

We left our bikes in the sand and crossed the dunes with our towels and packed dinner. The surf was white and turbulent and the waves were breaking far from shore, one on top of the other. No matter how many times we crossed from the absolute tranquillity of the ponds and stream behind the dunes to the sudden roar of surf, we were filled with wonder, as if we'd come across an altogether new world. That evening the slanting sun caught the salty vapor from the surf, raising a kind of misty fog that appeared blue because of the color of the sea behind it. By then, having been with Jack all summer, so many feelings about him had mixed with the colors and smell of the sea. We hiked far enough down the beach so that we could take off all of our clothes. We went swimming at the edge of the surf and then lay back on our dry towels without talking, feeling the vapor on our cheeks and chests—like talcum powder settling on your skin after a warm bath. We watched the colors softening, the smells becoming richer and the reddening light from the sky changing the color of the mist ever so slightly. Then stars were out and the sky was that infinite purple. The feeling of the ocean changed quickly. It became dark and frightening, beckoning us like a dare, and we hastened back to the tranquillity behind the dunes and got on our bicycles. We rode toward home, the lights on our handlebars reflecting off the mist. It was difficult to see the rocks on the dirt road, and we had to trust that we would not fall. The fertile fragrance of pines and oak rained down on us from the darkness. It brought us close to the earth and into our bodies.

Turning on the light inside our cottage after riding in the dark, looking at each other while our eyes adjusted to the yellow light, was a strangely welcome experience. We were back in the world. Our hair was dry but heavy with salt, and we were cool. I got in the shower and put the water just a little warmer than Jack could stand, so when he got in he turned it down slightly. Jack's skin became slick with soap, and I remember how his lips felt under the warm spray. Later, in bed, we were restless at first, as if we were still swimming under the sheets. Our pillows were damp from our hair. We made love and afterward we held hands.

"Cricket," Jack said. "How did we find each other—I mean, out of all the people on this earth, all four billion, how did we find each other?"

I laughed and then lay there drifting off to sleep, thinking about it. I had somehow found the one person on earth whom I could love the most.

There were tears in my eyes as I walked down the beach toward the cabins. I must have been looking at the sand for the longest time, because when I looked up I realized I was passing things that I didn't remember—rowboats turned over against the sand, the remnants of some sort of pier in the water. I turned around and walked back. As I reached the steps, I heard the sound of a boat horn on the water. I turned and saw the ferry departing and I had the feeling that he must be on it. I continued up the steps and then along the path to my cabin.

When I opened the door I stopped, frozen in my tracks. Jack was sitting on my bed looking up at me. He looked beaten down, his hair a mess and his shirt open. He got up slowly, walked toward me, and grabbed me firmly by the shoulders. His grip was strong. His eyes were so red and fierce that I suddenly thought he was going to do something terrible to me. I thought about his violent side in summer camp. I thought, This is it; this is where I am. But I didn't move. I stared into his eyes and did not try to loosen his grip. I only knew that my life was in his hands, as it would always be.

Then I saw tears well up in his eyes. He let go and pulled me against him. "Maddy," he said.

Kissing Your Ex

BROOKE STEVENS

This Conversation Guide is intended to enrich the
individual reading experience, as well as encourage us
to explore these topics together—because books,
and life, are meant for sharing.

A CONVERSATION WITH
BROOKE STEVENS

Q. Where did the inspiration come from for Kissing Your Ex?

A. I have no abstract ideas when I'm starting a novel. I write vignettes or scenes first, one after the next on varying subjects, anything that comes to mind when I sit down at my computer. I put these short pieces away for a few days and then come back to them. If a vignette suggests something more, I'll attempt to expand it. If I'm lucky enough, I will stumble upon an idea for a novel. I wish there were an easier way for me to start a book, but I can't seem to care about something until I can actually see a scene or two on the page. In the case of *Kissing Your Ex*, I started with a divorced couple on vacation in the Caribbean. They were having a superficial conversation on the beach. The couple seemed to care for each other despite the fact that they were divorced and yet there was some sort of unspoken tension between them. I became intrigued by the source of that tension. In this way, most of the novel was written backward from this initial situation and most of it was a kind of investigation into how they got to this point. Of course, many of the emotions and many of the situations in the novel are aspects of life that I've actually experienced. I am like Jack and Maddy in that I never give up on my past too; hence I have friends dating back to when I was three years old.

Q. Maddy and Jack are unable to express anger or displeasure with one another, and their marriage falls apart. This is just one of many insights into the nature of relationships that you seem to get just right. How did you prepare to write the novel?

A. Most of the insights in the book about relationships came about while writing the book—one scene felt truer than another and therefore the narrative followed one path instead of another. After finishing the book, I did some research into what psychologists had to say about marriage and I came across the quote I used as an epigraph: "A man is more likely to let a relationship suffer in order to hold on to his sense of self, while a woman is more apt to let her identity suffer to help strengthen it." I think that perfectly summarized what I was trying to write about without being aware of it. Men and women experience different pressures in life. Many men establish their identity through their work, whereas some women value a warm, communicative relationship above all else. This is certainly not a hard and fast rule, but it's often the hidden source of conflict between two people and it certainly is between Jack and Maddy. Their problem is compounded by the fact that they both tend to veer away from conflict and therefore the differences in the way they experience life never come out into the open. Their conflict festers and deepens and eventually they divorce without ever fully grasping the depth of each other's humanity. Fortunately, they both recognize that their divorce is a minor tragedy, which is why they take the trip together.

Q. The New York City that you populate with struggling artists and their friends seems very familiar to you. Have you lived in New York? Where are you from originally?

A. I grew up in a small rural town in Connecticut. Before college, I worked in Ringling Brothers' Circus for a year as a horse groom and then later as a steam locomotive engineer at the Cog Railroad in New Hampshire. I've held at least thirty different jobs in many parts of the country and I did so more out of pure curiosity than to prepare myself to be a writer. I came to New York City because it satisfied my restlessness and my curiosity about people. The city is its own traveling road show. In New York, people tend to befriend people like themselves, despite the city's diversity, and therefore many of my friends were struggling artists or writers who, like myself, held a day job. I did know one couple who were very much like Jack and Maddy. I met them in the bar that they frequented on the Lower East Side. Like Maddy and Jack they fell in love in college and later came to the city together. Many people in the neighborhood knew them. They had one of those symbiotic relationships that seems like it will never end. But sure enough, when they turned thirty, they split up. I could see the sense of tragedy in both of their faces; I could tell that even if they were to meet new people and remarry they would always be haunted by the closeness of their first relationship. I lost touch with them, so I don't know if they ever attempted to reunite, as the characters in my book did.

Q. Jack's desire to succeed as a writer is a contributing factor to his divorce from Maddy. As a married novelist yourself, do you struggle to give equal time to your art and your family?

A. Oh yes. I'm married to a wonderful woman and we have two darling, imaginative children who are straight out of a fairy tale. I've built a small writing studio on the property, where I really should be spending more time. But how tempting to stay inside and listen to my four-year-old son's adventurous stories about Mrs. Cuckoo and her best friend, Jelly Nelly. (Maybe I should become his agent when he's a few years older). I'm forty-six, quite a bit older than most dads of small children. The downside is that my children tire me out more easily than they would have ten years ago, but the upside is that I fully appreciate every moment I spend with them. There's nothing like being with a little person who lives right on the border of reality and the world of the unconscious. It's a state of mind that I tried to achieve in my earlier books, particularly *The Circus of the Earth and the Air*—a world that's right on the cusp of reality and fantasy. I've always loved children but I've never had the chance to live inside the head of one in the way my children have allowed me.

Q. Maddy gives up her art to focus all of her energies on the Puppet Garage. Have you ever considered giving up writing?

A. Yes. I feel responsible to the rest of the world and often wonder if being a writer is far too selfish, considering the state of things. I admire others who are doing things for people in need; they're the salt of the earth, not literary writers who are constantly worrying about their fragile egos. (I'm guilty of that too.) I wish I had the resources and the guts to start off on another career, to start a home in the country for underprivileged children, something like that. I'm politically aware and have considered political consulting, among other careers. But then I do love writing, particularly once I've created a fictional world—it feels like going someplace new every day. Maybe, as John Gardner believed, there is such a thing as moral fiction—that is, fiction that makes a positive impact on people's lives. I hope so.

Q. You're a teacher at Sarah Lawrence College. Can you talk a bit about your day job?

A. I love helping young writers, but I have to admit I'm not the font of wisdom that the teachers who have greater intellectual strengths than I do seem to be. My strength in teaching comes more from being a diligent, caring reader when it comes to reviewing student work. In college and in graduate school, I experienced both good and bad writing teachers. I felt so uplifted by the good ones and yet so let down by the bad ones that I swore that I'd quit teaching before becoming remiss in my duties toward students. One teacher in graduate school I found particularly helpful was Madison Smartt Bell. When he was helping me with my first novel, he told me that he had a dream about one of the images in the book. Madison is very insightful but that statement had a particularly strong impact on me—I knew that he was not only reading what I wrote, but he was allowing it to affect him as one would a published novel. That's the sign of a true teacher—somebody who gives himself to your writing as a reader, and yet can still steer you in a constructive direction.

Q. Near the end of the book, Maddy runs into Julie Berman, the Hollywood director reading Jack's script, which is the story of Maddy and Jack. When Julie says that she thinks the work needs a new ending, she is inadvertently commenting on Maddy and Jack's relationship. Have they come to a new beginning at the end? Did you know how this story was going to end when you began it?

A. Carl Jung said, "Seldom or never does a marriage develop into an individual relationship smoothly without crisis. There is no birth of consciousness without pain." I agree with this. I don't think there are too many things more painful to realize than that the person you are in love with is attracted to somebody else. Usually when something like that comes about in a marriage, the relationship may skid along for a few more yards but eventually it will end. That's because it's so difficult and painful and even life-threatening to grasp the full humanity of the person you're in love with. The easier route is to break it off or to vilify the person for betraying you. I think Maddy and Jack are right on the cusp at the end of the book of truly starting over, of more fully grasping the humanity of the other and of loving each other in a different, more mature way. I hadn't the slightest idea about whether these two would stay together or break up for good at the end of the book.

Q. You write so touchingly and convincingly from a woman's perspective in Kissing Your Ex, *as well as in your last novel,* Tattoo Girl. *How do you do it?*

A. Some of my favorite novels are either written by women authors or from a woman's point of view: *Anna Karenina, Madame Bovary,* to name a couple. One of my favorite books is *The Sun Also Rises.* I'm not a fan of all of Hemingway's work, but it is interesting to note that this one novel is written from the point of view of a man who is impotent. The best fiction I believe comes about when a writer challenges the very core of his identity in some way. Surely the macho Hemingway was meeting just this challenge when he was writing from the point of view of an emasculated man. He was turning his life upside down, so to speak. Most of Hemingway's other work seems to be a kind of wish fulfillment, the brave soldier, the brave hunter, etc. To me that's a great bore. But so are the many novels by men told from a woman's point of view that objectify the women they're writing about. The writers of such books are still seeing their main character through their own eyes rather than through the eyes of their character. I am lucky to have terrific women readers who have guided me in this area.

Q. Do you identify more with Jack or with Maddy?

A. There are aspects of both characters that I identify with. I've been in Jack's situation—I've never been in Maddy's, so I guess it's fair to say that I identify with Jack more and yet I do see the flaws in Jack's way of thinking about his marriage. Both Jack and Maddy have a great love of the past. They're deeply nostalgic, and so am I. I would much rather drive a crummy old car with tons of personal history than a brand-new Lexus. My four-year-old son is the same way. He's constantly talking about the things we used to do. He and I used to take long walks down some railroad tracks near my home with him riding on my shoulders in a backpack. He refers to those times as the old days and you can already see that nostalgic twinkle in his eyes.

Q. Would you like to discuss themes and motifs in the book that are important to you or significant in some way?

A. I think of all of my books as representing an individual's battle with loneliness. In my first novel, *The Circus of the Earth and the Air*, a man loses his wife and must find himself before he finds her. In *Kissing Your Ex*, it's Maddy's loneliness with Andrew that ultimately drives her back toward Jack despite all the pain accompanying that relationship.

Q. Describe your writing process. Do you have any specific or strange work habits?

A. Like most authors, I like to work in the mornings before all the little worries of life take over.

Q. What authors do you admire? Are there any that have had a particularly strong influence on you?

A. I worked as a security guard in my twenties and that gave me an enormous amount of time to read. I read the usual suspects one after the next—Dickens, Dostoyevsky, Chekhov, Tolstoy, Hemingway, Faulkner, Kafka, Woolf, Gabriel García Márquez. I loved *Le Grand Meaulnes* by Alain-Fournier and Theodore Dreiser's *Sister Carrie*. I'm always on the lookout for interesting writers whose primary concern is to tell a great story rather than to write the perfect sentence. A great book is like a great friend, I like my friends to be without affectations. Margaret Atwood is one of those wonderful writers who tells fascinating, complex stories without the prose affectations so prized in the literary world. I wish that the business of a telling a good story was not merely left up to the popular fiction writers.

Q. What are you working on now?

A. I am trying to write another love story, this one from a more mature point of view. I can't say much more about it because the story changes from day to day.

QUESTIONS
FOR DISCUSSION

1. Why is the rabbit house in upstate New York important to Maddy and Jack? How are the references to *Alice in Wonderland* by Lewis Carroll significant?

2. When does Maddy first begin to suspect that Andrew may not be right for her?

3. On page 107, Maddy is on the flight to St. Marie after fighting with Andrew when it occurs to her that Andrew and her old flame, Peter, are similar. How are they "connected" in Maddy's mind?

4. Julie Berman likes Jack's screenplay, except that the characters are "too nice to each other." She thinks they "need to get into it with each other" and have a real fight. How does Maddy and Jack's inability to "get into it" affect their initial attempts at reconciliation on St. Marie?

5. On page 247, in the brochure for the estate museum of Maggie Comane, Maggie is quoted as saying, "I've completed what I only started with Gwen. I've stepped into the world." What do you think she means by this?

6. Discuss the different ways in which the Puppet Garage is important, even vital, to Maddy's life in New York.

7. Why does the loss of Zuzu affect Maddy and Jack differently? How do they cope with the miscarriage together? Separately?

8. What does Jack reveal is the reason he did not want to try again to have a baby? How does he feel now?

9. There is constant contrast between old and new in the story— from relationships to clothes, engagement rings and the two different versions of the rabbit house. What is the significance to these contrasts? What purpose do they have in the story?

10. Andrew, Jack and Peter deal with money in very different ways. What do their financial practices tell Maddy about their different approaches to life?

11. Do you think Maddy and Jack will be able to repair and rebuild their relationship? How will their future be different from their past?